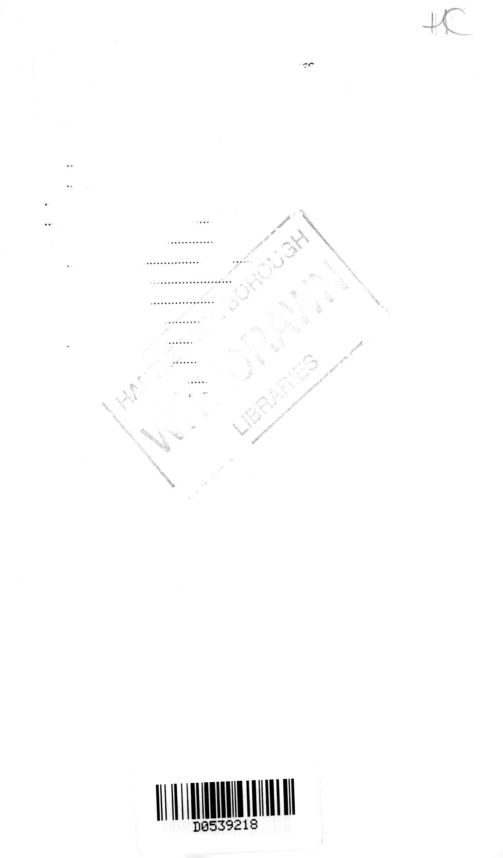

Alison Hoblyn lives in Oxfordshire with her architect husband and two daughters. After art college training she worked in the visual arts as a designer, artist and teacher.

THE SCENT OF WATER

History repeats itself, so they say. Perhaps it has to because no-one listens? Ellie, an artist in her middle age, needs to live her life in a new way after the death of her husband. She enrols on a garden course in Tuscany one spring. Here she begins relationships with fellow students Nerine, an eccentric character in her seventies, and the younger Max. Through the teaching of Salvatore — the owner of an ancient palazzo — who runs the course, Ellie finds that the universal truths, expressed in the Renaissance painting *Primavera* and the philosophy of Marsilo Ficino, are still potently relevant.

ALISON HOBLYN

THE SCENT
OF WATER

Complete and Unabridged

ULVERSCROFT
Leicester

First published in Great Britain in 2005 by
Transita
Oxford

First Large Print Edition
published 2007
by arrangement with
Transita
Oxford

The moral right of the author has been asserted

British Library CIP Data

Hoblyn, Alison
   The scent of water.—Large print ed.—
Ulverscroft large print series: romance
1. Women artists—Fiction 2. Middle aged women—Fiction
3. Tuscany (Italy)—Fiction 4. Large type books
I. Title
823.9'2 [F]

ISBN 978–1–84617–935–8

Published by
F. A. Thorpe (Publishing)
Anstey, Leicestershire
Set by Words & Graphics Ltd.
Anstey, Leicestershire
Printed and bound in Great Britain by
T. J. International Ltd., Padstow, Cornwall

This book is printed on acid-free paper

For David.
Impossible without you.

Acknowledgements

Thanks go to
My parents whose investment
and encouragement lives on.
David, Sarah and Louise for
always being there.
My sister Kate and the Friday Group,
for their prayers.
My supportive women friends;
especially in this case Jane Cairns
and Louise Rice.
Maggie Noach and Alison Coles
who helped me on part of the journey.
The Oxford Writers' Group for generous
sharing. Valerie Petts for showing me the
translations of Marsilio Ficino. Kieren
Phelan at Southern Arts who enabled me
to take a course at Ty Newydd where
I was well tutored by John Williams and
Anna Davis. John Arnold at the Diocese
of Westminster for information on
Catholic marriage. David Jackman for
legal advice. Marina Oliver for sorting
out my manuscript. Transita for being
such a good idea and to the spirit who
started and sustains the whole story.

1

April

You had no choice but to be content in the midst of such utterly ordered landscape; lines of mop-headed fruit trees and vines, lines of vertical cypresses, lines of ploughed fields — all casting deep shadow in the afternoon sunlight. Ellie had been driving in air-conditioned comfort through the Tuscan countryside. Alone and early, she had time to use as she wished. On a whim, she left the high winding road from Volterra and with stones skittering up into the car's undercarriage, plunged along a gravel track. At its end she found a deserted settlement. The French would call it a *domaine*, what the name was in Italian she didn't know. Ellie left the car, smiled and stretched expansively in the warmth. It took her ten minutes on foot to find the church; to look up a flight of steps into the darkness of its arched doorway; to be reminded of Andrew. She felt the pressure of heat upon her head; the spiky grass poking through her open sandals — and was overcome by loss.

Her mood so suddenly rearranged, she sank down on the wide steps and fumbled for a cigarette. The warmth of the stone through her cotton skirt was comforting. Inhaling deeply she tried to concentrate on the real, exterior world; the Magritte clouds in a cobalt sky, the bees clustering in the wild rosemary, the ants in the cracks of stone.

★　★　★

Ellie arrived at the Palazzo via a winding lane that climbed past terraced olive groves. It felt like home when she saw the silver-green foliage and the creviced trunks. Turning sharply right, away from the groves, she nudged the car through the open half of a pair of forged gates. Swinging hard right again, she came to a halt in the corner of a gravelled courtyard. Geese scratched and stabbed at the grit in the shade of the trees where she halted. In this veiled light even the shadows had colour, a singing violet-blue. Other cars were also parked in the cool — a battered Renault and a smart hire car, deluxe class; heat was still rising from its paintwork.

Silence always helped Ellie to move slower. She always felt compelled to respond to people; to smile the widest, to fill in the awkward gaps in conversation, to be seen to be doing. At this moment, however, she felt a joy that she had missed for a while, of being comfortable in her own skin. She walked past a small pool bordered with pots of rosemary. Someone had abandoned a pair of secateurs on the ground, had left midway through the task of shaping the plants into perfect globes. The clippings released a strong aroma into the still air of the courtyard. A small jet of water spurted from the middle of the pond, barely disturbing the outer regions of the basin but producing a lascivious dribbling that, coupled with the warmth and the scents, unexpectedly stirred Ellie. She raised her head guiltily to see if anyone had observed her. Far above on a balcony she saw the fleeting outline of a man. He was slipping out of a shirt as he walked back through some French doors. Ellie was conscious of her body freezing as she tried to make sense of the brief encounter; amazing, how a human was programmed to read so much from a passing glance.

She pulled her attention back to the long flight of stone steps up to the Palazzo. At the top was an outsize pair of wooden doors with several glass panels framed by timber mullions. She climbed. The doors wouldn't yield, so she squinted through the glass. At first the adjustment from sun to dark interior proved too great and she rested her eyes in blackness. A hazy amber light materialised like ectoplasm; it came from a silk lampshade set atop a marble table. By the lamp was an impressive flower arrangement — confident, beautiful but somehow not the emotionless confection of a professional florist. White lilies reflected the small amount of light back to the eye. Dark foliage stood, turgid and glossy, casting soft shadows on the wall behind. The wall, its undulating surface a mix of plaster pink and copper shades, seemed to rise up for ever, the ceiling way up where heaven should be. As Ellie gazed up her hand was on the bellpush; almost simultaneously a small dark figure crystallized from the shadows to open the door.

'*Ciao!*'

'Oh. Hello, I'm Ellie Carroll.'

'Ah yes, with the Garden Group.' The girl smiled widely.

'Yes.' Ellie felt relieved that as yet she hadn't needed to stumble through rusty Italian with this kindly girl — well, she was probably in her late twenties and most likely one of the family that ran the Palazzo. Hadn't it said in the blurb that the family had owned the place for more than six hundred years? What must it be like to have your home

4

invaded by B and B-ers, course-takers and retreat junkies?

'I am Francesca. It is my uncle who owns Palazzo Michele and will be teaching the course. You will meet him later when you have had time to relax. Have you some bags?' Ellie gestured down to her car, across the head of a young man who had now resumed the rosemary clipping.

'Good, Marco will bring them up for you. He's the gardener but he'll do most things for me.'

The whole domestic business was smoothly choreographed. Carrying her smaller items of luggage herself, Ellie walked past the once more discarded secateurs, up the steps and into the cool interior. She signed her name into a leather-bound book while Francesca smiled over her. Ellie's room was large and opened off the main hallway; the bed huge and draped in crisp white cotton. The windows were shuttered against the heat and a dim bulb glowed on the bedside table. Magically her cases were already there, placed reverently on a carved *cassettone*.

Francesca handed her the key. 'I'm afraid this one is a little stiff in the lock,' she smiled at Ellie, 'but most people aren't locking their doors. We hope everyone feels like it is their home.'

Ellie smiled back. 'Am I the first to arrive?'

'No, there was a man. He arrived just a few minutes before you. You can meet him at seven if you should like to have some tea or drinks on the terrace.'

Ellie nodded; while her mind was reviewing the earlier sighting, her body was ahead of her, her face flushing. Thank the Lord, the girl didn't seem to notice.

'I think I'll go and have a lie down then. I'm a bit tired.'

Francesca waved her off solicitously.

★ ★ ★

When Ellie awoke she had slept for an hour. In the crepuscular room she fumbled for the lamp and felt the click of the switch echo around the space. There was a comforting dampish smell to the plaster walls rather like the garden shed she'd retreated to as a child. To have slept so spontaneously was a rare event for Ellie; she was generally kept awake by thoughts of mistakes past or woken early by thoughts of duties ahead. Looking at her pale skin in the low light she thought of the 'lilies that neither toil nor spin' and smiled to herself. Pushing open the shutters she saw the light going, pausing at the moment where it would slip into darkness. As she showered to complete her renaissance she thought of what they'd be doing back at home but let the thoughts drip off her like the water. It was seven; time to venture out.

Perfumed and relaxed in new linen she stepped out into the darkness of the terrace. Chairs and tables were touched with pools of light from lanterns; there must have been places for a dozen or so people but, so far, only one was taken by the man. He was involved in pouring himself a drink from the tray beside him but looked up at the sound of Ellie's footfall and smiled.

'I was wondering how long I'd have to wait before I met one of my fellow intellectuals!'

Ellie watched his smile in the half-light, instantly measuring him by some lifetime system of calculation that she hardly understood. Early thirties, casually but expensively dressed, dark-haired like herself; the kind of good looks that in her youth had scared her off.

'I'd hardly call myself that. Fellow stumbler or fellow pleasure-seeker perhaps?' said Ellie.

'Definitely that,' he said raising the bottle to her and indicating another glass. 'Can I pour you one of these?'

Ellie lowered herself into the chair across the table from him and said, 'Yes you can — as long as I know who's pouring.'

'Max. Max Penman-White.' He didn't offer his hand but glossed his fingers over hers as he handed her the glass. It was so quick Ellie barely knew if it was intentional. But that touch moved her more than it should have.

She straightened in her chair. 'And I'm Ellie Carroll.'

'Well, I suppose this is our chance to find out about each other.' Max reclined and looked at her through lowered eyelids.

'I'm not giving out any confidential information like birth date!' Ellie tried to respond lightly.

He laughed. 'As if I would ask a lady that. You're obviously old enough to have seen life and young enough to see plenty more. Much the same as myself.'

Ha, I've a decade on you, thought Ellie. Nevertheless his chat-up lines were having a calming effect on her. After nearly two years when the only men around treated her in careful brotherly fashion she was enjoying his attention.

'That's about right,' she laughed.

As the wine went down the talk became easier. He was here to do the course on Italian gardens, History and Design, because it was going to be a relaxation from his pressured life in London. It wasn't a million miles away, however, from his work; he headed up a firm of florists.

'Sounds a nice romantic business to be in, doesn't it?' said Max. 'Not a bit of it. As I left the knives were really out — suppliers giving us a hard time. I can tell you I'm glad to be here.'

Now Ellie did recall the name, *Penman-White's*, the big society 'floral artists'. They'd done more than a few Royal functions. Max went on to say that given half a chance he'd ditch the whole business now, get out and design himself a nice country garden with an Italianate feel. Ellie watched him talking; he had a right to be confident but she didn't read him as showy. He was simply aware that he had achieved things. He reminded her of Dom somehow. Ellie would like it if her son grew into this kind of sureness.

And her? She swooped into the deep end and found strangely that she had breath to say that she was a widow; her husband had been rather older than herself and he'd died of a heart attack aged fifty-eight. And after Ellie had said all this, Max was sincerely interested. He asked her more details about Andrew and how she lived now. So she told him of her two children and her cottage in the Cotswolds.

'How old are your kids?'

'Twenty-two and twenty-one.'

9

'At least they knew their father when they were adults.' Max hesitated. 'I never knew my dad, gone before I was born. Dead,' he looked at Ellie with a bright smile. 'I've had a stepdad since I was eight, and worked for him since I was eighteen.'

Ellie didn't want to lead Max along the path of regrets, she feared it would take her too soon into her own dark territory.

'Oh, so he's the Penman-White of floristry fame, is he?'

Max laughed. 'Yes I guess you could say that. Although between you, me and the box of bricks he started life as a plain old White. The Penman got added for extra class.'

Ellie smiled. The slight superciliousness she had divined in their first exchanges seemed to have disappeared entirely.

'So, how long have you been on your own?'

There, he wouldn't let her evade the subject. Well, thought Ellie, he had shared a part of his life with her so why couldn't she? He listened quietly as she told him that Andrew's death had only been two years ago and that she was only now beginning to feel able to function alone. This was her first solo adventure. In fact she wasn't sure she would have come except a great friend said it would be good for her. She'd said something like 'Feel the fear and do it anyway.' Max was consoling and said how true it was what her friend had said. And wasn't Italy the land of the Renaissance anyway?

The silence had just congealed comfortingly around them and Ellie's senses had shifted to a position slightly to the rear of her when through the thick air there loomed a hat. A large hat decorated with iridescent feathers. And beneath it was a figure with the deportment of an Indian Runner duck; a wiry, agitated frame, beak lifted, eyes alert but rather distracted.

'Is this where we're meant to be?' she addressed no one in particular. Ellie felt later that she would look back upon that first meeting with Lady Nerine Temple as life-enhancing. 'Only just breathed in my room when that girl said I should come and have a drink out here before dinner. Seemed a sensible idea.'

Max was on his feet drawing up a chair.

'Sit down, let me pour you a glass of wine,' said Ellie, looking at Nerine's racehorse ankles and bony wrists. She had the pared down elegance the elderly sometimes possess.

'Oh thank you, but I'd quite like a nice whisky to pick me up after all that fighting with Italian transportation. Have they got any?' The beady eyes swept around the tables. 'Doesn't matter if they haven't, I have!'

Francesca appeared with perfect timing and a tray of bottles and tit-bits. '*Buona sera.* I know that there are more of you to come but I shall tell you of the arrangement for drinks from our bar now, I think. There is a place to help yourself in the library. When you have come and seen, you will be able to tell the others.'

'And when exactly are we going to see these others?' Lady Nerine squinted up at Francesca from under a trailing feather.

'The Dottor Hunter and the Signora Clements are arriving soon. The others will be arriving very early in the morning, it is a night flight they are getting.'

'So it's just cosy old us for now,' said Max. '*Very intime.*' He said it slowly and as Ellie turned to look at his face he winked at her. She smiled back feeling comfortable; the fears she'd had of new places, new people melted away.

At dinner, in a panelled dining room with doors open on to the terrace, they sat together and talked of nothing very consequential. Nerine was too much of a performance to be ignored and entertained them with her total enjoyment of things new. Max told them about his loft conversion on the river. He loved city living but he hankered after a bit of rural life; probably advancing age, he laughed, but also he'd spent some time in the country in his childhood. Out of the floating facts of the night, that drifted up on cigarette smoke, what Ellie remembered later was Max describing a log pile. He'd seen it on a trip to Bavaria and was struck by its orderliness; it filled a whole garage and was sorted and labelled according not only to size but also to date of harvest. What she saw was real pleasure in his face. Ellie settled back; she was savouring the badinage, relishing her first impressions of these people but — most of all — enjoying painting a picture of herself for them that was entirely within her control.

Later they met Salvatore Uccello. As they sat over their smoky *caffe* he asked if they would mind if he joined them. He probably wasn't much older than Ellie but he had that kind of reserve that is described as great 'bearing'. Ellie could not imagine him sharing confidences. He was tall and genteel; patrician — that was the word that came to Ellie's mind. In this case entirely accurate. The Palazzo had been his family's home since 1400 and he had lived there from birth, although he had obviously learned his immaculate English somewhere abroad. Oxford, whilst reading philosophy, it turned out. That conversation led to asking about everyone's educational background and Ellie had to admit to studying in Florence in the seventies, as part of her Art History course. Not only did that give her age away (she watched Max but there was not a flicker) but it also revealed that she had learnt some Italian.

'Ah, Signora Carroll, when I see you alone, the conversation will be of things artistic and only in Italian.' Salvatore smiled and laid a manicured hand briefly on her shoulder. She smiled up at him and agreed, saying that perhaps he could enlighten her on some philosophical points that she had never really understood.

It was Max's turn in the spotlight and he worked at getting them all laughing. With much expansive gesturing and crossing and uncrossing of his legs, he described his studies at the University of Life. Now, he said, he was thinking of stopping his many business interests to do some kind of degree for a while. Nerine simply tossed out that she had been to the Slade in the thirties. Ellie's antennae twitched.

'Do you still paint, Nerine? Because I do too. At least, I'm trying to find myself a style at the moment.'

'Lord no, I can't be carrying all that oil stuff around at my age. But I do have my sketchbook and I've just got one of those digital cameras. Great fun and very liberating, dear.' Nerine patted Ellie's hand. 'You should have a go, it might open a few windows.'

'We will begin tomorrow, not too early in deference to our fellow students, at eleven a.m. in the *salotto* — drawing room.' Salvatore said, standing up to leave. 'I shall outline your studies for you and then we will begin by understanding Italian people, a very important prerequisite.' He smiled, almost bowed and blessed their night's rest with a *Che Dio vi benedica*.

Ellie rose too, the harsh scrape of her chair on the terrazzo floor jarring the atmosphere. Everything had taken on a misty rose tinge; the polished plaster of the walls diffused the reflection of the candle flames like Indian red watercolour seeping across wet paper. She felt slightly heady; comfortable with Max and Nerine and simultaneously anxious that the dynamic might be changed by the arrival of the others.

'Good night then, fellow students!' She walked out into the entrance hall with their voices bidding her sweet dreams. She passed Francesca at the desk signing in a tired looking couple. His head was bent over a credit card slip. Maybe Doctor Hunter and Mrs Clements she thought. Not wanting to break the spell she just sent a glancing *buona sera* in their direction as she passed by. Out of the corner of her eye she could see Mrs Clements' head turn up sharply. Ellie felt the appraisal on her retreating back like cool fingers as she slipped into the sanctuary of her room.

★ ★ ★

Salvatore walked back through the olive groves in the darkness. This late in April there was still an edge to the temperature at this time of night, but in the day he'd felt the potential of the heat. It was his custom to spend time alone in reflection before he headed for bed. He got there around midnight. He took his notes with him to glance over before sleeping. Salvatore knew his subject well but always liked to refresh his mind or see if some new insights would come to him in dreamtime. The three students so far seemed interesting. He wouldn't have immediately imagined them as kindred spirits but they had become bonded expatriate English within a few hours of leaving home. He had a fondness for the race from his time there. The young man worried him a little. But maybe all young men did these days. What he might have called energy in the past he now labelled brash. He liked the ladies.

Nerine felt familiar; his mother the *Marchesa* had had the same spirit. Ellie was gentle. The way she pushed her trailing hair to peer out with those clear eyes betrayed a certain lack of confidence. No, that was not exactly right. His instincts told him she did have confidence, although buried deep, but she had no wish to assert her will on others.

Salvatore sifted his papers, written out in a careful longhand with the fountain pen given to him by his father. As he scanned the familiar words he hoped for some spark to ignite this group of people. He prayed this course would not become a chore; that this would not be a time when he went through the motions merely. Salvatore drew his hand over the top of his head, feeling the thinning hair. Life did have times when one just had to keep going but it could also bring surprises. This time, before a course began, was always filled with the excitement of anticipation. Would this group work as an entity? Would they be responsive participants? The dynamic of the course so depended upon the response when you were giving day after day. He often wondered if students knew what a responsibility they had; to give back, to pour water into their teacher's well. Salvatore laughed gently to himself; it was more like pouring water into a bottomless bucket in this place.

At last in his bed he sat upright against the mahogany bed-head, book in hand. It had been a while since he had read these letters by Marsilio Ficino. Something that lady, Ellie, had said about her studies in Italy had caused him to come back to them; she had been baffled by Neoplatonism. 'How,' she asked, 'could pagan and Christian philosophies be in harmony? Where's the link between Humanism and religion?' He wanted to give her the best possible answer and so here was his research. The heavy calf-bound volume of letters weighed in his hand; he turned the rough paper and read; the words were in elegant, rhetorical style, imbued with authority.

You have heard that proverb . . . Nothing is sweeter than profit. But what man does profit? He who takes possession of that which will be his. What we know is ours, everything else depends on fortune. Let small-minded men envy the rich, that is those whose coffers are rich but not their minds. Warn your fellow students to beware of . . . the attractions of pleasure and the noisome fever of the mind given to opinion rather than knowledge . . .
The tree of knowledge, even if it seems to have rather bitter roots, brings forth the

sweetest possible fruit. Let them remember too that there will never be too much of this fruit because there is never enough . . . In feeding the mind we ought to imitate gluttons and the covetous, who always fix their attention on what is still left. What is there further?

The Lord of life says 'No man, having put his hand to the plough, and looking back, is worthy of reward.' You have heard too of that woman who, because she turned back, was changed into a pillar. You have also heard how Orpheus, when he looked back, lost Eurydice; in other words his depth of judgment. Ineffective and empty handed is the hunter who goes backwards rather than forwards.

The last sentence was true, he thought, but fatigue was claiming him. He must sleep, for the rest of the group would be here early in the morning. Dousing the light he turned in the empty bed and welcomed oblivion.

2

There was the sound of the wind flapping the sides of the marquee. A muffled banging somewhere. A woman's voice was murmuring in the background, 'She's gone to sleep. I can't understand it, she's gone to sleep and her husband is dying.'

Ellie was making efforts to wake but she was rigid; paralysed but sentient. Under her she could feel the silk layers. Her white dress crumpled on the red damask of the Chesterfield. Her head nestled upon a pale satin cushion, which smelt of damp; the hair across her eyes soft-focussing the world beyond. With effort she looked up at the huge Gainsborough portrait of the fourth Lady Portham. She was a beautiful reproach; dressed in white satin with a red silken cape slipping from her shoulders. Then she was away, looking at herself through a camera lens. The soft young thing on the sofa with her shoes kicked off. Peaceful while all around was pandemonium. Andrew's ashen face and people beginning to scream, 'It's time for the burial and she's still asleep.'

A draught was banging her shutter. Ellie scratched around for the light switch as the geese outside her window squawked in the dark. It was only six a.m. and there was not a thread of light beyond the embrasure. She was sweating profusely; not that she wasn't used to that at her time of life. She was, however, surprised that her dreams had followed her here. Last night she had gone to bed with such a sense of renewal. What had pulled Andrew up from his grave?

Ellie went to the tiled bathroom to wipe her face and cool her damp body. She pulled her hair back and looked in the mirror. Only a few grey hairs and her face, although networked with fine lines, was still good; high cheekbones, deep brown eyes set in the pale and freckled skin. Andrew had loved her full lips, kissed them hard when he made love to her. She thought of herself at Benfield Hall all those years ago.

They had only been married a year and already Dominic was on the way when they moved up to Derbyshire. Andrew was thirty-eight by then and determined to have his children before he was forty. She was just a child of twenty-three barely out of college and with only a few months of work under her belt. They'd moved because Andrew had got a job as Land Agent at Crickwell, one of the large estates. The place had passed through many hands — from aristocracy to biscuit manufacturer and, in their time, it was owned by wealthy Americans. Now Ellie realised what an isolating time it had been. Andrew spent his time pacing the boundaries or communing with other estate owners and she was with the children at home. Sadie had arrived in short order just ten months after Dominic. True, they were invited to some lavish parties, especially at neighbouring Benfield, but whilst they weren't treated as labourers they were not entirely embraced as 'our kind' either. Andrew fared better because he was older and had had an interesting past. He'd taken his time finding a career, preferring to travel the world and enjoy life to the full.

Ellie didn't have the things that bonded men, like dogs or territory. The women she met were generally older and exasperated that she wasn't interested in bridge or Harvey Nics. After a few desultory invitations to coffee or tea they stopped asking. They certainly weren't that happy to have her brood sicking up over the Aubusson. So at gorgeous parties she would look too young, too slight, and be condemned to sleep upon a sofa in a corner.

She wasn't slight now. Actually she was rather glad that middle age had given her girth, both physical and emotional. At her more conformist times she took up diets or exercise but she didn't really like the feeling of being lightweight; it belied her experience. She'd had a friend at school who was small, petite. From her own height of five foot six she'd envied Penny then: watching the boys clustering around her desperate to protect and, she realised now, dominate. Perhaps that was part of choosing Andrew.

Ellie resolved not to wallow and determined upon a walk before breakfast. The light was now an apricot yellow at the horizon, the stars were put away. She wouldn't even shower and could look forward to that after her walk. There was no one by the desk that acted as reception as she passed through, pleased that her soft soles made no sound on the flagstones. She descended to the courtyard; there was only the slightest change of temperature as she moved out of the shade into the early sun. The way she saw that it warmed the colour of her skin and clothes made her perceive a heat far beyond the truth. She strode out of the iron gates and across into the olive groves, breathing in pulses and feeling lightened in her sturdy body. She had only managed a few minutes of this when she saw a figure coming towards her and she was irritated by the intrusion. It was the man she'd seen last night, white haired and gently shambolic in appearance.

'Ah, hello. Are you here with the garden course?' he greeted her in the Queen's English.

Ellie nodded.

'I'm Jonathan Hunter.' He extended a hand, pale and soft and nicely cared for.

'The doctor,' said Ellie

'Well, yes, but retired as of this year.' He smiled. 'And then I was more of a research scientist rather than a hands-on type of doctor.'

Ellie didn't really want to hear more of his CV at this point so she angled her body along the path and said breezily, 'That sounds fascinating. Perhaps you'll tell me more over one of our dinners. If you'll excuse me now I've just been longing for a walk.'

'Of course. So good to be out alone with one's thoughts isn't it?' He smiled again and almost doffed an imaginary hat. Ellie walked on with just a scintilla of guilt attached to her parting back.

★ ★ ★

That party at Benfield had started well, she remembered. At the door they were greeted by beautiful boys ready to receive the Burberrys and furs. The flowers in the entrance hall spouted up from an urn — the scale of which she had last seen in Trafalgar Square; it was massed with lilies pouring their scent over the incomers. But despite this grandeur she felt calm and unintimidated. When she came across her in one of the inner reception rooms Lady Portham even kissed her lightly on the cheek. It was a dream, not offered to many girls of her background, to sit on an embroidered chaise-longue and watch the beautiful and the rich slide past. They unsettled the piles of rose petals scattered on tables with the draught from their coming and going. Andrew was at her side as they sipped champagne and were offered canapés off silver gilt platters. The feeling of wellbeing climbed higher.

It was only later, when she had been divided from him by the seat planner — the pen is mightier than the sword, she thought — that things declined. She was seated next to a doctor, a little older than Andrew, who was very fond of sport. Ellie was neither of a scientific nor a physical persuasion and the conversation was like thick gesso falling to earth in static lumps. Soon he turned to the woman on his other side. He wouldn't remember her name or face, just as now, years on, she had forgotten his.

The sun did have warmth to it now as she took strong strides up through the olive terraces. It was like climbing a giant's stairway and her thigh muscles felt the unusual sensation of work. She began to talk to herself, or maybe it was God, a string of glorious drivel; thanks for the earth and the olives, the feeling of being alive and warm and independent. And then she looked up to see, sitting two terraces above her and smoking a rollup, Salvatore. While her face burned his was all disinterested calm. A braceleted wrist rested on one of his bent knees as he drew the smoky paper from his mouth with the other hand.

'*Buon giorno Ellie, dove vai?*' She knew enough Italian to know that he had used the familiar form of the verb. She clambered her way through the language foothills. At least her struggle covered her embarrassment. He patted the dusty ground next to him and she climbed up to sit by his side. The words continued, he seemed to understand, and her mind began to feel like her thigh muscles, loosened and grateful. Ellie asked questions too and learned that Salvatore worked as a garden designer, mainly for those who wanted instant history. He'd been running the historical courses now for seven years. He had grown up children with their own successful careers and a lovely wife who was away a lot, running a fashion empire. Francesca was his wife's niece and completely devoted to Palazzo Michele and to him. Wasn't that '*perfetto*?' Ellie, awed, unwashed, rumpled, thought it sounded pretty good. She watched Salvatore unwrap his long legs and raise himself from the ground. He looked perfectly groomed even after sitting in dust. Breakfast would begin in thirty minutes but, he assured her as he looked down at her, there was no hurry. She must spend some time alone with her thoughts. Ellie allowed a decent interval before she headed back to the shower.

★ ★ ★

Breakfast had been spent eyeing up the newcomers from the safety of a table shared with Max and Nerine. Doctor Jonathan didn't appear, however. By eleven o'clock in the *salotto* seats were arranged in a semicircle for Salvatore's first lecture. Now they were all to select name badges from a marble side-table and begin to find out more about each other. Salvatore appeared in the room and ushered them to their seats. As he greeted the settling company Ellie scanned the group; there must have been fifteen.

'It would be good to hear something about you and why you have chosen this course,' Salvatore began and deferred with a slight bow to the first on the arc. She was a lady in her mid-sixties who had come with another three women friends — who all beamed and shifted slightly as she talked — because they loved gardening. They belonged to the RHS at home and were eagerly anticipating the visits to gardens. More information flowed from more participants but Ellie only attended to the faces that took her fancy. She listened when Doctor Jonathan Hunter spoke of his need to fill retirement with stimulating projects and the marvellous interface between art and science that came with the study of gardens. Salvatore nodded and jotted down notes. Nerine and Max entertained the rest as they had done last night. Herself, she didn't mention Andrew, only her painting, the fact that she had a large and well-loved garden in the Cotswolds and that she adored Italy. Salvatore made no notes. Next was Mrs Clements. This morning she looked chic in a neat black dress and leather sandals, her sunglasses pushed up and sweeping back her streaked blonde hair. Ellie had felt good in her loose linen until she saw Jane Clements.

'I've always had a love of history.'

With a capital H thought Ellie.

'At home I have a development company in London and as you know,' she looked around at the assembled company, engaging them with her smiling mouth, 'gardens are such a selling point these days and I'm here to learn about formal design.' She pouted very slightly in Salvatore's direction and nodded towards the murmurs of assent. Ellie watched her exchanging some words with her neighbour and patting his arm after a shared confidence. She was probably just forty; not yet on the downslide of the big dipper of age.

Salvatore also questioned two married couples; they seemed to reply as a block. In fact later in the course not much of them was seen beyond the lectures and visits. It seemed the foursome had friends from their days in the diplomatic service living nearby. The remaining two men, Slater and Brad, were in their twenties, earnest about the integrity of design and on the threshold of setting up a Landscape Business back home in the States. Was it fair to label them as gay? Ellie fought the inclination. Salvatore was gracious and thankful for the information and now prepared to keep his promise of the previous night.

'And as for me,' he began and continued with his education, his family circumstances and how he had begun to teach. 'For us Italians our culture is very important. It is even a word that cannot be used lightly. For instance in England or America you might talk about a 'drug culture'. We could not and would not think of allying two such words. Culture to us is about all that is best and valued and that is what I hope to introduce you to in these weeks here.' He rested his arm upon the mantelshelf and lightly fingered a piece of porcelain. 'I will try to show you the very finest parts of our past and how good design remains relevant to our present: I also design gardens for clients here and abroad but they are hopefully not just pastiches. For garden design is more than plagiarism or physical lines upon paper or ground; it is a philosophy that engages your heart and your mind.'

Ellie looked around to see how this epiphany had been received. Max was staring at his own hands and she couldn't judge his reaction. Nerine was upright, attentive, an angel's smile on her lips. Jonathan looked thoughtful and the 'boys' were almost wetting themselves; they were straining forward like puppies on a leash. Jane Clements' hand was still; no thoughts were filling the pages of her designer notebook. From everyone else there was a gentle passivity.

'*Allora*. I would like you to go away into the gardens or grounds and write down what you think a garden is, what we need to make a garden and how we use our gardens. You have half an hour before lunch and after eating we will meet up again here for sharing ideas.'

They disassembled obediently and Ellie felt Max's hand on her back guiding her. 'I think we should have a glass of something to lubricate the mind, don't you?'

Ellie smiled up at him and nodded as they detoured to the bar. With crisp Pinot Grigio in their hands they walked out into the terrace garden. Members of the group were ranged along its straight gravel paths. The 'ladies' had realised that there was little respite to be found from the searing midday sun under the regiment of huge potted lemons that were casting shadows of pattern rather than real shade. They passed Max and Ellie on their way back to the drawing room.

'Too hot, dears,' they sighed.

'Not for me,' said Ellie.

'Nor me,' said Max.

Having settled at a table with their pens they began to brainstorm. The wine began to blur the edges rather pleasantly and Ellie had just come up with the thought that a garden is a statement of personality/fashion/wealth/status when Jane's voice interrupted the flow.

'How very clever of you to think about wine. Where did you find that?'

Max immediately volunteered to act as waiter while Jane parked herself in the third seat.

'I do so wish I had a gift like yours,' she said.

'What gift?'

'Artistic — the painting I mean!'

'Oh, that. Well it's a mixed blessing. It can be either wonderful or a real struggle. At the moment I haven't painted seriously for nearly two years.'

'I think I might be an artist manqué. I spend a lot of time with colour and form when I'm doing my renovations.' Jane delivered this whilst adjusting her dark glasses.

Max put a large glass down in front of Jane and elicited a vixen squeal of pleasure.

Ellie pulled her dress over her knees which now resembled a pond wherein a stone had been thrown; the rings of wrinkles radiated from her kneecaps. Jane had no such problem, she noted.

'OK girls, let's get some ideas down before lunch,' said Max.

And they did.

Back in the cool of the *salotto* after lunch, which she and Max had chosen to eat in the heat of the garden, Ellie felt the sun pricking in her skin and the wine's effects slipping away. She nestled into the same sofa as before. A headache was building itself behind her eyes and she closed them, better to hear Salvatore's voice.

'I hope you had time to think a little before lunch.'

She knew he was smiling from the way he was speaking.

'Ladies and Gentlemen, I only want to set you off along the right path, preferably lined with budding ideas, before this day ends.'

He explained how tomorrow they would be more serious and have a lecture and a visit. It all sounded blissfully passive and Ellie inhaled the frankincense scent of damp plaster.

'But now, what is a garden?'

A blank space and then the querulous voice of one of the ladies offered a place to grow flowers, a place to relax. Her contribution was followed by more and more, crossing and masking each other. Ellie decided she must join in and opened her eyes to find Salvatore looking directly at her. She struggled to sit straight.

'A show of wealth and power,' she said.

Salvatore gave a general nod as the voices petered out.

'Ellie's point is very interesting,' Salvatore said.

But many begged to differ. A female half of one of the couples bristled slightly as she drew everyone's attention to small town gardens or allotments which were purely practical places for food growing.

Salvatore nodded again but gently pointed out that it was true up to a point but originally allotments had been a Victorian invention of the Church to keep the working man out of trouble and gainfully employed. And how many allotment owners now were actually working men? In his time in Oxford, he said, most of those working the allotments were Dons. But of course she was right to bring in agriculture. Gardens developed from agricultural practices and the highest need of a growing plant is irrigation. Where the great pleasure gardens began, in the fertile crescent of Mesopotamia, irrigation was possible for those who had the technology and the wealth to put it into place. Ergo, they were the ones with power. And widening the point from the specific to the general, even if you thought of a simple thing like planting a new and different species of imported plant in your garden today it would mean you belonged to a culture with the wealth to provide the transport infrastructure.

Salvatore's words sparked off inter-group debate. Max wholeheartedly believed that the best gardens were the ones that cost money. Designers and hard landscaping and mature topiary all meant big bucks and he was all for spending his hard earned lucre on giving himself and others pleasure.

'Ah, almost an Epicurean.' Ellie heard Salvatore comment but Max missed it; he was warming to his subject of himself as a patron of the arts.

Nerine sighed as she recorded the passing of her family estate with its beautiful gardens. 'Bottom line is, we ran out of money, Duggie and I.'

Slater and Brad looked saddened, doe-eyed.

'But we had a bloody good time doing it!' Nerine burst into a laugh that temporarily left the boys in an emotional void.

'It is better for you to be free of fear lying on a bed of straw, than to have a golden couch and a lavish table and be full of trouble,' Salvatore quoted Epicureus.

Ellie thought she heard someone say 'shit'.

★ ★ ★

It had been a tiring day. As he sat at his office desk, Salvatore reflected that he always found the first day a strain. You were giving, giving, giving. Fifteen on the course; it was a large number to be able to attend to each one personally. That's why he liked to start the day in the olive groves gathering strength from the ground. It only looked like dust but it fed the ancient trees and he felt it fed him. He'd been a little irritated when first Jonathan Hunter and then Ellie had come across him but then he'd decided to give in early to his public role and quite enjoyed his conversations.

Ellie's widowhood explained her a little. He was always interested in the purposes of the group members. Some came with friends and his teaching was an interesting but dispensable adjunct to their holiday. Some came to suck every last piece of information from him so that they would become worthier people: others were there to demonstrate their knowledge to him. A few wanted to make sure they were his favourite student or the 'most popular group member'. He could see Jane Clements working on the latter and it seemed to be going down well with young Max. He'd watched the boy looking at her and later, even seen his eyes straying to the velvet seat on which she'd sat, her imprint clearly left there. The physicality unsettled Salvatore. Why he dubbed Max a boy he wasn't sure, for he signalled his manhood in every way he could. There was superiority too. Salvatore read the subtext of Max's words to Slater and Brad; he had to let them know that wealth outshone aesthetics every day. Then there was that little episode when Max debunked his quotation of Epicurus; no doubt that had made Salvatore see him as immature. Maybe he deserved to be deflated. Salvatore always wondered whether his garden courses roamed too far into philosophical territory. It wasn't to everyone's taste.

Lunch had been interesting; Max had found his way around the drinks swiftly. There was always one who made you regret the free wine policy. Salvatore knew the economics just about worked, and they certainly needed to: running Palazzo Michele was a financial struggle, but the fall out from well-lubricated guests was more difficult to handle. He had watched Ellie taking up with Max and he surprised himself by being just a touch offended by her drowsiness in the afternoon session. It was an unlikely coupling. He wouldn't have thought that either of them would be attracted to each other. Perhaps he could see Max's motivation; he was obviously someone who liked women and maybe Ellie's slight reticence was a challenge. But why Ellie should fall for such crude charm baffled him. He shrugged off the feeling. On the whole he was heartened by the group; a good spread of characters. Salvatore mentally edited them into a cast list. One day he'd write a screenplay; probably a murder mystery set in the Palazzo — and Max would be the first victim. Victims always seemed to have a lot to say for themselves before they were cut off in their prime. He'd have liked Maria to be here so they could laugh about this little fantasy; perhaps he'd telephone her later. Salvatore checked his watch; no, that would be no good, she'd be at a reception — or was it a fashion show — tonight? He imagined her, in her immaculate clothes, a glass in her hand, easy with the crowd. He could see her with her head back, the long throat stretched out and her red mouth opened wide to laugh. It wouldn't mean anything to her, his little joke; she needed to be here to understand.

He was grateful to her, he really was; without the money she earned there was no way they could have hung on to the Palazzo. The family home had always been important to them both. Maria had been so clever, so creative at stretching the budget.

And when the children were young the place was crammed with their friends. He was impressed by the way she could get them all to participate, to have fun doing the things she was doing. It was different for him. When he had a task to do he needed to do it alone. He tried to set aside time for his children when his work was through; it just seemed that when he had the time for them they didn't have time for him. He remembered their energy and the noise that echoed around these grand rooms. He saw a picture of himself walking in on a massive jam-making and tomato-bottling session where, above the children's voices, Maria supervised with ease the pouring of molten fruit while batting away drunken wasps. He smiled thinking of her then, in her sticky apron, her dark hair swept up into a band like a factory worker, but still the slap of bright lipstick at her mouth.

It had been his failure to provide enough income that had precipitated a crisis point. Maria hadn't buckled, she'd seemed more than happy to rise to the challenge. It was just breathtaking the way she didn't sit down when she was knocked back. And now all her hard work had created a business that employed people, hundreds indirectly. He knew she thrived on it and anything that made her happy was fine. All he wished was for her presence a little more.

Salvatore looked back to his books. He had taught this course so often he needed to enliven it for his own sake. And what were those words of Ficino? *In feeding the mind we ought to imitate gluttons and the covetous, who always fix their attention on what is still left.* This group might appreciate a little broadening of the subject matter. Salvatore had just rediscovered a book about the mythological Botticelli paintings and was once more captured by the artist's imagination. But it wasn't solely Botticelli's imagination that had created *Primavera* or *The Birth of Venus*, it was a layering of culture and ideas and influences that had brought the paintings to fruition. That was another reason to re-read Ficino. Some scholars were convinced that a letter Ficino wrote to Lorenzo di Pierfrancesco de' Medici directly inspired the commissioning of *Primavera*. Young Lorenzo was a mere adolescent when he commissioned it; he simply must have had guidance from a higher authority to do that. Salvatore imagined the boy sitting in the splendour of his Palazzo at Castello, visited by Ficino; the power balance would have been an interesting one, one man being courted for his brains, the other for his wealth.

Castello, of course, was one of the major gardens that he took his groups to see. Maybe it was a tenuous link to teach them about Botticelli's paintings on a garden history course but the humanist philosophy that inspired it would help them understand the broader picture; after all it had infused every type of creativity, including the garden design of the time. Salvatore felt happier, contemplating such ideas. He liked to live inside his head, which was not to say that he didn't like people, it was just that he needed space to be alone with his thoughts. But the aloneness he craved was subtle. Being without Maria to this extent was too crude and he felt the rawness of his state as he made for bed once more.

3

Later that first afternoon Ellie gave in to fatigue and went to bed. When she rose about five p.m. she walked into the Palazzo garden which commanded views of the city far below and the smudged hills beyond. The plan was formal. In the centre of the garden was a round pool, the water a soft green colour. It was the node of crossing gravel paths that created quadrants. Low box hedges made enclosed shapes within these segments and height came from citrus trees in large terracotta pots. The periphery of the garden was bounded by one path which, once you began to travel it, took you back to where you had begun. On one side the garden was shadowed by a tall retaining wall that stopped the wooded hillside above from tumbling on the perfect creation below. In the shade the stone glowed a ghostly blue from the copper sulphate that had been sprayed on the covering vines. The other long side of the garden merely had a flimsy iron rail to protect you from a drop down to the plunging road.

The focus of this place was the watery centre and, although some sentinels of cypress seduced you into searching for the garden's farthest end, when you got there it was a disappointment of clustered pots. Ellie imagined that in its prime there would have been more; steps down to another terrace and maybe yet another. Now it was curtailed by a balcony rail. The long view was to glass factory roofs and train tracks. But there was no doubt this was an ambulatory space. Walk and think. Walk and pray. Walk and listen. Walk.

'Ellie! That's where you are. Do you want to do a bit of sightseeing with me?'

Max broke into her reverie and for a moment she was irritated. Trying to work out where the feeling came from she computed rapidly. It was in her nature to say no first; she liked to reflect upon things at length; sometimes she reflected for so long that the time to make a decision just faded away. Here was an opportunity to say yes to a perfectly open request. He wanted her company, no doubt because she seemed a comfortable, unthreatening prospect. It was friendly. She could look back or go forward.

'OK, where do you want to go?'

There was a *monastero* nearby which according to the guidebook was worthy of inspection. Max drove confidently along narrow lanes. Once he had to pull over to let a local driver pass; the man did not raise his hand in thanks but while Ellie bristled at the lack of manners, Max didn't seem to notice.

They needed to climb to find the monastery and finally parked in a cobbled square on the side of the hill. The sun was declining and the warmth was just right as they stepped from the microclimate of the car. With her palm, Ellie smoothed her other arm from shoulder to wrist, enjoying the softness. Max followed her lead by tracing her arm with his fingers and she started at his familiarity. She was unsure how to interpret the gesture, but it triggered her imagination. He simply smiled, and followed up with a jovial pat on the back. He was nearly a decade younger — maybe men of his age just were more touchy-feely.

They climbed, labouring, stopping, admiring the view that receded from golds and greens to violets and blues; the horizon swathed in a mistiness that fused hills and sky. At the building, which glowed earthy red in the evening light, they had to stop and ring a cast iron bell. They were shown inside by a monk who spoke tersely in Italian, offered them a map in rudimentary English, directed them to a wall safe for donations and then left them alone. They set to walk the cloisters.

Ellie turned to Max. 'Do you know that

after all my studies in art history and architecture I've only now absorbed the fact that cloisters were designed for uninterrupted walking whilst praying. So the flow of devotion wouldn't be disturbed.'

'Oh, really?' He was unimpressed.

'Well, *I* thought it was a revelation.'

'Good for you.' Max laughed as they turned off into an inner courtyard, already being circumnavigated by another couple of tourists. There was a fountain in its centre and the periphery was planted with troughs of flowers. One or two of them had handwritten notices attached to them.

'What does this mean, Mrs Bilingual?' said Max, pointing to a note on some scarlet geraniums.

'*Non mi mutilate. Abbiate rispetti. Sono qui per lodare Dio.* Don't wreck me. Have respect. I am here to praise the Lord,' Ellie translated. 'And so am I,' she added.

Max glanced at her sideways and moved on.

After, they chose to have dinner at a local restaurant. In truth Max chose and tried to persuade her that they would have plenty more days to bond with the other course members. Ellie was slightly uncomfortable with this turn of events; she felt like a truant. But Max was the driver and she the passenger. The restaurant was on the edge of the city and filled with Italians engaging. Ellie usually found that word overused but here it was perfectly descriptive. It made her imagine a vast flywheel, its teeth meshing into the next cog, touching, both moving over one another face to face. These Italians were engaging with one another by patting and touching, pinching and kissing cheeks and talking up close; fat male hands were gripping female waists. Their language was paradoxically formal, youngsters adopting the respectful form of address with their elders whilst smiling coquettishly. Also physical was the relationship with their food. As Ellie and Max sat with their Punt e Mes waiting for pasta they watched. One man stuffed in his meat and potatoes so fast, so seamlessly he hardly had time to argue with his wife. An advanced gastronomic scoliosis made his body hunch forward over his plate. He never straightened up, even at the very end of the meal when he argued with the waiter.

'How long did you say you'd been widowed?'

It was a starkly intimate question to go with aperitifs and Ellie bridled.

'Two years.'

'Any parents still around?'

'No, my mother died in the same year as

46

my husband and my father died when he was just sixty.'

'That's amazing. So your husband died at almost the same age as your father.'

He'd remembered that fact about her life, she briefly noted to herself. Such a little sign of interest and yet she felt her confidence rising. The drink helped. Suddenly she was the class show-off.

'History repeats itself, so they say,' said Ellie, 'in fact I know a short poem about that, 'History repeats itself/It has to because nobody listens'.'

Max smiled a polite smile and nodded.

'So Max, what's your motivation in life?' Ellie wanted more of Max revealed.

'To be self reliant. To run a good business that enables me to do pleasurable things.'

'Like what?'

'I want to travel more. I collect art.'

She was surprised; for a moment her image of him was punctured. However it turned out to be serious investment art. Amongst the Frink and Picasso drawings was a lot of 'Brit Art' too. He talked of the White Cube Gallery.

'What is it that makes you buy art, Max?'

'I like to look at the stuff, or at least to know it's there. And I like to sponsor the young artists: it's a good feeling knowing that you're encouraging creativity.'

Ellie quizzed him about some of the pieces. There was, he said, a video installation of naked people aiming stones at a row of tin cans, over and over again followed by scenes of copulation.

Ellie struggled. 'Did you fall in love with this piece then?' she asked, trying hard to erase any overtone of disgust or sarcasm.

'Well. Not exactly. I'd say it's more an intellectual exercise; there's some impressive thinking behind it, you know.' Max stepped an inch or two away from her and, folding his arms, recited perfectly. 'The artist wanted to represent how wasteful it is for humanity to destroy or deconstruct when within there is the ability to be wholly creative.'

'And do you sit and watch this piece of work regularly?'

Max smiled at Ellie as if to say are you serious? 'No. Actually it's in a vault at the gallery. I let them show it when they want.'

She was quiet for a moment or two, fingering her glass. She was trying to crystallise in her own mind the reason for the existence of any art at all. It was almost impossible to put into words. Perhaps there was a place for crude ideas, for shock value in art, but she believed you touched the human soul most through beauty.

'And you think this is the best possible way an artist could convey these ideas. Do you?'

Max was watching her expression. He would see her waiting steadily for an answer. She could see him mentally gathering his cloak around him, ready for the onslaught. He was unable to say he really believed it.

'What are you getting at? Ideas not craftsmanship or something? I'm sure there was skill in making the video.' He tailed off and she felt almost sorry for him. Andrew had put her in positions like this. Disadvantaged. Feeling unsure that her opinion counted against the wisdom of the learned. But Max was a man. She almost counted the seconds it would take for him to rally. He didn't look at her as he talked; his voice a notch up in pitch and volume. 'Well. It's straightforward. It's using a medium everyone understands. Why not?'

'Would everyone understand that, Max? What would a child make of that piece of violence and sex?'

He tried to dismiss her. It was art, he said. It needed some discernment. It probably communicated a damn sight more to the person — yes even the child — of today than all these Renaissance canvases filled with Venuses and Graces. He looked at her in defiance.

49

'So what's your open-minded definition of good visual art, Ellie?' He was close to sneering. She just ignored the tone.

'I think it's the artist's duty to make art beautiful and I think you need technique and skill for that. OK, maybe the average viewer wouldn't understand the entire meaning of a Renaissance painting but most can appreciate the humanity of the faces in it, its loveliness of form, and the talent of its creator. Beauty endures. Will your video endure, do you think?'

She crossed her arms and sat straight in her chair. Finally she filled the heavy silence. 'I think not. It's not art; it's a temporary statement.'

Max was watching her with an expression between condescension and admiration. It fired her.

'The artist at best should uplift human feelings — at worst she should do no harm.'

Even as she was speaking Ellie reflected she was only now working out what she really believed. 'So you want my personal definition of Art? To me it's a spontaneous reaction to something higher than myself. The work expresses that first idea but only after I've gone through a creative process. So, although the finished piece is important it's the 'doing of it' that keeps me, or any artist, working.'

She'd gone off at a tangent and she'd lost him. Ellie watched Max trying to focus his attention as he finished off his wine. The fish had dropped the bait and swum downstream. She threw her napkin into the centre of the table. She half laughed. 'Oh I don't know!'

Max pulled her hand across the table, rucking the linen cloth. 'I'd rather hear more about you, Ellie.'

Ellie thought, if only you listened to what I thought you would hear more about me, but decided to shrug off the mismatch.

'Oh I'm very boring really. I suppose I didn't so much choose the path of being a wife and mother first, rather I just took a slip road and ended up on the motorway.'

'You've kept your skills going though. You paint. And I presume that you work to support yourself now.'

It was true. Ellie had tried to keep a thread of herself continuous. She'd even kept her own surname when they married, quite a feat back then. But what had seemed, at the beginning of her life, like a sturdy reel of yarn all ready to be woven, now felt like separate flimsy strands. She still couldn't see the whole broadcloth.

'Yes. I teach art. Adults mainly.' She heard herself going into a well-rehearsed set of lines that follow the 'What do you do?' question.

Paraphrased, it was how rewarding she found discovering the potential in people; how much more attentive most adults were because they really wanted to learn. What she didn't share with him was how she'd be unable to teach anyone young, because if she found talent in them she'd be so jealous that they were just beginning their lives and had the potential to really do something with it, she couldn't bear it. As she listened to the subtext in her head and watched Max, she felt pretty worthless. She believed she could see his mental judgment upon her in the way he lifted his glass and shifted in his seat. Written off as uninteresting and unenterprising. An ordinary life. The best strategy now would be to divert attention.

'But Max, you're in a creative line of business. What exactly is your job?'

Max inhaled, expanding his chest, spreading his arms, his face adopting the 'I know I'm damned clever but no applause please' look.

'I'm just much more on the number crunching side these days. It's a family business, you know. Begun by my stepdad. My mum's part of it too.'

'If I think of society florists I'd think the name Penman-White,' encouraged Ellie.

'Yes. All those smart weddings and parties

give us our high profile but actually we do a hell of a lot with property developers. It's long-running contracts that give us our money.' Max droned on about margins and P.W.'s property portfolio.

Can't get away from it, thought Ellie. It all comes back to crude figures. She offered her glass for the last of the wine as Max looked around for a waiter. So much for the romance of Italy and soaking herself in intellectual and creative life. She was talking about money. The grassy taste of the white wine seemed to bring her out of her self-pity. Who the hell do I think I am? Some teenager who's disappointed that the first boy I meet doesn't read me Elizabeth Barrett-Browning. Max is a straightforward man, generous — am I not enjoying his money tonight? He's entertaining and what's more, taking the initiative. Not unlike Andrew in many respects; what Andrew wanted he usually got.

'Penny for them.' Max splashed Pellegrino into a glass and the spume caught her cheek.

'Oh, I was just thinking that back home we'd probably never even talk to one another.'

Max composed himself as if to say don't be silly or some such then must have thought better of it and just shrugged. 'Tell me more about home,' he said while waving over the wine waiter.

'My mother left me the house I live in. It's as well she did because my husband hit the financial rocks and we had virtually nothing.' Why had she blurted that out? If it was an antidote to all that money talk it was pretty clumsy.

'What was the problem?' asked Max.

Ellie simply said, 'He was in property.'

Max leaned back and laughed knowingly. 'Say no more,' he said. 'Lots of people have caught colds in the property game. Were you bankrupt?'

Ellie was uncomfortable but didn't know how to avoid such a direct question. 'No. Andrew wouldn't take that route. Although I sometimes wish he had.' Ellie saw Max was waiting for more. She was disturbed by the upsurge of her feelings — maybe she needed some catharsis. 'I'll never forget the one solicitor from the American Bank that came after us, persistent beyond duty. He was cruel.' Her turn to laugh. 'At the time I didn't realise the irony but later I did; his name was Seymour Hopper.'

Max looked at her blankly.

'Hopper is another name for a locust,' she declared and they both laughed at the image of the voracious destroyer. After the tension release Ellie said, 'Look, do you mind, Max if we don't talk about all of . . . that?'

Max nodded and said, 'I grew up with no money.'

Ellie was faced with building up a new picture.

'But when was that . . . I thought you said . . . well, the business and all that?'

'When my mum was on her own with me.'

It figured, thought Ellie and felt warmer towards Max. In fact as they discussed which was worse, to have no money and then to come into it, or to be born with money and then to lose it, she felt Max was being himself for the first time.

Ellie wasn't exactly born with money, she told Max. She had a comfortable middle-class upbringing and was well placed to marry a professional man. Her parents hadn't exactly bet on her marrying someone fifteen years older at the tender age of twenty-three. To them she was still in her childhood. She'd not been a rebellious child ever. In fact, although she would have dearly loved to go to art college she gave in gracefully to her parents' wish for her to pursue an academic Art History course at university. They knew it was the closest they'd ever get her to a 'useful' degree, she laughed. But she also knew they only wanted the best for her and she was a cautious only child, not prone to following her passions. In fact she was not sure she had passions in her younger years and she certainly couldn't identify them now.

'You do yourself down,' said Max, strafing her with his gaze. 'Life has just thrown a few curves at you. Don't let the way you feel now rewrite your past. You might not feel it but I reckon I can see a very passionate woman in there.'

Ellie flushed, feeling like an unprepared adolescent. Maybe he hadn't written her off after all; this was an unexpected sensitivity. How many years had it been since a man had shown such interest and she was free to respond? She hadn't spoken, her jaw sagged.

Max laughed. 'Look at you! Don't you believe me? A woman without passion wouldn't talk about art like you just did.'

He paused and Ellie was aware she must be watching him hungrily, waiting to hear kind and good things.

'Nor would she talk about teaching like you just did. Whether you think you're just going through the motions or not, I think you really care about those people and want to give them the message of art. You're an evangelist!'

It was Ellie's turn to laugh. 'No way. Evangelists don't say 'this is what I think but then again I also think the opposite and of course it's up to you to decide, and I'd love to hear your point of view and I'm willing to be corrected,' which is what I do. They say 'this is what I think and you're damned if you don't think it too!' '

Max looked doubtful. 'You certainly don't come over as someone in two minds. And anyway, personally I've always found that the best road to winning others over is the path of gentle persuasion.'

And when he took her hand once again she felt more inclined to leave it there. After a while he spoke again. 'I just think there's no harm in trying to adapt yourself so that the listener is predisposed to listen.'

Ellie sat and tried to work out on exactly what level they were talking. 'How do you do that, Max?'

'Find things in common. Identify with the other person.'

'That's not always possible, is it?

'I think so. Just now you more or less said we wouldn't touch each other with a bargepole if we'd met at home. But here we are finding a meeting point.'

He raised her hand to his lips and kissed it. She was deluged with reactions; mortified that her hand with its veins and imperfect nails should be so closely inspected, guilty that when Max dug deeper she wouldn't meet his specifications and yet, at the polar opposite, flattered and grateful and ready to accept whatever affection was thrown in her way.

She retracted her hand. 'More like we're prowling around outside each other's front doors.'

'At least they're open a little. Ellie, I know you had me down for a smooth but money-loving peasant at the beginning of this meal, but I hope you might have got a bit beyond that now.' He raised an eyebrow and tilted his glass at her and all she could do was smile.

What was she doing feeling attracted to such a young man? She had to remind herself that she was 'on the rebound'. That phrase had always seemed to her quite benign; she imagined a figure slamming into a huge rubber ball and bouncing high into the air, the soft sides simply propelled the tossed creature into the ether, no sign of a landing place. Bereavement was more like being crashed on to jagged rocks; in a way it was safer to cling on to the rock than risk being swirled by a cruel sea onto even more piercing crags.

'What happened to the smile?'

'I'm sorry Max. I have to say I was thinking about my husband.'

Max leaned over and stroked her face.

'Come on Ellie, tell me all about him and then you might be able to look forward and not back. Just begin at the beginning.'

Her guts turned to liquid then, seeing his face so near hers. Finding comfort with Max would be just natural. The familiarity made her want to surrender, for, in the way he tilted his head and narrowed his eyes, she felt Andrew.

* * *

So, for Max, she recalled the day she'd met Andrew. She was out of the office with her boss, Nigel, to arrange a contents sale in the Cotswolds. At twenty-two Ellie's first job out of university was with a Sale Room in Cheltenham. Her degree had been good but somehow she hadn't had the push to scissor herself into those coveted jobs with Christies or Philips in London. She'd wanted to be near her mother and move at the pace of the country as a balm after Daddy's sudden death. Life simply continued. What she didn't share with Max was her feeling of numbness at the time. It was like walking on water; she could move forward but the water didn't touch her. It was a feeling she had to relive when she lost Andrew and then, cruelly, her mother.

'Go on.' Max was prompting her out of her reverie to continue.

So she described this day as June hot; remembering to herself how she had driven through countryside that was a cliché of Englishness — green and curving with a lush topping of trees. The villages and towns looked like an extension of the land, she told Max; the buildings not built but grown. All immaculate in their livery of honeyed stone. It was remarkable how she remembered every detail of that journey; driving up the main street of the market town and seeing the Cotswold hills as a flickering backdrop in the heat.

In the cool stone barn that acted as salerooms she had labelled her last lot just as the public had begun to press in. Nigel always called them the 'hoi polloi' but these first were a group of equine ladies with cut glass accents. 'Don't get excited,' Nigel had winked and said under his breath, 'Asset Rich and Cash Poor.' Max laughed at this. Ellie remembered how she had been smiling to herself when half a dozen men in suits walked in. They could have been dealers. They certainly had the swagger of the professional. Two were smoking cigars, probably the legacy of a business lunch. The tallest man hung in the bright doorway like a daytime bat.

Contre-jour she had thought as she watched his silhouette moving towards her. As the light on him adjusted she took in his face with the flesh carved to his cheekbones and the crow's feet that radiated from translucent eyes as he laughed. His pale summer suit glowed in the gloom. Light had clung to him like some Verocchio angel. Ellie didn't share all the details of this memory with Max but did describe how she had watched him pumping Nigel's hand and hailing him like a long lost friend. Just fleetingly he had looked her way and their eyes met in the middle of this performance.

'You don't forget the very first words of your future husband,' she said to Max.

He was amused by this. 'So what were they?'

'Nigel, good to see you. Come round for a drink after the sale and bring your lovely assistant with you.'

That was their meeting. Later as Nigel walked her round the corner to Andrew's offices he had filled Ellie in. Andrew was a Chartered Surveyor. No he wasn't married. She smiled, remembering his paternal warnings. Lived a full life if you know what I mean. Been around. He was only here because he was helping out an old friend in his business. Couldn't quite see him ever staying in one place. Seemed happy on his own but not without his share of pretty young things on his arm.

'I suppose I should have been warned off by this,' she said to Max. What she didn't go on to tell him was the immediate sequel to this first meeting. Even now she recalled it with some pain — and shame.

★　★　★

Andrew had a flat above the offices that were in a Queen Anne House; its perfect, symmetrical front elevation punctuated by sash windows. The workspace extended to the rear in what had been Victorian schoolrooms. It reminded Ellie of song lyrics 'With a Queen Anne front and a Mary-Ann behind'. As her mood bubbled after several glasses of wine and became even more liberated by Nigel's departure, she quoted them to Andrew. He laughed along with her and complimented her on her own lovely bottom. By eleven they were in bed together. That was totally, absolutely out of character for Ellie but her need to be enveloped, to have the physicality of a man close to her, was too strong. Now, she knew she had justified her actions by believing it was love at first sight. In the morning he said did she realise he was fifteen years older than her but she shrugged off the comment. Her head was filled with the idea that Andrew was 'the one'.

No, what she told Max was that the meeting led to a gradual falling in love. She knew she was massaging the truth into an acceptable version — mainly acceptable to herself. Growing up had made her realise she had begun in the wrong way. If she ever fell in love again she would want a measured start to a relationship. But loving Andrew had been different. All through the marriage, whenever he'd wanted her sexually he'd called her Mary-Ann. It was as though she was severed into wife and whore. Although there was always passion there was little kindness when they had sex. In other respects their interests and backgrounds were compatible and they blended aesthetically. The façade was perfect. Ellie often wondered whether other people's 'being in love' in any way equated with hers. That was the nature of love; it couldn't be quantified. Was it like pain thresholds? We all had different ones and some people could put up with more than others. Were some people also designed to be satisfied with a lower threshold of love? When they met, no doubt Andrew felt it was time to settle down but what compelled them both to take the risk — and partner for life — she couldn't say even now. So many years ago and she could barely recall that first attraction; the flare of salt on a fire. Until today. Until Max.

★   ★   ★

The bathroom French windows were open wide on to the balcony that overlooked the private courtyard. As Salvatore shaved he squinted into the mirror, glad that its silvering had mellowed with age and now reflected back to him a softened image. Because of his height he had to stoop a little to see his face properly. He didn't really mind the bags or the wrinkles; what he didn't want to see was the tiredness or, sometimes on a bad day, the signs of defeat. He mused on last night's dinner. It had been a spirited gathering, *jolly* the English would call it: Almost a full complement, although Salvatore noted that Ellie and Max weren't there. Nerine had conquered the American boys' hearts and they now wanted to do anything they could for her. She was busy trying to persuade them to find some nice Italian girls and this they took in great good part. Salvatore watched Jane Clements as she sat on the sidelines surveying the antics with a world-weary amusement. She was an attractive woman. Stylish. If she'd been walking through an airport it would have been hard to place her nationality; sophisticated European would probably sum her up. She'd stayed up late, drinking and talking on as each one of the group faded away. Her room was adjacent to the private apartments and eventually Salvatore walked her alone to her room where he bade her goodnight with just a stroke of pity in his heart.

Salvatore walked through to his drawing room and pressed a few buttons. The strains of Donizetti floated through the room as he sat down heavily on the sofa in his dressing gown, wiping away the last specks of foam on his face with a towel. As the words penetrated his mind he stared at the painting over the fireplace. He let the warmth of the colours seep into his mind; the ochres, warm yellows and terracottas always had a calming effect upon him. And yet there was an energy and spark in the work too that didn't allow somnolence. Such a simple subject, almost crudely painted; flowers in two vases and pomegranates in a glass bowl all set in front of a landscape of rolling earth that came to a climax in the distant range of mountains and sky. It was the restrained use of cool violets and blues in shadows, flowers and mountains that made him notice the warmth all the more. And the way the artist's hand had overlaid scratched lines on the landscape gave a compelling sense of perspective.

In truth he never knew whether the painted fruits were oranges or pomegranates, but their name figured in the title so they must be. He studied the layers of paint and let his mind unpeel; it took him to his parents. His father had acquired the piece, he was not sure how but from a London gallery he thought. Of the painter he knew only a little more, but he had always felt she must be a good woman. He was probably making the fatal mistake of allying a painter's personality with their work; Ficino had words to say on that. *A painter who makes corrupt use of his art is not necessarily a bad painter because of this, but a bad man. Thus a good painter is not the same as a good man.*

Perhaps it was that she wasn't actually such a good painter, more a sincere one, that he felt drawn to it. When his father had brought the canvas home his mother merely tolerated it but Salvatore took his father's side. He loved the painting. It was only after his parents had both died that he'd been able to move it to where he could see it every day. And there were those enigmatic fruits: As a recalcitrant twelve-year-old he had trailed around the Uffizi with a cultured aunt who bristled with an educating zeal. She had taught him about symbolism. Pagan inter-pretations appealed to his imagination most. The pomegranate was an 'attribute' of Proser-pina; the sweet and seeded fruit symbolised the goddess' return to earth in the spring. Of course, as with all good pagan ideas, Chris-tianity took it to itself and made this representation of spring and rejuvenation into a metaphor of hope in immortality and resurrection. Rejuvenation. Hope. Salvatore felt a dullness of heart and set his unconscious the task of swimming up a layer, into shallower water. He concentrated on the abstraction of composi-tion, pattern and colour; trying to enjoy the merely visual as he had so many times before. In fact the room had been decorated to give this one thing its correct setting. Maria had chosen the ochre colours well. None of them were clear and clean, all had a dull edge to them. But now and again there were punctuation marks of bright lavender and blue.

It reminded him how much he was missing Maria. She'd been preparing for the fashion shows in Milan for over a week and had phoned to say that she didn't have time to get home before another trip to Switzerland. This time they'd hit some huge problems with the collection and she was needed. But after several months Salvatore had become almost resigned to these absences. Maria had pulled off a huge coup and partnered with a Swiss manufacturer to produce her designs. In the end, when work took her away so often, she rented an apartment in Locarno, near the factory. She was talented and good at business and Salvatore had long since allowed her to take over all the financial organisation of their life. She'd had to do a lot of separating out of accounts when her business expanded, and although she'd explained it all meticulously it made his head reel. This year she had domiciled in Switzerland in order to get huge tax benefits and Salvatore had trusted her business sense. Running courses at the Palazzo had been her idea too. A great idea, but sometimes Salvatore wished the teaching didn't tie him to the place so much.

Still, today they would be getting out. He was going to take the group to see Gamberaia. It still had the power to move him even after so many visits. And in the afternoon, when they all had time to rest, he would take the opportunity to go for a swim in the river. Life could be worse, he thought. Which was exactly the point. Life could be dramatically worse. He was living in a beautiful place, running his own work and was as financially secure at the moment as he could possibly be. He wondered why then his spirit was not content.

4

Ellie awoke early but without dreams. Her head was woolly, her tongue furred. She had drunk more than she'd realised. Reminders of Max seeped through. Last night he had delivered her back to her room with a goodnight kiss on her cheek. It confused her, these echoes of young emotions intruding into her middle age. Breakfast was a gift. Bread that bound everything together once more. Bread and no wine. The sweet and liquid jams, the astringent tiny coffees that she drank like a penitence. No Max to face, just the welcome sight of Nerine bobbing in through the tall garden doors.

'Ready to be enlightened darling?' she asked, whooshing her straw hat from her head on to the table beside Ellie.

'Not really.' Ellie smiled up at her. 'I feel rather passive this morning.'

Nerine looked hard into Ellie's face as she sat down and began to brush crumbs from the linen cloth. 'Beginning of the end. Passivity that is,' she said. 'No point in being alive if you're not going to participate.'

'Well, thank you, Nerine, for that bit of

social lubrication!'

They laughed; Nerine with her head back and her throat juddering. 'Come on darling. After lectures I'll give you a crash course in digital photography. You'll be a natural.'

Although Ellie demurred she was glad to be swept along in the wake of Nerine's enthusiasm and she felt the wraith of Andrew's memory loosening its grip. She watched as Nerine gobbled her breakfast, slapping her lips and tongue around the food as though it was manna, and was delighted. Nerine seemed to have such a love for the world it spilled over and touched Ellie. It was a good solar-plexus feeling.

'Don't you want to paint again?' asked Ellie as Nerine wiped her mouth.

'Why should I?'

'I don't know. With photos your creativity is limited by the technology and well, painting's just a much more direct and permanent way of expressing yourself, isn't it?'

'It's obvious you haven't tried working with a computer. You've just bought into that crap about having very little intervention between your creativity and the finished artwork. And permanent? What do you mean? Are you hoping that art will bring you immortality, Ellie? Because I'm not.'

70

In truth Ellie did not know what she thought. The way Nerine spoke her mind would have knocked her back a month or two ago but now the challenge made her see a strand in herself. She needed to hold on to things, to make things permanent. She wondered fleetingly if that was what her religious faith was all about. Life insurance.

'I admire you Nerine. For holding everything so lightly. You just so obviously enjoy the *process* of life.'

'Only because that's all that's left now!' She laughed and rose. 'Come on. Time for edification.'

Seats were arranged for the lecture in the wisteria-covered loggia to one corner of the courtyard. One or two flowers straggled on this late in April. Salvatore gathered them under the wings of chartreuse leaves. Max sauntered in last and nodded proprietorially at Ellie who tried to ignore the intimacy. He sat down next to Jane who, Ellie noted, shifted stylishly to welcome Max's arrival.

'Good morning.' Salvatore's body arced around as he bestowed a smile upon everyone. 'Today we have a treat in store. It is a visit to a garden which rightfully I should probably show you later because it fits better historically.' He watched his audience, giving some kind of acknowledgment to each one.

'But I want to start with it as it will grab your attention, perhaps even your hearts.'

★ ★ ★

The minibus took a sharp turn right amongst tightly packed houses. As the bus swung Ellie looked at Salvatore but he was studying some papers on his lap. Max and Jane were in raucous conversation. Ellie watched the tableau; Jane caressing her own hair and neck as she talked into Max's close face. The driver shifted gear abruptly and the bus juddered and struggled. They were climbing steeply up a winding road with a drop down to olive groves on their right and a high terrace wall on their left. The horn shouted out every few seconds to warn oncoming drivers who, she imagined, would have to be the ones to back up along this terrifying track. Andrew would have driven here. It was only by great force of will that she was driving in Italy.

Nerine, who had been dozing next to her, began to attend. 'How frightful this road is. Nice to be driven isn't it?'

'I'd be terrified if I had to do this,' said Ellie.

'Course you wouldn't. You'd just get on with it. After all everyone would be travelling too slowly for a major crash. The worst thing to happen would probably be a prang.'

'Nerine, I wish I could look at things like you. But if I dented the car I'd be in an agony of shame, especially as it's a hire car.'

'But that's perfect! You're insured and they sort it out. I've had lots of cars in my time because I have little arguments with posts or bollards or other drivers and I've come to the conclusion that cars are simply things to be used and thrown away, like soap!' As they laughed the bus drew into a semicircular lay-by below a towering wall.

Together they saw the garden of Villa Gamberaia at mid-morning, when the sun was high and casting hard shadows. For Ellie the impact of the garden was immediate but she tried to restrict it that day to an intellectual exercise; she listened hard to what Salvatore had to say but she didn't want to let her heart go out to it. She kept under wraps her excitement at its effect upon her. It didn't escape her that she was paralleling her relationships, with Max and with the garden.

Salvatore walked them around for the first hour; pointing out the rationale of the design, the journey of life that was taken by walking the garden. It worked as a place to inhabit but it also made nods towards the landscape beyond. An opening in one hedge framed a view of an olive, a cypress and the distant church. You were meant to pay attention to these symbols of life, death and God. Nor were you unimpressed by the sight of Florence shimmering in the heat way below. Ellie was glad that Gamberaia existed; she knew before she had even left that the beauty of it would sustain her in the future. It gave her joy and pleasure not least because she had no desire to possess it except in her memory.

Later the group splintered and retraced their tour singly or in pairs. Ellie and Nerine were in the lemon garden, on a terrace that was level with the *piano nobile* of the villa. As they were looking across to the windows, shuttered against the searching sunlight, Max found them.

'Hello girls,' he said as he slung his arms around both their shoulders. 'This is why I came on this course. I need look no further, I just want this garden copied back at home, right down to the last detail.'

Nerine slipped her shoulders from under his arm and dipped out of his grasp. 'Do you think a garden like this is likely to integrate with the architecture of your house?' she asked in her bird voice.

Max looked at her, unabashed. Ellie watched the conversation unfold, watched the polarity of the two people who were beginning to mean a lot to her. Max just enjoyed going out and taking what he wanted from life untortured by how he might appear. Ellie feared she could never be like that.

'After all,' Nerine went on, 'This garden was made for the building: it would be almost impossible to recreate such perfection.'

Max shrugged. 'Well, isn't it just great that some classical garden designer has done all the hard work? I'll only have to find someone to adapt perfection. Do you think old Salvatore would be interested?' And saying this he went off in search of him.

Ellie looked at Nerine who was studiedly involved in looking at the paving beneath her feet. 'He's not so bad, Nerine. Not when you talk to him on his own. He just gets a bit carried away in front of the group.'

Nerine batted away an insistent fly and looked at Ellie from under the brim of her huge straw hat. 'I'm sure he can be a sweet little boy but I think he'd be capable of consuming anything within his orbit. Just remember that, my darling.'

Ellie linked arms with Nerine. 'All right, I will!' she smiled as they set off down steps through a sunken garden that linked them back to the long greensward that travelled the length of the house. It was a deliberately stark length of grass, unplanted with anything that might detract from the architecture. Nerine had her reservations about it; she wasn't sure she agreed with Alberti who had demanded that architecture needed to be 'read' without the distraction of growing things.

'It's like a firebreak, seems to me it excludes passion.'

Ellie on the other hand liked the openness and felt that she had need of that kind of clarity. She thought of her own home, every wall clad in some kind of creeper and shrub; well stocked beds to 'soften' the cottage, and thought how unreadable it was.

It wasn't long before Max found them again. Ellie didn't know how to behave in his presence; what degree of intimacy was appropriate at this point? It was strange because she felt the same surge of familiarity that she'd experienced the night before; this sense of coming home comforted her, more, it was leading her on. Or was Nerine right to warn her off? Did she see her clearly as another sad widow succumbing to a clichéd holiday romance? As they wandered the grounds Max wanted to know how she saw the place — he was like a child keen for her opinion, delighted by her approval of things he liked. He pulled her gently along the gravelled paths of the water garden and his touch on her arm was heightened. She'd never taken drugs — all right, maybe smoked a little pot at university and willed herself to be unaffected — but she imagined that this was how they would affect your senses. Everything became important; it was as though every touch or sight or sound was in existence just to fill up some internal reservoir of good feelings. Ellie knew Nerine sensed the rising light in her and guessed that she only wished it might be directed at someone other than Max. But Nerine said nothing beyond that one comment in the lemon garden.

By now the sun was high and hard and Ellie knew she wanted to come back to paint when the light was softer. She sought out Salvatore to see if he could arrange it for her and, with his usual charm, he did. Max overheard the arrangements and wondered if he might come along as well. Perhaps it was partly a reflex action — Ellie generally said no to things to give her time to think — but she tried as gently as she could to impress upon Max that when she was painting she would rather be alone. He equally gently tucked a strand of her trailing hair behind her ear, a small intimacy that made her almost relent, and gave in to her wish.

'All right, I give in. But as payback, I'd like you to do a portrait of me sometime. What do you think?' said Max.

Ellie smiled. It seemed a reasonable *quid pro quo* and it would provide her with some legitimate time in which to observe Max. Jane and Nerine were watching to see how she would answer; Jane positively egging her on to agree, Nerine impassive.

'I don't see why not!' She laughed. 'How about later this afternoon at five-ish?'

* * *

The journey back in the bus was quieter, everyone taking time to reflect or doze. Max and Ellie did not sit near each other, he once again with Jane and she with Nerine, but Ellie felt his presence almost crackling across the space. Salvatore was at the microphone:

'Ladies and gentlemen, there will be a light lunch back at the Palazzo and then you are free to do as you wish this afternoon and tomorrow morning. However, there are selected books and materials for you to view in the library. We will resume formally with a lecture tomorrow afternoon.'

There were few words after that and even fewer after eating, when most of the group took off for their rooms. Lying on her bed Ellie half wondered if she would hear a knock at her door but she did not. Neither did sleep come to her and she lay without rest, her head filled with thoughts, her body restless.

★ ★ ★

Later, walking through the pedimented doorway of the library she felt small. The wide panelled door was wedged open by a brass gryphon and, displayed on the massive oak table beyond, were some nineteenth century folios. They were illustrated with contemporaneous plans of Gamberaia. Ellie had her head bent over them and was taking notes in her sketchbook when Salvatore arrived.

'They are beautiful, are they not?'

Ellie started and nodded vigorously at him.

'I'm sorry to have startled you. I expect you'd rather be alone.'

Ellie demurred. Actually she felt completely at ease when Salvatore was around. It was surprising as she had always been intimidated by obvious intellect; it was just that Salvatore didn't seem to want to impress as much as communicate.

'Perhaps you could just translate some of this for me ... it's a bit beyond my vocabulary.'

Salvatore would be delighted he said and he would now talk to her in Italian once more, he'd momentarily forgotten his pledge. That was how Max found them at five; talking quietly and animatedly over plans and books. Ellie had the distinct feeling he didn't like the exclusion of the language barrier.

'It's five!' he said, laying a warm hand on the back of Ellie's neck, 'and I've come to keep you to your promise.'

Ellie blinked back, her mind still within the pages in front of her; it was a moment before she answered.

'Oh yes, I lost track of time. Let me get my things.' She turned to Salvatore and in rapid Italian explained her promise to Max that she would paint his portrait. The men looked at each other, expressionless. Then Salvatore nodded to Max and began to order the documents.

As Ellie walked out of the library she could hear Max asking Salvatore to show him the plans of Gamberaia. In turn she heard Salvatore's gentle voice warning Max of the fragility of the papers and asking him not to touch. Ellie was now too far away to hear more, but as she looked back from the hallway, through the giant doorways of the two rooms that now separated them, she saw the rigidity of Max's body and how the two figures were sculpted by the light. The vignette was like an interior scene by Vermeer of merchants in parlay.

'Hello darling.' It was Nerine. 'I was thinking about you.' She kissed Ellie on her cheek. 'Do you think it would be fun if while you did a portrait of Max in good old fashioned paint I had a bash at one with my digital camera?'

Ellie laughed. 'I should think he'd be more than flattered at all the attention! You go and set him up on the terrace and I'll be back with my things in a minute.'

The heat was kinder now and the light had mellowed to the red end of the spectrum as Ellie and Nerine worked. In the cooler air was the sifted musk of green leaves. Max sat relaxed, with a bottle and glass on the table beside him. There was little conversation; Ellie had decreed that. The soft silence was furred with the sound of distant traffic from the town below. Now and again it was punctuated with birdsong, occasional clicks from Nerine's camera and her footsteps on the gravel. As Ellie went deeper into her drawing she felt her skill and her vision of Max begin to coalesce. The fear of not being able to transfer her perception of him on to the small piece of paper began to recede. She did sit for moments just watching him. As she observed the flush on his cheek that moved between coral and copper she felt it was time to add the colour. There was a dull green shadow below his eyes, blue highlights in his dark hair and a violet penumbra below his left ear and down the side of his throat. She wanted to reach out and blend the hues, press her thumb to the pulse in his neck. It returned again — that sense of knowing him, as she laid down the washes of colour.

Nerine excused herself. She wanted some time to work with her images on her laptop. 'You are not to show Max your painting until I've finished too. We can look at them together just before supper.'

Max protested amiably but when Nerine finally left, that was the agreement of them all. Ellie worked on for over an hour; she was glad that she had all but finished by the time others came wandering out to the terrace for drinks. Jane Clements leaned over Ellie's shoulder, the smell of her warm flesh barely concealed by a powerful scent. As Ellie continued to watch Max, she saw his eyes appraising Jane's body, sleek and brown, and the cleavage she was offering to his gaze.

'My, you really are clever, aren't you?'

If the paper had been dry, Ellie would have covered the painting; as it was she said, 'Thank you, Jane,' gathered her things and got up to leave, pleading some final adjustments in the privacy of her room.

Max whined slightly in a teasing tone and put his arm out to Ellie as she passed by. 'Remember, you, me and Nerine in the *salotto* at seven-thirty.'

★　★　★

Ellie hadn't expected to be shocked; certainly Max seemed oblivious to her reaction but Nerine had been seeking it, she knew that. When the portraits were unveiled Max was cock-a-hoop; he just loved them both. They seemed to Ellie completely without a common thread. She looked at hers anew. She had painted Max to be open and sensuous. His lips were fuller and maybe his jawline was stronger than in reality it was. The colours gave him a vigour and presence that was totally present to her just hours before. She felt naked: her feelings were laid upon a piece of paper. Nerine's work shone another light upon the subject. The way she had manipulated the bare photograph was stunning, but was it more truthful than her painting? There was far less definition to the head and whereas Ellie had chosen to fill the page with just Max's face, Nerine had taken his whole figure and marooned it in the centre of the frame. His body language was arrogant and yet he seemed smaller, less powerful. They could have been different people.

Ellie was searching back in her mind to recall where she had seen such disparity before. She remembered. Two portraits of David Garnett; one by Vanessa Bell and one by her husband Duncan Grant. During their marriage Grant had taken Garnett to be his lover. Ellie could see the paintings clearly now: Grant portraying Garnett as sublimely physical whereas Bell conveys him as a pink-cheeked, thoughtless youth. She looked down at her own painting; as Ellie's unconscious lust faced her in technicolour her conscious decided there would be no further travel along that path.

Supper was a communal affair. Max insisted on showing his portraits to all. And he was blatantly freer towards Ellie, taking more opportunities to touch her and speak conspiratorially to her. What price her divine inspiration, her ideological cant about art now? She had fashioned a sad come-on to a near stranger. Ellie winced inwardly lest it should be apparent to all. But no one else, aside from Max and Nerine, seemed that enlightened, except perhaps for Jane who said Ellie had made Max a bit too gorgeous, hadn't she? Despite all Max's wheedling for her to stay and have some drinks, as soon as she could Ellie went to bed, reminding everyone that she was going to be up very early to paint at Gamberaia. Max pantomimed desolation, blowing her a parting kiss as he settled to entertaining the assembled company, glass in hand. As she left, Ellie felt the love and goodwill in Nerine's good-night hug.

★ ★ ★

Salvatore judged the group's visit to Gamberaia a success. They were entranced as it brought theory to life for them. He knew an English audience were hard won as they were used to filling their gardens with so much colour. Here were few flowers but the structure was so strong, it made such an impression. It had upon him when he'd proposed to Maria here thirty years ago. He watched Ellie as he told the story of Princess Ghyka who had lived at Gamberaia in the early nineteen hundreds. She had been responsible for the curve of dark cypress hedging. It was as monumental as a castle wall with arched entrances and exits carved through it. Her idea too, to flood the gravelled parterres so they became still pools of water; water that doubled the sensations with its reflection. By all accounts she had been a great beauty but as her looks faded she ventured outside less and less. As she grew older she left the villa only to paddle in the parterres at dawn and walk in the avenues mainly after dark. When Salvatore's mother was a little girl she had seen the Princess wandering the garden very early one morning, her face veiled with swathes of pale net.

Salvatore liked the way his story had appealed to Ellie's heart. He found himself looking forward to telling her more fables. Before their visit to Castello he planned to show them all images of the Botticellis; she would enjoy that. Salvatore reached across his desk for a volume of letters and thumbed the pages. This was what he was seeking, the letter from Ficino to the young Medici. Salvatore inclined to the view of the authorities who believed *Primavera* had been executed for the boy. In fact he was more convinced by every reading that it must have been inspired by this letter from the philosopher.

For Humanitas herself is a nymph of excellent comeliness born of heaven . . . Salvatore could see the face of Venus conjured up in the painting, her enigmatic beauty subtly altered by her surroundings, and felt her presence almost physically. But *Primavera* appealed to his intellect as well. That was, after all, what it was intended to do. Was it not a visual aid to the young Lorenzo di Pierfrancesco, an exhortation in paint for him to turn his back on the transitory pleasures of the world and to embrace 'Humanitas'? What definition would Salvatore give that word? The closest he could come was refinement. Yes, he understood it to mean human nature at its most refined or cultured.

It would surely be hard for a youth, so materially endowed, for he had inherited the splendour of Castello and its lifestyle, to be able to see the good of such philosophy: *her soul and mind are Love and Charity, her eyes Dignity and Magnanimity, her hands Liberality and Magnificence, the feet Comeliness and Modesty. The whole then is Temperance, Honesty, Charm and Splendour.* Botticelli's Venus then was a vivid illustration of virtue rather than a pagan goddess of pursuing love. Perhaps Ellie knew this from her studies or maybe she would like to know. Salvatore leaned his head back and closed his eyes. As he contemplated her reactions he lifted his uncapped fountain pen, feeling the smoothness of the barrel as he touched it to his lips. He opened his eyes as his thoughts moved on to the others. Max the Brash could probably do with a *Primavera* set in front of him each day. Salvatore could not come to any conclusion about him but there seemed to be more than a little of the adolescent lingering in the man.

He'd seen him early that morning, setting out for a run to the village below, his face determined, the muscular limbs pounding. And later, as Salvatore had gone down to pick up some papers from the bank he'd seen Max again, sprawled, sweating, on a plastic chair in front of one of the cafés. Salvatore had registered the image of the café owner sweeping her pavement around the slumped figure; pouring water in front of a stiff broom and shirring the rubbish into the gutter.

Now it was late, but for once Salvatore felt relaxed in the quiet of his home; there were no lectures until tomorrow afternoon. He had set everyone some tasks to do and Ellie had asked to go back to Gamberaia to paint in the garden. He had helped her to arrange things to leave by five a.m. She said the early light would be better for her. In the hard light of midday the eyes failed, pigment was leached from the hedges. The next morning, she said, the cypress would still be black but the box and bay would reflect back more colour. He needed the reminder; despite all his experience and years designing gardens, sometimes he forgot about the transfiguring power of light.

He made ready for bed with a feeling of satisfaction. A feeling that he had been able to open eyes and had his eyes opened too. A thread of this thought jolted him into remembering an instruction he had failed to give Francesca. Salvatore scribbled words and, wrapped in his dressing gown, walked into the hall to leave the note at reception. As he did he saw Max, bottle of wine in hand, disappearing through Jane Clements' door. Half an hour later the night noises drifted to his open ears.

5

Ellie reached Gamberaia early the next morning when long shadows were lying lightly on the grass. *Prato di giardino*; meadow of the garden. As she understood it, it was the nearest Italians came to describing a lawn: what very different overtones it had compared to the English patch of grass. Yes, she could come back with her sketchbook and paints they had said. Nerine even lent her the digital camera. Ellie had gripped the wheel as she negotiated the last hill, fearing she might have to back down. She had driven here alone armoured by her hire car; only daring at all because she knew the roads would be empty this early. But what was it she had come to capture, or at least hold hostage? Emptied of people, the garden had such an effect upon her. Its *endurance* struck her. Here it was still; the stage set for hundreds of lives and, not entirely unaffected by those lives, it had undergone alterations with each owner. But there was a permanence that spoke to her soul.

This early she was the only one in the garden and she shivered slightly in the blue air. In this light, as she wandered in the formal garden, she appreciated even more the flooded parterres that had once been filled with roses and scented herbs. Now the sheets of clear water reflected the verticals of cypress and the vast globes of box in their shallows. They were so still and untroubled; she couldn't work out how they remained clean and weed free when no water appeared to run in or out of them. She'd like to know the secret. These last three years she'd been very still, trying to prevent the ingress of life's water. It had worked, up to a point, but she'd felt herself stagnating. Today was another small movement for her and not just a ripple on the surface, more a rumbling spring emerging. Ellie longed to find life easy. Before last night she'd thought perhaps Max could teach her how. She was glad that he'd acceded to her need to be alone here today.

She wandered the course of the garden along the wide bowling alley that Nerine had not favoured. She respected Nerine's taste but she didn't always have to agree with her. Today she felt as though she was on a quiet street, peopled by statuary, that led her to the grotto at its terminus. But she also couldn't help feeling that she was being directed rather forcefully to move along this vista. Without the element of chance discovery, somehow, part of the mystery of the grotto was removed. This morning the water that trickled over the shell and stone-encrusted figure of Neptune was turned off and sad damp marks betrayed its path. Ellie was cold and turned to walk back through the trees of the *boschetto* and up into the lemon garden.

She now knew, for Salvatore had explained it, that for the Renaissance garden maker this little bit of contrived 'wild' woodland was an important symbol of nature's lurking presence. No matter how he might design and control, Nature was there to remind him of its power. Ellie felt a sudden readiness to bow to the forces of nature, to submit, to relinquish. Was this how she should feel at her age? There were grains of her twenty-two-year-old self pollinating the present. Emerging from the dusk of the *boschetto* to the light in the highest point in the garden she'd travelled a long path.

There by a lemon tree in its man-high pot sat Max, smoking; his face up to the early sun.

'Hi!' he turned to her without embarrassment. 'Want a cigarette?'

'No. Too early for me.' He must see her perturbation.

Max stubbed the butt out on the gravel path and extended his arm to Ellie. 'Come and sit down. The grass is quite dry here.'

The grass was speckled with daisies like some *mille fleur* tapestry; she crushed them with her body and the heavy basket of paints. Ellie could smell the damp of the grass.

'Why did you come?'

'Ellie, I wanted to be with you and I don't give up easily.'

'But why me?' She couldn't understand.

'Because you've got style. Because you're not boring. Because you intrigue me. Because you know as well as I, there's chemistry.'

And Max pulled her shoulders towards him and kissed her on the mouth. A probing metallic kiss which declared its intentions.

At the time she noted her response without any judgment. A long-absent sexual jolt. A delight in being sought out. A comforting sense of being alongside a warm male body, someone who cared about her. They were the sensations which almost prevailed throughout their morning together. She recalled Nerine's words about being consumed.

After the kiss they'd spent the morning in the garden; Max encouraging Ellie to get out her paints. She'd tried to put down a few watercolour sketches but she couldn't seem to link her hands to her vision. And she couldn't capture the required state for painting. It needed to be almost meditative.

Her painting came out of an equilibrium that gave her the confidence to dare to create. Instead her mood was wired. Her stomach fluttered like an adolescent. So they'd roamed with Nerine's camera. Ellie hoped she'd be able to manipulate the images later. Photographs never satisfied her; the colours, the contrasts of light and dark were all somehow changed. So she took pictures and wrote some notes in her sketchbook of how she felt things to be. Cerulean seeping into gamboge. A warm mist of ultramarine with light red. A dark corner of green muddied with violet. It was unsatisfactory to have Max there. He romped like an animal. He intruded. His attitude was click, click, click. It's done. He couldn't see the way ideas processed through her. Prematurely she'd brought things to an end in the garden.

He'd bought ciabatta, ham, olives and a bottle of *Prosecco* for an early lunch and they climbed up a warm hillside to have them. Ellie knew she shouldn't have the wine but refusal would have seemed priggish. In a few minutes her head was light and her body aware of every point of heat and blade of grass that touched it. When Max rolled across the warm ground and stroked and kissed her again and her body ached to respond, she felt out of control. She felt his hand brush her breast, his thumb pressing almost imperceptibly upon her nipple, the action not undeliberate. She should have laughed about it with him; brushed him off like a cheeky boy but, in middle age, she experienced that gut turning teenage feeling of having got in too deep; of having 'let him go too far'. It was amazing how the ancient humiliations blended with the shock waves from that touch. She couldn't speak of how she felt while her body fired a circuitry that she thought was defunct. For months before his death Andrew had almost left her alone; the times he touched her were few, the times he desired her were even less. When they did have sex she felt like a vessel into which he vented himself physically and emotionally: there was release and rage in the act and not much more. Certainly not this touching designed to give her pleasure.

Max was looking into her eyes to see the effect he was having. No subtlety here; with his index finger he traced a route from her lips, down her neck and to the crease of her cleavage. It was too much and she backed away.

'OK!' Max was laughing. 'I'm sorry, Ellie but you make me want to do that.'

Of course, her fault again. Max was unembarrassed. He linked his arm into hers, brotherly fashion, leant into her and kissed her cheek. 'I rather like a bit of reticence, it's quite a turn-on!'

Ellie disengaged her arm and mustered up as much maternal distance as she could. 'Max, I'm in a different place in my life to you, apart from everything I'm that much older.'

He was dismissive. 'Older women have so much more to offer.'

Yes, once again the 'she' was to offer and the 'he' to take, Ellie thought.

Max was still speaking. 'Anyway, age should give you freedom to choose what you want to do with the rest of your life. Haven't you had enough sadness, Ellie? Don't you deserve some unadulterated pleasure?'

Why, she wondered, couldn't she just give him a straight answer? Instead she changed her approach and bubbled with banter, brushing off the incident with jokes that kept away more intimacy. Max seemed unaware that she was now holding him at arm's length.

The sun was piercing when Ellie prompted their departure. 'We need to get back for Salvatore's lecture.'

Max groaned. 'Must we? It's just some stuff about Botticelli. Nothing directly relevant.'

She laughed again. 'Of course we must, I'm really interested. I've always wondered what the story is behind those paintings.' She was rearranging things in her basket with unnecessary purposefulness. 'We could miss out on learning something really good.'

She followed his smart car the twenty kilometres back 'home'. As they walked back into the cool hall Ellie's face was burning from the sun and she knew Max was on a very different imaginary path to her. He was running with the scent and she had not disabused him. Nerine was sitting in the half-light reading an old copy of the *Telegraph*. She glanced up and it seemed to Ellie that she read the entire situation immediately. Her face affected disinterest in their arrival together.

'So, how did you get on with my camera?' She talked straight to Ellie.

'I'm not sure I'm good with anything so new. It took me a while to settle to it.'

'Well, you haven't begun yet. The next stage is the best. You never know you just might end up with something that is completely and utterly different from your starting point.' Nerine flicked her a look and Ellie just nodded. 'Come back to my room tonight and we'll have a little play on my laptop,' she said with raised eyebrows.

Ellie nodded and her smile fixed into a gape, hiding the laughter that was rising. Nerine, stealing Max's line. The comfort of women was extraordinary.

'Let's go and get good seats for the lecture.' Nerine linked her arm through Ellie's and marched her off.

Salvatore had a full house.

'I wanted to show you slides of these two paintings, *Primavera* and *The Birth of Venus*, because they hung in the Villa Medici at Castello, our venue tomorrow. I go along with the scholars who believe they were commissioned by one of the occupants, Lorenzo di Pierfrancesco de' Medici.'

His words were calming, coming out of the darkened room; the bright images of the Botticelli paintings began to speak to Ellie as if they had been painted for her, for today.

'He was a young man, a cousin of the great Medici leader Lorenzo the Magnificent, and by all accounts as naive and unpolished as his cousin was learned and sophisticated.'

Max slumped lower in his seat, his eyes closing. Salvatore's voice in the shadows now exhorted them to go and see the originals in the Uffizi if they had time. He described how they were really visual morality tales, particularly *Primavera*; exhortations to a young man capable of choosing the wrong path to live a good life.

'I've always wondered what that painting was about,' piped up a diplomatic wife. 'I did a bit of a course on the Renaissance but we didn't get that far.'

Salvatore made a slight bow towards her. 'Historians have constructed many different theories about the meaning but I shall try to give you a simple version.' He smiled at her. Ellie was charmed by the way the words could have been patronising but were delivered without arrogance. 'At its heart it is about Platonic Love.'

Was this a special lecture for her, thought Ellie? Love without sex. It was probably where she would be happiest now.

'I suppose we understand a Platonic relationship in its popular sense,' Salvatore was continuing. 'That is, a complete disengagement from earthly passions.'

Ellie enjoyed Salvatore's avoidance of the word sex and she could see Max had too, he was smirking at her. She looked back at Salvatore studiedly.

'But this painting is saying more. This is about looking beyond the here and now, towards a divine inspiration. And when the 'lover' has gazed into the Beyond, he or she is moved to return to the real world and, in the light of insight, make a difference to other mortals here below.' With a pointer Salvatore traced the figures of the three circling women in their diaphanous drapes to the left of the painting.

'One meaning that has been attached to these figures is that they are a metaphor for the Cycle of Grace: one Grace looks toward the Beyond and receives divine blessing; she freely passes this to her sister who receives it courteously, and the last figure in the triad makes grateful thanks.' Salvatore looked out at his audience who were trying to digest his words. He was adding that there were of course other layers of meaning to each figure but he would not digress now.

'Simply, these Graces are an illustration of what is going on in the central figure of the painting; Venus, goddess of Love, in one sole figure represents that endless cycle of giving, receiving and thankfulness.' Salvatore paused and looked up at the illuminated figure on the screen, the momentary silence bringing drama to his final sentence. 'She is Love Brought to Earth.' There was quiet as everyone absorbed the imagery. Max shifted in his seat.

'So what about the dude in the loincloth?'

There was a ripple of laughter; even Ellie found it a welcome relief and Salvatore didn't look at all discomfited.

'Thank you, Max. The 'dude' is actually Mercury, or Hermes, the messenger of the gods. In fact I think dude's a rather good word as he was the shrewdest and swiftest of the gods; eloquent, able to bridge the gap between mortals and the deity. He's the revealer of secret mysteries or 'Hermetic' knowledge.'

Ellie watched Max who, although he was arranged in a pose that parodied indifference, was keenly attentive.

'In this painting he's looking to the Beyond for those secrets and turning away from the world. He's had a relationship with the three ladies though — his role in mythology was as leader of the Graces.'

Ellie almost expected to see boredom on Max's face but he continued to watch Salvatore neutrally.

'His opposite, on the other side of the painting, is the Zephyr; as much as Mercury turns away from the world so the wind blows back into it with passion. It's another way of showing the same idea of looking up for divine inspiration and then returning to the world to use the gift for the benefit of others.'

'So, who is the figure being chased by the Zephyr?' Slater had raised his hand like a schoolboy.

'That's Chloris: in mythology she's an innocent earth-nymph. She tried to escape the Zephyr but, at his touch, she becomes transformed into Flora, the herald of spring.' Salvatore pointed to the tripping figure with flowers tumbling out of her mouth. 'So by a breath of wind from a higher world, let's call it a gale of passion, Chloris is turned, against her will, into Flora. I suppose you could say she was ravished. And she certainly undergoes a complete *change of nature*.' Salvatore rustled through some notes in front of him. 'In fact there's a quotation from Ovid where Chloris says of herself that she was so plain she hardly dared look back at her old self after her transfiguration. However, she did admit that it was her plainness that attracted her a 'proper' husband.'

'Sort of 'what you see is what you get'?' asked Brad. Salvatore smiled gently at him.

'Exactly. The Zephyr responded to her lack of artifice.'

And brought her flowers, thought Ellie. She looked at the two figures, drab, diffident Chloris and the colourful Flora. She wanted that metamorphosis, she wanted to be garlanded with flowers. But there was a modernity, a wordliness, to Flora's face; she had a come-hither look that Ellie couldn't quite see in herself. Under cover of the darkness she stole a look at Max and metaphorically shivered in the teeth of the passing gale.

The atmosphere was warmed up again by Vera, one of the 'garden ladies', saying, 'I do like that sweet little Cherub up in the trees. Is it Cupid?'

Salvatore smiled. 'Yes, he's also called Amor, another aspect of Love, you see.'

Max chipped in, 'And as you can see, my dear Vera, he's blindfolded, makes him a bit of a random shot, doesn't it, Salvatore?' He didn't wait for an answer. 'Yup, there's no telling where Amor will strike.' Ellie looked hard ahead as Max fired a grin in her direction.

The exchange hadn't gone unnoticed by Salvatore, she could see, but he simply went on talking for some minutes. He was pointing out that the painting amazingly depicted forty *species* of flowers and he linked some to the garden design at Castello. He showed slides of the contemporaneous plans and warned them that what they would see tomorrow was a mere ghost of the past. Then he checked his watch and turned up the lights.

'If I go on you'll have no time before dinner, ladies and gentlemen, but I can tell you more on the coach tomorrow.' He looked around and caught Ellie's eye. 'If anyone wants to know any more, please come and talk to me. I've hardly scratched the surface.'

As they all filtered out into the late

afternoon's dying sunlight Max found Ellie. 'Just my kind of lecture that. A quiet snooze in the dark and waking up every now and then to see a naked woman.'

'Didn't you listen to Salvatore at all?' asked Ellie, smarting at his disingenuousness.

Max put his hand on her neck and made to kiss her. Ellie turned her face and his warm mouth found her cheek. He grinned at her. 'Joke, Ellie! I'm not a total peasant, you know.'

Feeling like a schoolma'am caught with her knickers down, Ellie blustered. 'That was interesting, all that stuff about Primavera. The mythology of the figures and the philosophy behind the Three Graces, didn't you think?'

Max nodded, smiling at her embarrassment. 'Yes, yes it was. Let's have a long talk about it over dinner. I'll order us some bubbly to get us in the mood for some intellectual wrestling.' Max stroked her cheek with a finger. 'And maybe we'll have to wrestle on long into the night.' He licked his lower lip and wiped his brow with a handkerchief. 'Look, I'm off to shower now but I'll keep a seat warm for you. Don't be late!' His hand glided over her hip as he left.

Nerine came up behind her. 'Need a chaperone?'

'You know he followed me to Gamberaia this morning?'

Nerine nodded. 'No doubt wanting a little more than drawing lessons.' She smiled.

'I feel so stupid Nerine. Me, the widow-lady, getting myself entangled.'

'Don't be silly. He's a determined boy and it's an unequal struggle against all that testosterone.' Nerine pushed a strand of hair under her little cap. 'And you're vulnerable.'

'But I could have just told him straight out I'm not after what he has to offer. I've got a tongue in my head.'

'Yes, I'm sure he found that out.' Nerine smiled slyly and Ellie opened her mouth in unbelief.

'You're so wicked for an old lady!'

'Let this wicked old lady take you out for some supper.'

'But Max, he thinks we're . . . ' Ellie trailed off as Nerine watched her without comment. There was just a little time fighting her conscience before she took the yellow route. 'Thanks Nerine. Let's go now.'

★　★　★

Another evening, another day gone by without mishap. Salvatore liked to eat alone; as much as he got on with them, he really needed time away from people. So it was his habit only to venture out to circulate the groups around coffee time, in order to gather feedback. When people were relaxed after eating, their inhibitions softened by the wine, it was a good time to pick up the undercurrents of any brewing dissatisfaction. He certainly sensed some in the corner by the window where Max sat alone, an empty wine bottle at his elbow. Salvatore always found it strange how the English felt compelled to finish any alcohol in front of them; to carry on drinking after the meal was over. And in return he knew he'd surprised many an Englishman in his time in Oxford, by not being their image of the libation-loving Italian. It was a false image. Italians did not drink to get drunk which is what Max was doing, it seemed.

'All right, Max? It doesn't seem like you to be on your own.'

Max squinted up at him. 'I'm a bit pissed off with Ellie. We arranged to eat here and she's swanned off with Nerine, Francesca tells me.'

'No Jane either?'

Max waved his hand, the joints flopping. 'Gone off with the dancing boys somewhere.'

The air felt stagnant. Salvatore couldn't think of much to say. 'Well, it'll give you a chance for an early night. We've got quite a day looking around Castello tomorrow.'

Max looked back at Salvatore, and the expression on his face was contemptuous. 'Yeh. Sure.'

★ ★ ★

Back in his study, wrapped in a dressing gown, Salvatore pondered the contempt. It had told him a great deal, that one glance. *Yeh. Sure, Old Man. That's OK for you with your pipe and slippers mentality.* He couldn't say he wanted to live Max's life, in fact he was sickened by the superficiality he'd already seen, but he did admire the energy, the activity he displayed. It reminded him of something. An image of the bustling, juvenescent Amor in *Primavera* came to his mind. There were such different faces of Love in one painting, he mused; Amor's energetic figure, with his bow tensed, hovered above the calm form of Venus. Salvatore carefully leafed through the volume in front of him, found the passage he wanted; Ficino's translation of *De Amore* by Plotinus.

If the soul is the mother of Love, then Venus is identical with the soul, and Amor is the soul's energy.

What a clear picture Botticelli had painted of these two faces of Love; the placid goddess and her restless son. Ellie's face crashed into his imaginings. Would she succumb to this cupidity; would she allow herself to be felled by an energetic arrow? Love, brought thudding to earth. Salvatore definitely sensed something between Max and Ellie. Perhaps he should warn her about the boy's nocturnal activities? He snapped the book shut. None of his business; they were both consenting adults after all.

Salvatore got up and filed the volume away but his mind would not close on the subject as easily as the pages. So he set himself a task; Slater had questioned him about the Graces and Salvatore had promised him a book. Methodically he searched the shelves, fingering the worn spines, lifting the volumes gently and scanning their pages until he found what he wanted. Here it was, some explanation of the Graces' dance. *The precious choreography of the Graces is both sustained and moved by these contending forces, the two gods* (Venus and Amor) *conveying to the triadic dance their proportionate characters of passion and restraint.*

Salvatore looked at the colour plate of *Primavera*. It was genius the way Botticelli had conveyed motion in the static figures of *Chastity*, *Pleasure* and *Beauty*. Three characters with entirely different natures had been

108

blended together. There was harmony in the discord — it was a dance of balancing opposites. Was that what Ellie saw in Max? Her balancing opposite? His passion, her restraint. Salvatore marked the book and pushed it aside. He stood up and walked to his bedroom. What was causing his imagination to fire this way? It was immaterial to him, surely, what his guests chose to do. He felt his face burn with shame — shame that he'd conjured up such images of physical passion. But he was a man, wasn't he? A man deprived of his wife too long. He sat on the bed and slipped off his dressing gown. Alone again, he repainted the dance of the Graces in his mind; his place was with *Chastity*, Ellie stood by *Beauty* and Max — Max was energetically seeking *Pleasure*.

6

Coincidentally Ellie and Nerine found a restaurant called *Il Rifugio*. The front room was mellow, lit by candles and filled with Italian families tucking in to platefuls. They, by contrast, were ushered into an empty back room, tiled like a public lavatory. They sat under the glare of strip lighting trying to work out the menu. The obvious snub didn't worry either of them and they even promised each other that they would not check the bill at the end. The wine came first. They treated themselves to a pseudo-champagne which the waiter uncorked quietly and professionally.

'Listen to that,' said Nerine 'it sighed like a contented cow!'

The meal could have been sawdust by the time it arrived and they wouldn't have cared. But it was delicious.

That evening Ellie was, for the most part, the transmitter. In receptive company she felt free to speak of herself as a widow. Ellie said she felt unpropped; alone but not solitary. She had been driving past a school one morning and seen a young teacher standing by herself, probably on bus duty, and all around her were kids walking, cycling, cars turning, motorists passing. Her body just looked so fearful, so alone in her space as if she didn't know what to do among all this activity, all this purpose. Ellie's eyes met hers in the instant she drove past and she knew they felt the same things.

Nerine had been a widow for twelve years. She said the edges were less sharp these days but she knew Ellie must be in the stage when she could still cut herself on the severed rocks; the time before the reality of her state was firmly embedded in her subconscious. Ellie, safe with Nerine, feared that her marriage had not been as good as others felt it to be; the negatives kept reaching out and haunting her. Nerine consoled her by talking about her own past. Duggie had died slowly from cancer and she had tried so hard to cope, to be normal, almost breezy, that after he died she wondered if he knew how distraught she had felt. As she wrenched over the possible misunderstanding she began to pick at the bones of miscommunication between them over the years. It had taken a whole year before she had spiralled down into depression that took away the next two years of her life. Perhaps she would have coped better if she'd had children to watch going on with their futures?

Ellie listened and tried to untangle her feelings on the subject. She wasn't so sure that was the case. Her own children, Dominic and Sadie, were nineteen and eighteen when their father died. For three years before his death they'd had to learn that things don't always go the way you want or expect them to. They'd had a pretty idyllic upbringing in Derbyshire on the fringes of aristocratic life. Andrew was making himself invaluable to the Estate and with his expertise and charming ways began to get himself involved in some successful property dealing. Dom and Sadie went to good private schools and came home to hob-nob with the kids of the old wealthy. They wanted for nothing; Andrew always made sure they had all the material things they needed.

'That's important for a man,' Nerine commented.

Ellie thought she should have looked upon these years as her happiest. As the children became more independent she was beginning to be well known locally as a painter. She felt an impostor as she'd never had formal training. Nerine snorted at this and waved her cigarette holder dismissively. The paintings sold at local exhibitions but the clientele were well able to afford to buy and buy they did.

These were years when Ellie painted like a

factory hand; she churned them out. She sometimes enjoyed the process and had a certain satisfaction in conquering the technique but she often stopped and wondered what it was she was doing. She made copies of nature mostly. She'd gone to London rarely at this time but once she visited the National Gallery and was brought up short by a still life in a Caravaggio painting. She'd squirmed at the sensuality of the fruits and flowers. Her own renderings were often faithful but pedestrian, she felt. These were the few paintings that remained unsold as they didn't touch the heart in anyone. The ones that pleased her walked out of the door. Nerine nodded in recognition. Ellie bemoaned not being able to entrap the extra dimension; the special quality came and went along with her belief in herself, what she was doing and why she was doing it.

'That's the definition of an artist isn't it?' said Nerine.

In their privileged bubble, Ellie's children seemed to have no such problems with their confidence and Andrew, to all intents, was riding high. So the tumble was a hard one. Andrew had concealed just how deep into property investment he had been.

'Not an unusual story for that time.' said Nerine.

What had angered Ellie the most was how Andrew had been seduced by wealthy partners; to them it was a flea bite. When, to crown it all, the Estate was sold and his job went too everything was lost.

And the children took it the hardest. Uprooting to rented accommodation in the south and being pitched into new schools just before exams was no picnic for them. She'd watched their anger as they reeled with the punches and then gradually built up layers of protection for themselves. They both worked hard, Dom to get into university and Sadie to start as a journalist on a local paper. That's what they were doing when Andrew had his heart attack.

'You know, Nerine, when he died I felt that Dom and Sadie just accepted his death as one more betrayal of trust. And I was guilty by association.'

'Are they living with you now?'

Ellie shook her head. 'They both left to set up their own lives as soon as they'd satisfied themselves I wasn't going to fall apart. There's not the closeness I'd hoped for with my children.'

'Well, this is the time children like to exert their independence. I shouldn't blame it on anything that happened in the marriage.'

Ellie reached out for Nerine's hand,

grateful for her solid words. She smiled back at her.

'But do you find it hard living on your own, darling? I mean are you one of those nervous types?'

'No, no not at all.' Ellie paused. 'I say that but actually, just before I came away . . . '

Nerine leant her head like a wren on a wire.

'You know I live in a little village, well more of a hamlet really; it's quiet and out of the way. And of course my mother was there for years before me and I've just always been used to leaving things unlocked. When you've got such good neighbours it never occurs to you to worry about things like that.'

'Not the case in the environs of wicked Ladbroke Grove,' sighed Nerine.

'I'd just popped out to take some cuttings to a friend down the road and, you know how things go, she invited me in for a coffee so I was out for nearly an hour. When I got back it was strange.' She hesitated, trying to recall her feelings. 'There was nothing missing but things looked different.'

'What do you mean, looked different?'

'Just rearranged. Family pictures on the bookcase, documents on the desk. You know how it is Nerine, when you are so tuned into visual things as we are, you just know when a line isn't straight or something's composition has changed.'

Nerine nodded.

'And I'd been looking at all the material for this course we're on, that morning. I particularly remember where I'd had to break off half way through the reading list page, to go out. Yet, when I came back the papers were back in the order they'd been sent originally.'

'Are you sure, darling? I don't quite get the point of a burglar who wants to tidy up your papers!'

They laughed. 'I know, it sounds dotty but I can say it put the wind up me for a few days, especially as another neighbour said she'd seen a smart car parked up the lane for a while. Thought I had a visitor.'

'I bet it made you lock up after that.'

Ellie smiled. 'You're right! I suppose I've tried to bury it a bit but, when I'm not thinking it was all a figment of my overheated imagination, I wonder what it was all about. I fear, Nerine, there are things still lurking in the woodwork, things that Andrew didn't share with me about his business dealings.'

'Do you think you've forgiven Andrew for his disastrous speculation?'

Ellie jumped in. 'Oh, yes, yes, I did that before he died.' Ellie certainly felt she had. It was a question she often asked herself and always answered in the affirmative. She was silent for some moments.

'But, you know when Salvatore was telling us about *Primavera*, about the way the three Graces represented an endless cycle of giving and receiving blessings, the thought did come to me, why was it that Andrew could never see that kind of . . . ' she stopped to search for the word, 'consequentiality.'

Nerine inclined her head to hear further explanation.

'Just that, he couldn't see that everything that you do in life leads to some outcome for which you are ultimately responsible. He'd always act first and think about the effects much, much later, if at all.' Ellie sat back. 'The problem, as far as I see it, Nerine, is that we can't see in advance where the end result of any act will take us; I mean, we, pitiful humanity, cannot ever hope to see the bigger picture. But if you submit your life to some higher authority . . . ' She stopped to think. 'If you're guided in your actions there's more likelihood that you will . . . ' she searched for the ending, 'do less harm.'

'But we all fail, dear. With or without God, we all make mistakes and get it wrong. Don't you think the messes sometimes make us learn things?' Nerine was quiet in her reasonableness.

117

'I know, you're right. In fact I don't really regret all the financial problems, except that I was sorry for the kids. I was almost thankful that it happened.'

'What do you mean?'

'I think, Nerine, it gave me a real purpose — and for the first time in years Andrew and I worked hard alongside each other, as equals, to recreate a life. And when you're left with little materially that's when you begin to discover other parts of yourself.'

'You found comfort in your faith did you, dear?'

'Maybe my beliefs made it easy for me to withdraw from a lot of difficult stuff, but I don't think so. I know they helped me face things. What I find so difficult now is trying to be part of the world and not seem like some censorious freak. So many of the values around me just don't accord with my beliefs.' Ellie pulled her hair back from her temples and looked hard at Nerine. 'I'm not sure that anyone who doesn't have a faith can understand what it is that motivates those of us who do. It's a kind of madness to the outside world. Asking anyone to put their total trust in a metaphysical entity and to live by a completely different set of rules does seem potty, doesn't it?'

'Well, that's the nature of faith isn't it? It's

just faith, not proven science,' said Nerine. 'Whatever you believe, my darling, you stick to your guns. You won't be happy if you try to act against your convictions.'

They toasted their convictions before the conversation changed to dissecting each member of the course part by part. With more than one bottle of champagne inside them, Max, Doctor Jonathan and Jane Clements came in for close scrutiny.

They parted in the entrance hall of the Palazzo in the early hours; it wouldn't be long before Salvatore's scheduled visit to the garden at Castello. The thought of such activity made Ellie feel weak. She stage whispered to Nerine. 'I don't know whether I'll make it after all that champagne. What is it about Italy that completely changes my nature?'

Nerine laughed, her voice erupting into a bubbling cough, and assured Ellie that it was good for her to be different here where nobody knew her. With luck no vices could follow her home.

When Ellie awoke it was to a line of bright light across her face and a firm knock on her door. She sucked herself up from unconsciousness like a stone in a muddy lake bed.

'Ellie, are you there?'

It was Max's voice. She tried to keep as

quiet as she could while turning her wrist watch to scan its face. No glasses, no sense.

'It's ten o'clock and we're all off to Castello.' More knocking. 'Ellie, are you coming?'

She held her breath and waited for his departing footsteps. She heard him talking to Salvatore. Although their voices were dimmed she thought Nerine was telling Max that she had seen her go out for a walk. Grateful, she stayed inert until she could hear the doors of the minibus slamming.

★   ★   ★

Around eleven-thirty she went to help herself to a cold drink and, with her basket full of painting gear on her arm, stepped into the sunlight of the terrace. She was surprised to see the figure of Dr. Hunter dozing quietly, panama tipped over his face. He came to and fumbled for his cup of coffee as she pulled her chair across the gravel.

'So what's your excuse for not going on the trip, Jonathan?'

'Old man's privilege,' he said without irony.

He must have been almost a decade younger than Nerine but his demeanour did spell old man.

'Rubbish.'

'No, Eleanor.'

'Ellie, I prefer Ellie,' she said but he didn't really hear and just continued.

'I'm quite happy in my role as elder. I feel I've had a long and successful career and been in a position to change people's lives. I've had a good marriage and raised responsible children who are now happily making their own contribution. Time to choose my own timetable. Time for rest.'

How smug was that? Somewhere, buried very far down, Ellie knew that he was not the legitimate target but she couldn't help herself. An explosive exclamation of disbelief escaped from her. Jonathan, again, didn't react. She thought, don't I even do anger noticeably? Hardly worth trying to get through to this man, she supposed, with such a gulf between them. He'd had such freedom from the day-to-day grind of family responsibilities that he could make a career and still take the credit for raising his children. He hadn't always had to follow in another's footsteps. No, he initiated whilst Ellie merely reacted. She thought of her own creative life; a mess of part-time fragments, shaped by her life behind Andrew, forged in the space left after the time and emotions lavished on her family. What had she got to show for it? No professional qualifications, no uninterrupted

CV, no money and no one waiting to write her obituary. Perhaps a few students who appreciated her teaching, but no doubt Jonathan would say they were just ordinary people who melted into the background.

Ellie spread out her painting things. Rattling the metal paint tin. Slapping down the board. Sharpening her pencils until the lead snapped.

'Jonathan, what do you think about artists? I mean do they change people's lives, or would we be just as well off without them?'

'I think it depends what you mean by artists. I'll assume you're talking about painters like yourself.'

Ellie gave a faint nod.

'The world would have been impoverished without Leonardo or Rembrandt; they had consummate skill; they made people look in a new way, and they created real beauty.'

Ellie read between his lines. As she fiddled with her paint things the pressure of her thoughts built up inside her. Genius in art is OK; only excellence is allowable. My dabbling makes no difference to the world whatsoever. Is that what he thinks? She didn't want him to confirm her fears. Instead she had a need to keep winding up the tension.

'So you think beauty is a prerequisite for any art?'

'I suppose I do.'

'How do you define beauty then?'

'Tricky. In some ways it's indefinable because it depends upon the subjective stance of the viewer — what his background has taught him to understand and appreciate.' Jonathan adjusted his hat and traced the table top with his fingers. 'I suppose there needs to be some kind of symmetry or pattern as a framework for the viewer.'

'So would you call a Mondrian beautiful?'

'I think it has a kind of order that makes it satisfying. But then, as a scientist, I know that straight lines appeal to a certain part of the brain.' Jonathan relaxed in his chair and smiled. As he uncrossed his legs the neatly pressed trousers resumed their creases, the silk socks flared pale in the sunlight. 'In fact it would be rather good if painters researched the ways the brain responds and gave it what it wanted, a sure fire way to both aesthetic appeal and sales!'

Ellie shifted upright in her seat, hands pressing on the wooden arms. 'Tell me you don't mean that, Jonathan. I couldn't paint something just because I know someone's brain will respond to it. How can you believe that feelings are only neurological responses?'

Jonathan smiled faintly. It was a smile she recognised: the smile that came before dismissal. She wouldn't be dismissed.

'I mean one day I can look at a Mondrian and be calmed and another day all I sense is empty space and desolation. People are not invariable and logical. When I paint something good it's come from my heart and that's where I want it to land in the viewer.' She could feel the pulse in her neck as she pushed on. 'Please tell me that you've stood in front of a Matisse or a Fra Angelico and you've felt part of a creative force far greater than mere humanity, something that transcends a collection of firing brain cells!'

Jonathan looked bemused, almost hurt. 'Well, I wasn't being that serious Ellie, but I can see you are.' He took a fortifying swallow of coffee. 'In answer to feeling part of something greater — if I'm honest I would say that what I feel when I hear great music or see a Rembrandt is more akin to pride in the achievement of man.'

Ellie looked down at her feet, circling the toes of her espadrilles in the dusty gravel. She still had enough insight to know that her anger was misdirected, but she was irritated by his arrogance, his utter belief that man was in charge of everything. There was no convincing him that he might need to answer to any higher authority. And certainly that was way outside Max's experience. She felt herself flush. How could she have opened herself up? The portrait of him: the fumblings in the garden. How could she have had such a totally different view of the same things? She began to replace all her things in her basket. Leaning over to pick up her glass from the table she made an effort to fix eye-contact with Jonathan and smiled at him.

'I suppose that is where we agree to differ,' she said.

'Well, thank heavens for that. Life *would* be boring if we were all the same.' Jonathan rippled with a laugh, splashing his poplin shirt ever so slightly with fallout from his cappuccino.

'I think I'm going to find some shade to sit in.' Ellie rose self-consciously and squinted towards an imaginary view. She could feel Jonathan watching her, probably in bewilderment.

'Yes. Good idea.' There was a hesitation before he went on. 'You know, I'm sure now that I've met you somewhere before but I can't place you at the moment.'

Ellie turned to look down at his quizzical expression. 'Let me know if your memory returns,' she called back over her shoulder.

★ ★ ★

It had been a frustrating morning for Salvatore. The minibus had broken down on the way to Villa Medici at Castello. It had been two and a half hours before they could leave the roadside. It didn't take long before Max was expressing his views of Italian inefficiency and strutting the hard shoulder stabbing at his mobile phone. This worked only intermittently and brought forth another tirade. Salvatore didn't understand it all but some of the interrupted calls were to do with Max's business; not going too well by the sound of the one-sided conversation. Jane Clements remained slumped in her seat in the bus, looking tired and uncharacteristically rumpled, her expression not quite penetrable behind her Gucci shades. The diplomatic couples were resigned but not best pleased at the interruption to their schedule. Only Nerine seemed totally untouched, clambering along the grass verge collecting wild flowers and grasses.

During the wait Salvatore attempted to continue yesterday's lecture in an informal way. In the circumstances there was not much enthusiasm for the topic, the concentration absent. Salvatore found it interesting that, as time went by, even the most so-called civilised members of the party seemed to have lapsed into blame-laying. Unable to do anything Salvatore sat in the bus reading his pocket Ficino. The words seemed remarkably apt as a background to bubbling anger and resentment.

Mortal men ask God for good things every day, but they never pray that they make good use of them . . . They think that they can be at peace with others, yet continually they wage war with themselves . . . They believe they can find a faithful friend in others, but not one of them keeps faith with himself. What they have praised they reject; what they have desired, they do not want; and contrariwise they claim to know about everyone else's affairs, although they do not know about their own.

What more my friends? The magistrates forbid murder and allow instruments for killing men to be made everywhere. They desire an excellent crop of men, yet they do not take sufficient care of the seedling, that is the child.

Salvatore watched Max in full flood and thought that he was still a child, petulant and self-absorbed. He tried to dampen his judgmental spirit; perhaps indeed Max had been a seedling trodden underfoot, but it was no good, Salvatore just did not like the man. What good was it doing anyone to make such a fuss? It was simply wasting the present moment.

People always live badly today; they only live well tomorrow. For the sake of ambition they strive against each other with evil deeds, but the path to glory would be easier to tread by doing good to one another.

Even after they had been rescued from the roadside a further hour was spent in Poggio ai Caiano before new transport could be arranged. The consensus over coffee in a tired bar had been to abandon the whole visit and reschedule it for the next day. By the time the sweating group returned to the Palazzo Salvatore had pledged compensatory free champagne and, looking at Max, had mentally calculated the drop in profit. Maria would have handled this better. It was times like these that he missed her acutely.

As everyone filtered back into the cool hall he'd watched Ellie walk in from the garden and come face to face with Max. Their body language was a mismatch; he bearing down on her, damp and effusive, she stepping slightly back, protected by a basket breast-plate and repelling his advances.

Behind them, slightly out of focus as if in the background of a news photo, Jane Clements took off her glasses and observed, seemingly unmoved. She faded from the edge of the picture, 'Can't hang around, I'm off to stay the night with some clients from

London,' she had said as she disappeared past him.

★ ★ ★

Probably he should have spent the whole evening with the group but when he saw their mood after dinner seemed amicable, obviously bonded in their adversity, Salvatore gave way to his fatigue and decided to go to bed. He noticed that many of the women had gone before him, Ellie included. As he left the knot of people in the bar the thought did occur to him that he ought to stay to keep an eye on Max who was getting progressively more drunk, but if his spirit was willing then his flesh was far too weak. Besides, if one was not also fortified by the vine, Max was beginning to be very boring; he was starting a long rant about business and how 'the bastards couldn't wait to stab you in the back'. As Salvatore walked to his apartments he could hear Max singing very loudly — that Beatles song *Day Tripper*. Very subtle Max, he thought. He was half singing, half shouting that line about being taken half the way there. He sang it over and over, virtually spitting out the word 'she' as he began again. It looked as if he was settled in for a late night session and frankly, Salvatore was too tired to care.

7

It had been an uncomfortable meeting with Max. After her conversation with Jonathan, Ellie had spent a quiet few hours drawing in the garden. She had rejected the blatant colours of her paintbox and was calmed by the flow of pencil on smooth cartridge. It was not sketching — a word that made her think of hasty assessments and things half observed; for Ellie drawing felt like a marvellous structure, a firm foundation. Thus walking into the hall to be confronted by the tide of returning people — and Max's physical presence, jarred her. The whole group were hot and irritable, bringing their sweat into the coolness. They fell upon Ellie as a good audience for their frustrated outbursts. Especially Max, who wanted to metamorphose his grievances over the breakdown into a performance. At the end of it Max had tried to hold and kiss her, make a public claim on her, and she knew she had equally publicly rejected him. She had watched his face souring, transforming into an angry mask. He turned away from her and headed for his room, cursing the wasted day.

Nerine rallied her, pressing a large bunch of wilted flowers on top of her basket, and pleading for a nice cold gin and tonic. Arms linked, Ellie had walked with her to the bar. They laughed, in a determined affectation of lightness of spirit.

★   ★   ★

In the dark of the night, at first nothing was seen — only felt and feared. Waking to the dread was like drowning: a presence in her dream — or was it in her room? The latch chattered in the dead silence as her door closed. Ellie clawed her way upright in the bed, awake, straining to hear. She had chosen the wrong sense and failed to see until the dark form was nearly upon her. But even in this absence of light he took away more. He pushed her down, his heavy body and breath were pressing on her, his hand was pulling up her nightdress and he was swearing in her ear. Fear was the knife that cut through confusion and brought response.

'Max? What are you doing? Get off! Get out!' Ellie's breath was constricted. She heard the weakling voice as though it didn't belong to her. The sound was shrill, the edges breaking. From Max there were no words, just the insistent weight and the oppressive

131

reek of alcohol. His face hovered above her but even this close, in the catacomb dark, it was shifting and barely distinguishable. It felt to Ellie as if there was a vacancy — a space empty of humanity.

'You have no right . . . ' She was pinned down, so she only had words and the words came from somewhere outside herself. 'You're drunk. You're a drunk, pathetic, unloveable *child*!'

Max pressed his hand on her mouth. His breath was foul as he lowered further down on to her. His shirt was open so his bare flesh met her exposed skin, adhered by his sweat. Now his body was still and he seemed to be waiting. Ellie lay inert beneath him, hardly allowing breath to continue. In the stillness, thoughts and pleadings of desperation raced inside her head. Then, without words, he levered himself off her and spat in her face before stumbling away.

As the door banged shut Ellie was islanded in the rumpled bed, knees drawn up, white sheet gathered around her. She was trembling. Outside, she was just the same but inside — it felt as though every part had been rearranged, put out of order; the everyday description 'being shaken up' meaning something at last. She wondered at the force of such aggression in Max. The worst part was feeling that his anger had transferred to her, was boiling up in her, and she wanted to resist that with every conscious sense she had.

Much later as the moon moved around she cried. It must have been her fault. What was it in her that invited violation? She shed tears for the tenderness of sex she had never known. She cried for Andrew who failed to protect her. What a fool she was to trust anyone. Nobody could help her. From now on she would lock up, her doors, herself. Before dawn, she prayed. She called upon her God to care for her. How long she had sat so still in her soiled bed only came to her along with the first strains of light. Then she rose like a sleepwalker. His smell was everywhere and she was pulling off her nightdress before she reached the bathroom, throwing it away to the far corner of the room. Under the steady stream of the shower she wept and prayed some more as she washed away all trace of his presence, thankful for her deliverance. At last, with the water, some peace descended and she felt a little of herself stealing back into the place that had been sundered by Max. Ellie understood now that she did not have to fight back with the same weapons. His actions were not going to taint her.

★ ★ ★

Turning up to breakfast took an effort of will and make-up. Max was there, eating heartily. He bade Ellie a cheery good morning and asked if she had slept well. Ellie was underwater. Her mouthful of bread stuck fast like a communion wafer.

Nerine lowered into the seat beside her and murmured, 'Well, I'm surprised to see him up this early when by all accounts he was packing it away in the bar till late last night.'

Ellie just nodded, concentrating on chewing each mouthful, willing herself to swallow.

Nerine was alerted by the silence. 'Anything the matter, darling? You look a bit pale.'

'Just didn't sleep well.'

'No, can't say I did either. Never mind. At least we've got a treat of a garden to see today. Clever you missing out on yesterday's breakdown.'

Ellie felt the irony of the words but made a decision then to keep quiet, to face up, head on. After all, she was physically unharmed. What good would it do to dwell on the night when the day was here? 'New every morning' — the words came to her, ironically from Lamentations. *Because of the Lord's great love we are not consumed. For his compassions never fail. They are new every morning* . . . It was a verse learned in childhood. She would not be consumed.

★　★　★

The journey to Castello was uneventful, Max sitting with Jane Clements, sometimes leaning over the back of his seat to draw the others into his expansive conversation. He was working hard at being on good form. Ellie listened to his laugh winging around the bus and slipped down in her seat, eyes closed. Nerine dozed next to her, occasionally coming to with a disconnected word.

They disembarked and as they clustered by the bus, breathing in both the cool exhalation of trees and the smoke of those deprived of their cigarettes, Salvatore sought the group's attention.

'As I've already reminded you, this palace, the country estate of Cosimo de' Medici, was later the home of those marvellous Botticelli paintings. Our main purpose today is to look in detail at the gardens but I'd really urge you to go and see the paintings in Florence if you can. The companion to *Primavera* is *The Birth of Venus*, which has to be seen in the flesh.' It was a feeble joke; Salvatore was trying to lighten the atmosphere. In her mind Ellie clearly saw the new-born Venus, vulnerable in

135

her nakedness. Half-heartedly the goddess made some effort to conceal her body but her gaze was strangely resigned; propelled so abruptly from her birthplace of the sea she was not yet part of the world. It always seemed to Ellie that Venus was unconscious of external life, unaware of the impact of her beauty and, being without the fear that is born of experience, unresistant to both good and bad influences. Ellie longed for that kind of equanimity.

'They are interesting paintings because they look back to classical mythology but try to interpret pagan stories through Christian eyes.' He seemed to be directing this at her, but Ellie didn't want eye-contact. 'As I touched on yesterday, Venus is more like the Madonna than a pagan goddess of love.' A strange tension, thought Ellie, no wonder her expression hovered, remained unreadable. Venus didn't know her place in life either. Perhaps she too was lost between faith in one God and a pagan world.

Salvatore went on. 'As we have discussed, Humanism was the great intellectual movement of Renaissance Italy, when classical writing, the plastic arts and architecture were being rediscovered.'

On the edge of the group Max and Jane Clements were grinding cigarette butts underfoot, their concentration flagging. As Salvatore talked they led a small breakaway group into the garden, through metal turnstiles, and began talking amongst themselves.

Salvatore chose not to notice and continued. 'Humanists believed that the Greek and Latin writings contained all the lessons one needed to lead a moral and effective life. Of course, moral and effective living was meant to be the province of the Church, so the Humanist scholars had to convince most of the Popes that they needed their skills. Unfortunately the relationship between scholars and Popes was never simple because the Humanists had their own take on theology. Remember, new Greek translations of the Bible were being researched at this time, and there was a return to teaching as laid down in the text. Some scholars were very critical of Church doctrines that didn't arise from the Word of God. And others even argued that pagan philosophers like Plato basically agreed with Christian revelation.'

'Was that Neoplatonism?' chipped in a diplomatic wife, and confided to her friend that she'd 'done it' in her art history course last year.

'Exactly,' said Salvatore. 'In fact Cosimo's grandson Lorenzo de Medici encouraged a school of Neoplatonic philosophers who met in the garden of his villa. The garden was an important place for exchanging ideas: I suppose the Medici were remembering the habits of the ancient philosophers.'

'Sure, Plato and Epicurus taught their followers in their own backyards,' volunteered Brad. Salvatore directed him a nod of agreement and began to lead them all into Castello, only briefly paying heed to the splinter group that had wandered ahead.

'Now this garden, although undoubtedly a place where philosophy will have been discussed, was more a testament of ideas. In its construction Cosimo de Medici set out to concretely illustrate both his position as head of government and the magnificence of Florence, the city over which he had such influence.'

Salvatore's words were lost now and again as he moved ahead of them, but Ellie could make out him saying that the garden was somewhat changed from Cosimo's original vision but nevertheless still clearly told a story of wealth and power. The garden wasn't as glorious as its original conception, it was now state-maintained and had a municipal air about it, but it still had a confidence that she admired. Many trees and hedges were long gone and the garden had lost its compartments. Ellie's imagination was taxed trying to conjure up water flowing through the now dry fountains. The water had been the greatest achievement at Castello; in the hills behind the villa Cosimo constructed two magnificent aqueducts to serve fountains and plants.

The advance party, now consisting of Max, Jane, the 'garden ladies' and Jonathan Hunter, had moved well ahead to explore the terraces that climbed the gentle hillside behind the villa. Ellie watched Max and Jonathan in close conversation, wondering what on earth they had in common. As Ellie, Slater and Brad, Nerine and the 'diplomatics' were soothed by Salvatore's words they saw Max and Jonathan peering down at them from the summit of the garden.

'Hey, there's a statue of a poor old geezer up here in the trees,' shouted Max.

The 'geezer' in the *boschetto* was a fountain representing the spirit of the Appenine mountains, explained Salvatore. Castello was a representation of Tuscany. Water once cascaded from the crouching figure of Appenino down to the next level of the garden into a grotto lined with a parade of sculpted animals and birds. Max and the others reappeared at this lower level, jostling to gaze into the dark space. Salvatore rearranged them all so that they should get an equal view. Large beasts in stone and marble at the rear of the grotto became distinct as they squinted into the gloom.

'Ideally a Renaissance garden would have had a representation of every type of plant in it and here in the grotto was an attempt to gather a spectrum of the known animal world. There's just one mythical beast, a unicorn, which represents the purity of the water from the springs in the hills behind. Originally water would have spouted from mouths and claws and beaks and then run on down, watering plants in its course, to the fountain of Hercules and Antaeus lower down the garden. Rather like the water flowing from the hills to Florence. As you can imagine, in this climate, water is a precious commodity and vital in enabling the community to thrive.' Salvatore gestured at the animals, suspended in an heraldic dance. 'You may think that these are just wonderful pieces of sculpture but everything in the garden was carefully chosen to reinforce the power of the Medici family and its close association with Florence. The lion here in the grotto was a longstanding symbol of Florence. You can see how close it stands to the goat, and Cosimo used the Capricorn symbol as his own device. And although on first sight the fountain of Hercules and

Antaeus seems just to illustrate a mythological tale it's probably an allegory too.'

Barbara, one of the diplomatic wives, volunteered her recall of mythology. 'I seem to remember that Antaeus was a giant who was invincible as long as he kept his feet on the ground. Hercules just lifted him up in order to squeeze the life out of him.'

A lesson for us all, thought Ellie.

'Just right,' nodded Salvatore, 'and here on the fountain he not only squeezes life from him but forces out a jet of water. Some say this parallels Cosimo lifting water out of the earth.'

Max was attentive. He turned to Jane. 'So, if you were going to have your own fountain, Janey, what would it be?'

Jane puckered her mouth and smoothed her hair. 'Was it Diana who was a huntress? Yes, I fancy a fountain of Diana.'

'With a device of cut lemons perhaps?' Ellie couldn't resist it.

Jane Clements turned a cool smile upon her.

'Well, Clements, you know . . . um, perhaps oranges too?' Ellie was no good at carrying through her intended slight; it all seemed so pointless.

'I suppose I should have Flora,' mused Max. 'Yes, Flora and Bacchus *in flagrante delicto* perhaps.'

Ellie walked away from the conversation, arms folded, head down, causing a glance from Nerine.

Behind her Max went on. 'What do you say to designing me a garden for my country house, Salvatore? You'd have plenty of material for allegories or allusions — after all I've associated with more than a few rich and famous.'

Salvatore said of course they could discuss it but Ellie was grateful to hear the flatness in his voice.

Meanwhile the garden-loving ladies were meandering around the terrace inspecting the orange and lemon trees planted in shoulder high pots. They had cornered Bernie, one of the diplomats, who was making use of his training, and were muttering about the lack of colour in the garden.

'I mean, I do like all these statues and gravel paths but it's a bit monotonous, isn't it? Give me a nice English herbaceous border and the shade of an ash tree any day.'

'Well dear, they can't do it in this climate, can they really?' And so it went on; the superiority of British plantsmen praised in ringing tones. From a distance Ellie saw Salvatore, gently amused, answering their questions on species and propagation with endless patience. Ellie attempted to hide herself away in one corner of the *boschetto*. Not easy, as the trees were set well apart with proper paths between them. In no way did it replicate nature. But she liked the ordered plan of the garden. Andrew would have liked it too. Andrew. How would he deal with Max? She needed some support here. Someone to tell her how to behave after — she couldn't even think it, let alone talk about it. All she knew was she was not going to accept it; not going to absorb the tiniest portion of his violence into her. However, she needed to lick her wounds.

Feeling keenly the lack of private and secret areas she was ready to steal back to the olive groves at Palazzo Michele and for the first time she felt a tug of home and wanted the familiar around her. She could see the shade of the ash and her own herbaceous border. At least coming this early to Italy meant that her own garden would be coming into its best as she returned. Perhaps she could persuade Nerine to visit when they got back? Here, Ellie felt unplaced, it was as if she had no life, never had had a life with Andrew, never had children. It came to her then, what a construct our lives are. Cosimo and succeeding Medicis chose to build themselves into a garden; to tell the world how they lived, who they were, in art and ordered nature. Of course they had the backup of history — lives recorded by historians. But these days when history was being rewritten so often, who was to say that there was any truth to these pictures of their lives? In lives with such power there was doubtless the potential for as much evil to be perpetrated as good. Yes, seemingly magnificent lives would have to be judged.

And how would Andrew's history be remembered when she and his children were gone? What was the meaning in an ordinary life? It was here she took refuge in her faith. Here where the cinder path shuddered to a halt on the cliff top. For her there would be absolutely no meaning without a God who saw her as part of a divine plan, a plan that continued and gave her time to work out whatever it was she was created for. This was true especially now when her children had grown and there wasn't the same daily motivation of fledging the young. As she rehearsed her beliefs she could hear a maniacal chorus in her ears; of course, the empty nest, the reason why so many middle-aged women turn to God and Church. Sex gone. Passion is reinvented. Ellie was shaking her head and speaking out, 'No!'

Salvatore touched her arm. '*Perche no*, Ellie?'

He was asking her, why? Ellie's shock at this blurring of her inner and outer worlds broke across her like a wave, but she rallied.

'I'm sorry. Just talking to myself!' Once more she was behind the façade that she had polished over the last two years. She had hoped that these weeks were going to see an end of it. Now her hopes sank into unlit depths.

He spoke again. Had she translated it right? She thought what he said was, 'It's all right, Ellie. You can talk the truth to me whenever you wish.'

Then, it felt like an impossible option but later she did speak to Salvatore. And she spoke in his language, grateful for the freedom and privacy it gave. She didn't talk of Max but she talked of her fears and her faith and he understood; he didn't mock her. It was like a homecoming. After her 'confession' they shared some dreams; dreams in which life was unencumbered by responsibilities. When he began to talk, Salvatore's vision was modest and it varied little from the reality of his life. He was contented, he said, to be a link in the chain and to steward this wonderful Palazzo for future generations. It was just that at this moment he felt like he was on the deck of a huge liner, watching the point where that massive chain disappeared through a housing, out of sight and into the depths below. He couldn't see the links but he knew that they led to an anchor that had halted the ship. Ellie took time to assimilate the image and when she had, she told Salvatore that she felt they were in similar places. The life plan that seemed so self-propelling was simply in hiatus and it was best just to admire the horizon for a while.

★ ★ ★

At the start of the day Salvatore had felt refreshed after an early night. He was not someone who easily put difficulties behind him despite having the intellectual capabilities to rationalise, so he was pleased to feel that the trials of the previous day were properly displaced. Castello proved to be an easy tour; so many good, concrete facts to impart although he knew he hadn't engaged the attention of the whole group. Castello didn't often capture imaginations like Gamberaia; perhaps it was because it was no longer home to a family and that air of a defunct history with no future pervaded people's consciousness. Ellie had been distracted and he'd speculated about her mood. What he hadn't foreseen at the very beginning of the ordinary day was the unexpected manner of its ending.

After dinner he had walked into the olive groves. There was little moon and the fireflies flickered and faded in metallic points of light like a time-lapse constellation. He walked amongst them, scattering their phosphorescence, and reached his favourite place. The soft earth was dry and still filled with the day's heat and his body relaxed into it; he stretched out and sand and dry leaves worked into his hair. It was barely ten minutes of repose before he heard another body approaching; he had stiffened, willing whoever it was to leave him in peace. Then he heard his name being called and knew who it was.

'Am I disturbing you?' asked Ellie.

'No.' He had lied but surprised himself at the way his resistance to company had melted away in her presence.

'It's just that I came out here to be alone and realised it was the last thing I wanted.' She gave a small laugh; he had noticed this habit of derision before.

Salvatore smiled encouragement; perhaps he was to be a listening ear. She sat beside him, her knees drawn up and enfolded by her arms.

'What do you think we should do with our past, Salvatore?'

He didn't understand and asked her to explain.

'I know if it's been bad, common sense tells us to put it behind us. But it's not that easy, is it?'

Salvatore nodded. 'That's true — but in the same way, if it's been good we shouldn't hold on to that too tightly either. After all, there's nowhere else we can live except in the present.' He paused and traced lines in the dust. 'Are you thinking of your husband?'

It seemed an effort to her to simply nod her head. 'Everything of value came out of that marriage, my children, my homes, my freedom to create. But . . . ' she looked as though she was forcing the words, 'with time to analyse things, I wonder what would have happened to us if Andrew hadn't died.'

Salvatore listened. He assured her that she was not disloyal, merely honest, as she told him how she felt she'd been overshadowed by Andrew's brilliant energy, his needs, his selfishness. He knew no authority but his own. She was shattered to think the marriage may not have worked in the years after the children left; that if it had not been death that parted them then it might have been her own wish to live.

'I feel a complete hypocrite at times. The mourning widow. Sometimes I can't bear the sympathy. If only people knew what I was thinking.'

Salvatore had said to her then that this loving and not-loving was the basis of any long term marriage and wondered whether he truly believed it. How was one to measure a marriage? How did one know if it could be better than it was? That other people found depths that were inaccessible to you? It was unfathomable and it was the point at which he found comfort in the fact that there was God in his universe; a God who had placed him where he was meant to be. When he shared that with Ellie he felt she had found a part of that same solace.

'I'm sorry you should have to listen to this, Salvatore.' She tried a laugh. 'You were just the poor soul who happened to be here!' Lowering her head, she went on. 'But I've been struggling with these feelings by myself. I can hardly discuss it with the children, they just need to cherish the good things about their father.'

How we always want to go on protecting our children, thought Salvatore. 'I wonder when children can start to see us parents as humans who make mistakes?' Salvatore touched her briefly and spoke into the warm darkness. 'What's the English phrase; Forgive and Forget? The first part is essential for the last and you may have to keep doing that over and over again for the rest of your life.'

★ ★ ★

Alone again in his bed he reflected on Ellie's trust in him; why she had chosen this evening to confide in him. Was he really just in the right place at the right time or had she singled him out as her confessor? People who didn't know him were not usually inclined to use him as confidante but those who did knew of his ability to keep confidences. It had been a very long time since Salvatore had talked to any woman the way he talked to Ellie that night. He propped himself up against white pillows and picked up his book; it was a comforting ritual. Ficino would have some sage words where he often failed.

You say that one of your relatives felt injured the other day by the insults of some impudent people.

He who accepts injury receives it from himself and not from the offender.

You will perhaps say that it is difficult not to desire vengeance. But be in no doubt that if men forgive, the most just God will settle the balance a little later. Socrates, the wisest among the Greeks, practised this virtue alone, and Christ, the master of life, practised it

150

above all others. Indeed it is said that He descended amongst men virtually just for this.

The magnanimous man in his greatness sets small value on small things. Trivial and fleeting are temporal things, for the past is no more, the future does not yet exist and the present is indivisible; it starts and ends at the same time.

Read this letter to your relative and tell him to find his remedy in reason and not expect it from time.

Yes. Good words for Ellie. She would have to find her remedy in forgiving and not expect time to heal the wounds she was nursing.

8

The next morning at breakfast Jonathan made a purposeful approach to Ellie and Nerine's table. Whilst fingering the brim of his panama like a concert pianist he asked if he might sit down with them. He settled directly opposite Ellie and fixed his gaze on her.

'Do you remember me saying I thought I knew you from somewhere?' Ellie nodded. 'We sat at the same table once at a magnificent party at Benfield. Lady Portham's fiftieth, I believe?'

Ellie sat mute, trying to salvage visual memories. The dream she'd had. The doctor she'd sat next to. 'That was you?' was all she managed.

'I fear so. A little less grey then. I did feel sorry for you that night sitting next to an old bore like me. You seemed so *fresh* compared to the rest of us.'

Ellie demurred. 'I do remember not being a very good conversationalist.'

Jonathan laughed. 'Hard to be scintillating with people with whom you don't have much in common.'

'So how did you work it out?'

'Do you know, I think it was the fountain at Castello, just reminded me of the one in the middle of the lake at Benfield and I suppose a train of thought got going. There it is. Marvellous how the tides of life wash in and out, isn't it?'

Maybe, maybe not thought Ellie. No more making up my own story to tell here. This man may know a large part of it — but what exactly, she wondered?

'So did you know my husband?'

'No, not really. Wasn't he the estate manager for Crickwell?' Ellie nodded. 'That's what I thought. I said as much to Max and Jane yesterday!' He was triumphant. 'Only I couldn't remember his name — until Max reminded me.'

The silence was gelatinous. Ellie offered nothing.

'That Max fellow tells me your husband died two years ago.'

'Um . . . that's right. I'm sorry. I just want to go and get myself another juice.' Ellie rose, scraping the chair back on the tiles, gripping her glass hard to match the tightening in her chest and belly. Her teeth were clamped down against each other. Leave me alone. Everyone gossiping about my life. What else had Jonathan and Max been sharing about her? She spent a while pouring the drink, willing herself to be as insentient as the orange juice. When she returned, the topic of her past had obviously been dropped and Nerine was regaling Jonathan with hairy descriptions of the old times with Duggie out in Ceylon. Had she been in a better frame of mind, Ellie might have added that Andrew did the same to her — told her tall tales of VSO out there in the sixties. The difference was, when you told your own story you could edit it; right now she wanted no more of her history to be recounted and shared.

'Well. It's a small world,' said Jonathan and got up awkwardly, tipping his hat to them. 'See you ladies later.' And he was gone.

Nerine knew better than to probe. Instead she understood Ellie's need to leave the walls of the Palazzo and scooped her up. 'We're going into Florence. And we'll take the train.'

Ellie smiled in relief. 'That's a bright idea, Nerine.'

★ ★ ★

Walking in the vast marble cathedral that was Santa Maria Novella station brought back a kind of peace to Ellie. As they weaved through committed travellers, she felt thankfully anonymous and liberated; from here she

154

could go anywhere, no questions asked. Nerine and she hadn't spoken much on the train; they'd mulled over their guides and window-gazed. Nerine had said they must go and see the Gozzoli frescoes in the Medici palace chapel and so that gave them somewhere to begin.

As they walked past the bare brick façade of San Lorenzo, Ellie tried to catch her bearings. She had stayed in a small *pensione* a stone's throw from the church in her student years. Thinking back she couldn't believe how much she'd taken it all for granted. She'd walked past San Lorenzo every day and was only once attracted in to look at Michelangelo's magnificent library by the cloisters. Ellie then was more interested in searching out cheap pizza than exploring the treasures on her doorstep. And it was easy in Florence to treat the exceptional as common-place. Until recently she'd felt somewhat ashamed of her lack of cultural curiosity. She now realised that she was simply responding to some inbuilt personal attraction. She found more pleasure in the plain brick façade of the church than the mad Mannerist pomp of Michelangelo. At eighteen she couldn't own up to that but now she could. Who knew where or when those preferences are actually forged?

One thing was sure at the moment, she had more faith in her ability to discern good art than good men.

'Why do we respond to some art or buildings or people and not to others, Nerine? I mean, what makes us 'like'?'

Nerine looked amused at this question after such a silent progress from the station.

'You might as well ask what gives us discernment of any kind. Education, observation, exposure, instinct — I don't know, Ellie! Probably scientists would rationalise it down to nerve stimuli whereas no doubt you would want God in there somewhere.'

Ellie laughed. 'You're damn right I would!'

Palazzo Medici was relatively quiet and the queue for the chapel a mere fifteen minutes long. They filed past the *Journey of the Magi* fresco with a murmur of foreign voices around them. Ellie couldn't say that the painting was simple, for it was richly coloured, patterned and gilded, but it was direct and unashamed. She loved the confidence of the faces that stared out at her as though it was today. Gozzoli had painted his patrons into the scene — and seemed to have turned the biblical into something completely secular.

Later, with a glass of red wine and blistered pizza before each of them, Nerine confronted

Ellie. 'I know there's something wrong and I'm giving you this opportunity to talk about it.'

Ellie didn't speak for some moments. She'd been wrestling all morning with the decision but now this ultimatum had emerged, decisiveness deserted her. She looked helplessly at Nerine with her mouth half open.

'And I am not going to talk to anyone,' Nerine added.

So Ellie told her. Amongst the clatter of cutlery and laughter, with interruptions by the efficient waitress, in the ordinary *trattoria*, she told her about Max. About his attempt at violation. She didn't invite comment and she told Nerine of her decision to make no issue of the experience. Thankfully, Nerine in her wisdom offered no advice; she knew that she was there to act as a passive minister.

'I just want to go forward now. It's interesting, isn't it? I came out here to see if it gave me a clue about taking my life in a new direction. This wasn't quite how I expected it to be.' She smiled wryly.

'And are you any clearer?' asked Nerine

'Yes. Strangely I think I am. I've had to face myself. What my purpose is. Where I think my security lies. And you, Nerine, you've taught me a great deal.' Nerine raised her eyebrows. 'You just live life and don't look back.'

'Well, except to learn from my all too frequent mistakes, darling.'

They laughed and clinked glasses. For a while they bent to their food, and when they'd filled up, Ellie's mood was lighter. They decided to ditch art appreciation and go shopping. Ellie wanted gifts for the children and neighbours; also a little something for one of her elderly students. Nerine wanted to take Ellie to *Pineider's* to find some handmade paper.

'Did you know you can keep company with the ghosts of Stendahl and Shelley there? My dear, it's the only place to go. If you can't afford anything you can just drool over the beauty of it all.'

They walked past the duomo, watching tourists photographing each other against the Baptistery doors and then turned, with the sun in their eyes, towards the Piazza Signoria. Then Nerine checked her watch and let out a grunt of irritation.

'It won't be open yet. Come on then, we'll go from the sublime to the ridiculous . . . ' and headed off in a westerly direction with Ellie in tow.

The Mercato Nuovo cheered up Ellie no end. Within half an hour she was laden down with plastic Davids, card boxes covered in cherubs, Leaning Tower of Pisa candles and Venus fridge magnets. She had been tempted to buy Dominic an apron adorned with a screen print of part of David's anatomy but curbed herself because Nerine told her it was not the best thing for a mother to buy her son. They gloried together in bad taste, giggling like teenagers. They both couldn't resist the plastic snow-filled domes; Nerine's mini blizzard fell upon a tiny duomo while Ellie imagined she could see the *Three Graces* shiver under their layer of snow.

'I honestly don't think I could cope with any good taste now.' Ellie was breathless with a laughter that was quite out of proportion to the joke. She was grateful for the feeling of air rushing into her chest as she bent over and breathed in greedily. Nerine thumped her between her shoulder blades.

'I really didn't take you for such a peasant!' she howled.

'I am, I am. It's such a relief!' Ellie straightened up, her eyes running, and hugged Nerine, sending bags flying.

When they'd reassembled they walked on, crossing the Ponte Vecchio against tides of students uniformed in jeans and designer rucksacks. Ellie was glad to have Nerine steering her, for she only dimly remembered the geography of the city from her teens. It was more the emotions she remembered; the fear of being independent, the joy of wandering in the quiet galleries of the Uffizi early in the mornings. Now the queues were hours long. She'd meant to come back to the city with Andrew but something had always prevented them. In the early years it had been a lack of will. Andrew had no great desire to travel, his wanderlust having been sated before she came along. For holidays he was happier to walk in Yorkshire or Wales, Ellie and the kids always trailing well behind. In the few years when they might have had both money and opportunity Florence didn't seem the ideal choice for children. And latterly the budget was directed at survival merely.

'Did you ever come here with Duggie?'

'Oh, lots of times. We had friends in Via Tuornabuoni. Long dead sadly.'

'Isn't it strange to come somewhere without the people who made it special?'

'I didn't come for years. And then the first time was awful. I didn't know one could have such resentment for inanimate objects . . . all these buildings that outlived my loved ones.'

Ellie leaned over the side of the bridge and looked down into the Arno, watching detritus drift in eddies. She listened to Nerine's voice above the hum of the city.

160

'But then as more and more of our friends began to die I turned to places for consolation. Knowing we had been here, walked here at a particular moment in time, gave Duggie a reality that was beginning to slip away. Otherwise it was like a hole in time was beginning to heal over with no trace.' Nerine turned to Ellie. 'I know you were mad at Jonathan this morning for discussing Andrew with the others, but really you shouldn't be. Be grateful he's alive in someone's memory.'

Ellie put her hand lightly on Nerine's shoulder. 'I know you're right. Perhaps I was just never any good at sharing him even when he was alive. And most of all I don't want the wrong memories to be bandied around.'

'You mean difficult memories?' said Nerine.

Ellie could only nod, head down, her hand dropping to her side.

'Accept them, Ellie. Assimilate them and get on with the rest of your life.'

'OK! Isn't this where I came in?'

They laughed and headed, bags in hand, back to the station.

*　*　*

It had only been one week since their arrival but the Palazzo felt like home as the taxi crunched on to the grit of the entrance courtyard. Nerine took time getting up the flight of steps to the reception hall where she immediately flung off her shoes. Ellie followed the small damp footprints that marked her progress across the flagstones to the bar. Nerine hailed Francesca as she slumped into one of the large wing chairs.

'Gin and tonic, darling,' was all she said as she unpinned her hat and dropped it, like a dead bird, on the floor. Two couples, in quiet conversation in the gloom of the half-shuttered room, turned at her voice. Max and Jane, Slater and Brad. Max stood and came over immediately. He was affable, loquacious, solicitous. Could he find Nerine a cold compress? Hardly stopping the flow of his words he turned to include Ellie in his conversation, asking her about her day and offering her a drink. This total lack of acknowledgment stirred her up again. She heard Nerine's words ghosting — *accept, assimilate, get on with the rest of your life.* Why was she no good at this? For all her thoughts on the situation Ellie could not then, nor later, make up her mind as to whether Max truly did not remember his assault upon her. The alternative was too vile to contemplate.

He didn't stay long but ushered Jane out with apologies of other arrangements; Ellie stared after their retreating backs. She watched Jane's walk, too consciously relaxed, and Max's hand firmly guiding her by the elbow. Nerine tripped off too to have 'forty winks' and the boys regrouped on the sofa. They were keen to hear about the day in Florence; desperate for information with which to add to their store of knowledge that they hoarded like nervy squirrels.

'What did you think of the Gozzoli frescoes?' asked Brad.

The fresco became the new target.

'Group photographs of the Medici family. Not so much the adoration of our Lord as the adoration of the Guild of the Magi or the commemoration of the stunning wealth of its patrons. Propaganda for the Medicis just about sums it up I reckon.' Ellie knew she was doing it again, misdirecting the anger. She made efforts to unstiffen her body in the chair.

Brad continued. 'I see that, but even though the Gozzoli fresco is blatantly political that doesn't mean it's not a wonderful work of art, does it?'

'No. It's supremely well crafted . . . but for me true art has to be connected with the spiritual life. It has an extra dimension. Something that takes the viewer beyond the frame.'

Slater interrupted. 'So Gozzoli was just a journeyman working for gold.'

'I suppose if you had no charity in your heart that's how you'd look at it . . . '

Ellie wasn't sure she believed this harsh approach but the sharpness of her words released the tension she felt. She softened.

'Mind you, his pay was hardly magnificent. Few artists got as rich as their patrons.'

'The gap's closing today though, isn't it?' said Brad.

Ellie rubbed her eyes and sat for a moment head in hand before replying. 'It seems to me that the wealthiest artists are the furthest away from producing true art.'

'OK, who's a true artist?'

Ellie didn't hesitate. 'Fra Angelico. He may have been as subject to his patrons as Gozzoli but he never worked without praying to God first and I think it shows. And some might quibble about the painterly skills in a Winifred Nicholson painting, but the spiritual emanations from her images go beyond the craftsmanship.'

'I would never have taken you for a religious person,' said Slater.

'Oh good. Continue not taking me as religious please. I hope I'm just one of those people who is trying to live life with a spiritual dimension rather than manipulating it to serve my purposes alone.'

Ouch. How arrogant that sounded even in her own ears. But she might as well go the whole hog now. Ellie spread her arms and tipped back in her chair. 'Actually, I'd like to BE a Winifred Nicholson painting — rather rough and spontaneous but sincere!' Ellie caught a movement in the corner of her eye; Salvatore advanced from the doorway where he must have shadowed the conversation.

'I am not entirely in disagreement with you, Ellie, but I don't believe that even the manipulative are untouched by art. No matter what his initial intentions, be they just to selfishly demonstrate his wealth and power, I think the patron could be moved beyond his earthly concerns by the beauty of the artist's interpretation of his commission. And I think you're a little hard on poor Gozzoli. His skill was surely God-given and his vision takes me beyond the frame.'

Ellie responded to the smile in his eyes. 'I'm sorry. I sounded rather black and white there, didn't I? I'm sure he did have a gift, I'm just questioning whether he always used it well.'

'That could take us into the depths of a conversation about being human and not always getting it right.' Salvatore smiled at her.

Brad was barely listening to Salvatore's contribution. 'But what about all this modern conceptual art today? The pieces that make people so mad they can't call it art. Why the hell do we pay so much for that?'

Ellie jumped in. 'Back to my schism between the manipulative and the spiritual . . . that's head art not heart art. Artists who strut around being clever think there's nothing as good as rejecting the wisdom of the past. And those who pay think it's clever to be iconoclastic.'

Salvatore nodded in agreement and added, 'The sad thing is that most of those 'modern' artists are just going to be fixed and dated by their vision. Artists like Nicholson, Morandi and de Chirico will be timeless because they reinvent the ordinary and . . . ' he reached for the right words, 'invest it with mystery.'

Ellie thought that Salvatore was right. What was the point in destruction, in knocking down? In art, as in life, the only way was to build on the good things that had gone before.

★ ★ ★

Saturday. It could be a leisurely start to the day and Salvatore was still in his robe as he ate breakfast. A week since the group had arrived. It was a relief that he could leave them alone today. The learning process, he found, was so much better when they had time for their own explorations. He wondered most about Ellie's and pondered her brittle conversation about art. There was a change in her but he could not understand it. Salvatore drained his coffee cup. What he needed was a day away from this place too. A phone call put everything in place. Thank heaven for friends.

The road to Bagno Vignoni ribboned through the countryside. As he made his way further south into the valley of the Orcia, fields of young wheat trickled across the soft hills, punctuated by the striations of vineyards. The green was luminous; the freshness welling up from the waters beneath. Salvatore considered how many had taken this road before him. Ghosts of warring Guelphs and Ghibellines bent on destruction flitted ahead of Santa Caterina, who like him had travelled to the waters to refresh her spirit. Salvatore conjured up the portrait of her that hung in Pienza cathedral, fashioned as a Christian nymph, watching her reflection in the clear water of Bagno Vignoni.

Salvatore arrived at the spa to warm welcomes from his hotelier friends, another husband and wife team.

'Sorry to leave you to it, Salva, but we have a conference to look after. Here's the key to our apartment, just help yourself. You know where everything is,' he said, and she urged him to relax and take advantage of the mineral baths as he looked so tired. It was true he was — and this was just the place to address it. The last time he'd been here was when he brought his uncle Ercole for a curative weekend for a bad back. The old man had basked in the spa waters with such a grin on his face — but that may have had more to do with the two bottles of wine they managed over a very long lunch. It made Salvatore smile to himself; Ercole had helped him so much, it was good to be able to give his uncle something he enjoyed.

Before he went to the pool, Salvatore wandered into the library and noted with pleasure that he was the only one there. He pulled a book out on the healing properties of the Bagno Vignoni waters and leafed through. There was something about the flora too and its use in herbal remedies. *Adiantum*, the pale fern that grew in the crevices here, was meant be good for restoring hair loss and, not only that, it made cocks and partridges 'bolder in battle'. Salvatore smoothed his own thinly covered scalp and meditated on such a wonder potion. Perhaps he should invest in some — he was needy in the area of courage too. Why, he wondered, couldn't he talk to Maria about their life, or absence of it, together?

Salvatore replaced the book; enough of these thoughts, he needed some physical action.

Soon undressed, Salvatore stepped down into the baths where the warmth of the natural springs touched his body and mind. He floated on his back. Il Magnifico, Lorenzo de Medici, used to float in these very waters for relief of his rheumatism. Even the best of us need help with our weaknesses, Salvatore mused. For some reason he began thinking of Ellie, thinking of her conversation about her husband. It had brought things to the surface for him; her sense of things unresolved, the difficulty of being suddenly alone. It was probably the first time he felt he had been inside someone else's grief and he marvelled at how she had made him understand. He moved on to his front and dipped his face into the water. How would he function if he lost Maria? Gently, he swam to where the water cascaded into the pool. The temperature here was hotter and he lifted his face to allow the rush to flow over his head. With the water came an unexpected sob and he felt his body shudder under the jet. He was glad that no one was watching.

9

The two weeks that followed were structured by Salvatore's lectures and visits. Ellie was thankful for this as she could concentrate on the work in hand and almost deny Max's presence. She was pleased when he chose to cut lectures, which he seemed to do regularly.

There were times when they couldn't help but meet, like the day they were touring the Botanic Gardens in Florence. The guide from the university had just led them all into a greenhouse and most of the group had their heads bent over plant labels, listening greedily to his words. Max came up behind Ellie and laid his hands on her shoulders. She reacted as though electricity had shot through her and turned sharply to look at him. Max had his hands in the air.

'Whoa, steady. It's only me.'

'I know,' was all she could muster. His neutrality towards her bewildered Ellie. She wavered between wanting to challenge him and simply reflecting back his charming veneer.

'Don't seem to have seen much of you lately.'

'That's probably just as well, don't you think?'

He looked quizzical. One thing she was thankful for was the way he lowered his voice when he spoke. 'Ellie, I thought experienced women like you could handle a little dalliance.'

He must have read her face. Why couldn't she mask her feelings? As the rest of the group moved between them she must have had her mouth open. She was glad of the physical wall of bodies as the anger built up in her. Max simply receded, a smile on his face, his hand across his brow as if in some kind of salute as Ellie fought to deal with her feelings.

Nerine was more transparent. As Jane and Max walked into dinner one evening, he hailed Ellie and Nerine. 'We haven't talked to you girls for a while. Come and share a table?'

Before Ellie could think how to respond, Nerine cut in. 'Sorry Max, dear boy, we've got a date with Jonathan and Barbara and Bernie. Seems we've sorted ourselves into the mature and not-so-mature!' Her laughter rattled in the marbled room like rhinestones. She smiled sweetly at Jane who tried to respond but didn't do too good a job.

Max's jaw clenched for a fraction of a

second before he made a mock bow and said, 'Ah well, we will have to share your wisdom another time.'

Ellie watched his arm go around Jane as he took her off to the far side of the room. They spent a lot of evenings together. It produced in Ellie a surprising mix of reactions. It certainly kept Max away from her but a tiny part of her felt disappointed. It was as if some relationship with him had been strangled before its birth. It disgusted her that she could even think about him in this way. But no matter how hard she tried she couldn't suppress the unlikely attraction she felt for him. It was like a dead body that would not sink to the depths of the sea but kept returning to the surface, ever more damaged.

The days continued and the cliques hardened. Max drew the younger members into his orbit simply because his energy attracted the energetic. To be honest, Ellie was rather saddened that she was now sometimes cut off from them by her avoidance of Max. But thrown into company with Jonathan, Ellie was surprised, especially after their bad start, to find how fond she was of him. He was perhaps too happy to hide behind his image of elder statesman but she'd done him a wrong when she wrote him off as insensitive. Jonathan was kind and courteous to her in those last days. Although she probably would have been able to talk to him of Andrew he didn't again directly talk of him. He was happy to compare notes about Benfield and talk about the upstairs gossip in the Portham household. Lord Portham was well into his seventies now; in fact his son was older than Ellie. She remembered him as a rather pompous twenty-something who'd gone into banking.

'Yes, done rather well with an American bank,' said Jonathan. 'I talk to him quite regularly at Benfield gatherings, especially those shoots they have.'

Ellie was grateful for Jonathan's sensitive disinterest in her emotional life. They kept the conversation to jobs and homes and hobbies. He didn't care to play a part in her psychotherapy and he was gallant to her and Nerine. Over subsequent dinners with them he proved himself to be a cultured man with a great deal of love for his family. Ellie, listening to him talk one evening, couldn't help but muse on how it might not be such a bad fate to be married to a man like Jonathan. He would take care of a wife. He would probably spring no surprises financially or emotionally. She smiled at herself for entertaining such thoughts but also allowed the feelings of need to come to the surface. She'd been coping for so long and not given herself permission to lean on anyone.

On the days they had to themselves, Ellie often escaped to Florence and spent time alone — as alone as you could be in the bustling Uffizi — in front of the Botticelli paintings. She tried to understand the place of Venus who also looked apart in the midst of so much activity. In *Primavera* the goddess appeared to be pregnant; Salvatore had not said anything about this, nor had she thought of it before. Perhaps it was some image of fecundity: the painting was, surely, partly meant to be an allegory of spring with its new birth. She would ask him. Philosophical discussions were what they had these days; somehow they'd drawn back from talk of feelings and any further intimacy. What she did remember him saying about Venus was that she was a summation of everything else going on in the picture.

Standing inert amongst the crowds, Ellie focused on the still figure of Venus. They mirrored each other. A blur of bodies passed between Ellie and the unmoving goddess, each of them quiet amongst the activity. The Graces whirled in their dance between the divine and the earthly. They were receiving blessings from above. Surely that included forgiveness for any wrongdoing too. These blessings they were passing on to those here below and then thanking creation once more: All in an endless cycle. Venus stood in quiet balance at their side. She was their metaphorical full stop. All that was bad was absorbed and disabled by her; all that was good grew in her. She was placed as the symbol of Love on Earth.

For Ellie this was the moment of clarity as the painting took her beyond language and into the eyes of her heart. She often struggled to work out what her beliefs actually meant in practical terms. She often despaired at how she mulled over things endlessly and couldn't act. She wanted her beliefs to lead her somewhere. Looking at Venus' feet planted firmly on the flowery ground she thought about the paths she, Ellie, had trodden. She had survived so much. Where had that strength come from? Her friends without faith would say it was hers alone, her strength of character, but she knew it was not. It was by the grace of God she was still standing. Ellie looked at the raised hands of the Graces and ideas melted into her with the same fluidity as the dance. Salvatore had talked about the Christian concepts within the classical stories but she had not understood until now, and certainly not seen the relevance to her. She inclined her body in mimicry of one of the dancers and thought of the Christian graces, faith, love and above all, hope.

Ellie stepped back from the painting. For moments it was hidden from her by the rush of bodies. Students walked past, heads sideways, to tick it off their list. Couples in anoraks stood, consulting their guides, matching the picture with other people's words and views. At that moment she wanted to have her own authentic understanding. It was a desire that was granted. Later, the only way she could describe the sensation of love and hope was to say she was drenched. The outpouring was so strong she almost buckled under it.

★ ★ ★

She didn't make verbal sense of it until she was sharing lunch with Nerine.

'Where did you get to this morning?' Nerine asked her after they were served their food.

'Back to look at *Primavera*.' She paused to sip some rather good Chianti. 'Before Salvatore talked about it I thought it was so familiar that I'd 'done it', if you know what I mean?'

Nerine nodded.

'But that's the thing about good art, it's got layers. It keeps telling you more.'

'And what did it tell you?' Nerine was knotting creamy tagliatelle on to a fork in elegant crochet.

'To live what I believe.'

Nerine chewed away, eyes wide. Seconds passed before she was able to wipe her mouth on the sky blue napkin and say, 'What's that?'

Ellie liked the dramatic effect and the pause. A moment of silence was needed before this. After all, it had taken her years to get here and mean it.

'Because we are forgiven, we forgive others.'

Nerine waited for more, face impassive but not unkind.

'What's the point in God if he's up there and we're down here? I believe in a God I can have a relationship with, every day, every moment. And you can only have that if there are no barriers — everything needs to be forgiven.'

Nerine still didn't speak. Ellie wanted to laugh. It was a bit much for a gentle lunch. She put out her hand and covered Nerine's long fingers. 'Sorry if this is a bit heavy, Nerine, but it's nice to not feel like a wave tossed by the wind at this moment.'

Nerine smiled. 'I think it's lovely, dear. And

even if I can't understand exactly where you are, I love the idea that everything came clear through that painting. It's a kind of synaesthesia,' she put down her fork, 'and I approve of that linking together of everything.' Her hands moved as though piecing together an imaginary chain.

'Synaesthesia, that's a good way of putting it, Nerine. I couldn't work out what sense was coming at me, was I feeling love or seeing hope or tasting life?' She laughed and made her voice ghoulish, 'or maybe hearing voices?' Nerine joined in with the laughter. 'Whatever, at last, I just felt I knew what to do and where I was headed.'

Nerine picked up her hand and stroked it. 'My dear girl. I just want you to remember that you are human and that we humans are all fragile creatures. Don't expect too much of yourself.' Her eyes were clear, her grip on Ellie strong. 'And remember the fleetingness of feelings. Feeling something is one thing, living it is quite another. You may be asked to do more than you can.'

Ellie was touched by her concern. She tried to see herself through Nerine's eyes. For heaven's sake, she didn't want to come over as a flaky visionary. Nerine must be assessing her. In fact her silent reception of Ellie's rapturous outburst spoke volumes. But it wasn't like that at all. True, Ellie had watched this kind of euphoria in others who'd suffered: sometimes it seemed like a mad compensation. But this . . . this knowledge was different.

'Don't worry, Nerine. I've got my feet firmly on the ground, I promise.'

'Good. And if you threaten to lift off I'm right here to pull on your balloon string!'

They laughed and ate in peace.

★　★　★

On the final evening, there was a last supper. Everyone attended and by placing herself as far from Max as possible, Ellie found she was enjoying the end of term atmosphere. She tried to imagine going back to a place where these people were not on hand each day. She'd even become quite fond of Vera and her friends. Jane wasn't actually too bad either, if you severed her from Max, and she'd noticed they were spending less time together latterly. And Nerine, well, Nerine was her salvation. The relationship gave her something of everything; Nerine was part mother, part counsellor, part mischief-making sister. There was no way she would not continue to see Nerine and she told her so. At the end of the evening, of course, everyone swore to keep in touch and Ellie felt she really must learn to embrace email at last.

* * *

In the morning they all filed out into the hall, weighed down with luggage to say their goodbyes to Salvatore. Ellie was thankful for these weeks, she told him, and so pleased to be able to fill up her creative 'tank' with all the beauty he had introduced to them. She wished him well. As she drove alone once more to the airport, she thought about him and smiled. A good man. And a good man like him deserved the good life he had. The thoughts brought up in her a wistfulness she hadn't expected. So, as the winding roads of Tuscany gave way to a motorway route she reviewed it all, the good and the bad. And she was grateful for the concentrated taste of life that had been given to her. She had been shaken but her roots were deep. She had to believe the essence of her was stronger as she returned home.

* * *

When everyone had packed up and gone home Salvatore did not always feel a sense of bereavement; sometimes he felt a relief and a restoration. This time, however, he was surprised at the emptiness he was feeling. Maria was to be away for another four days and Francesca, having helped with the housekeeping, was off to stay with cousins in Sardinia for a day or two. He walked the empty rooms, remembering their occupants. Their farewells had been interesting; Max had bound him in a boxer's hug, saying, 'And don't forget, when I find a site, I want you to design me a garden.'

The diplomatic couples had been diplomatic to the end. They politely thanked him; making reference to the salient parts of his course, expressing their interest in the philosophy — ah, so it had not been lost upon them — and carefully pressing their printed cards into his hand, hoping that he would find his way to Surrey on his next trip to England.

Jane was flattering. 'I've learnt so much that's going to be such a help with my projects. I think I'll try to find another course back in London. They do lovely ones at the Chelsea Physic Garden.' Then she'd taken off her dark glasses and leaned to kiss him on each cheek, her scent enveloping him. 'Thank you, Salvatore, you're an inspiration.'

Salvatore watched as she made her goodbyes to the rest of the group; heard her say to Max as their faces touched, 'Be sure to look me up in Town. You've got my number.' And knew that it was probably the last Jane would see of Max.

Brad and Slater had already plied him with addresses, their own, and names and numbers of Institutes on the East Coast. Now they pumped him enthusiastically by the hand.

'Salvatore, they'd die for your lectures in the U.S. of A. Say the word and we can arrange a tour,' said Brad.

'It could be a brilliant add-on to our landscape business. We mean it!' enthused Slater.

Salvatore had spent a happy evening letting his mind wander over the possibilities of this but in the end he'd brought himself back to his responsibilities and filed the notion.

As the 'garden ladies' tweeted their goodbyes — he wasn't sure how much they had truly enjoyed — Salvatore had tried not to be distracted by Ellie's presence, hovering at the back of the queue with Nerine.

He watched as Max bade the two of them a formal farewell. Shaking Ellie's hand and giving her a brief kiss, Max said, 'Well, Ellie, it's been very interesting to meet you. I wouldn't be at all surprised if our paths didn't cross again.'

Ellie's expression was under control but Salvatore sensed this was not a reunion she would relish. She made light of the remark. 'Oh, I don't know, you're such a city boy and I'm a country bumpkin through and through, it may not be too likely!'

Max had just raised his eyebrows and moved on to say goodbye to Nerine.

It was only then that it consciously touched Salvatore that he would miss Ellie. He wanted to have more time.

'Ladies, it's been an extreme pleasure to get to know you.' He'd bowed slightly to kiss their hands. 'Perhaps,' he said, watching Ellie's expression, 'I might be able to visit you both in the autumn when I come on business to Oxford.' Salvatore caught the smile on Nerine's face and knew that he had not quite effected the casualness for which he'd been aiming. They both nodded at him.

'That would be nice. It's going to be strange being alone at home after having got to know everyone so well.' Ellie was bright but impersonal.

Francesca hugged her. 'I am one who hopes you will come here again.'

And so am I, thought Salvatore.

★　★　★

It was another three days before everything was prepared for the next course. Maria came home on the eve of the new session. She was tired and Salvatore was distracted by the preparations. He knew that both of them recognised how much anticipation was attached to these times when Maria returned home after a long absence. Salvatore was beginning to accept that it would always be anti-climactic. She positively shunned his attempts to make the event special. It was as though she just wanted to slip back in to their joint life with no fuss and certainly no celebration. He watched Maria try to not to show her irritation as he made her sit and accept the drink he'd made for her. She called him Darling and told him she could get her own. Conversation was stilted. Each was caught up in personal orbits of thoughts and it was hard to coalesce. Salvatore had an image of his girls playing skipping games with friends; they had to jump in as the ropes were turning. He remembered how heart-stopping it had been when the timing was wrong and the ropes and bodies collided, causing howls from the children and putting a sudden and final end to the predictable rhythm.

Maria went to bed in the guest bedroom: she'd asked Francesca to get it ready so as not to bother him. She hugged him and hoped he understood she desperately needed to sleep in, whereas she knew he would be up at dawn to prepare. And of course Salvatore understood that and hugged her back, feeling her release herself too soon.

Alone in his bed once more he willed himself to think forward and not look back. There would be more people here in the morning; all of them with their own lives, their own needs, their own problems. If teaching had taught him anything it was how different people's views on life could be. How everyone learned in an entirely different fashion. You could never take it for granted that another person was seeing the world as you were.

10

It was May and the drifts of cow parsley took over the sort of no-man's land that spread out from the end of her planted garden, forming a barrier between mown lawns and the fields beyond. Straggling elderflower bushes masked the wall between her and the meadows so, from the house, it may have seemed that her garden flowed into the countryside. When you walked there it was obvious it did not; the stones marked a pure and definite boundary.

Ellie was glad she had gone away so early; she had caught the freshness in Italy and returned for the best month in an English garden, or so she thought. Her garden was pale toned in its foreground, pinks and whites overcoming the greens of foliage, setting up a connection with the nacre white sky of morning. The plants further down the southerly slope first increased in colour to vermilions and madders then declined gently into violets and blues, the colours enhancing the recession. Ellie had thought hard as she planned, scribbling out, writing diaries of ideas she never continued — the diary nor the idea — and yet the result, or rather work in progress, was more a consequence of abandonment of these well laid plans. Sometimes a perfect outcome sprang from nature overriding her; she liked to think that the poppies in the terraced rose garden arrived, unbidden, out of a sense of congeniality.

She couldn't say that she would use any of the things she'd learnt in Italy in her own garden — this garden was in another language. The cottage itself was almost unreadable under its covering of creepers and climbers. Now Ellie had the perspective, it occurred to her that this camouflaged façade could be a reflection of herself. Come autumn she'd make good use of the pruning saw. The cottage was small: the garden disproportionately large, nearly three acres in all. She had moved in with the children after Andrew's death, hardly expecting that she would be nursing her own mother in the succeeding months. She may have been eighty but the event was not expected and not accepted. The strokes had been cruel, the first taking away her mother's reason and turning her into a stranger. There was almost relief when the second took her away just weeks later. As fast as her mother's illness moved so also had nature taken over in the garden. It had been a strange solace to Ellie to reclaim the flowerbeds from the virulent weeds in these years after her mother's death. And coming so hard upon Andrew's heart attack it almost crushed Ellie. Her comforter had been taken from her and she had to become strong again too soon.

Now, over two years on, there was a spring of anger returning to the surface; why did you have to be so reckless, Andrew? Ellie had seen the hurt it had caused her mother to watch them struggling in a financial midden. Who knows how the stress must have affected her? Out of habitual loyalty to Andrew, but more to protect her mother, Ellie didn't tell Ma the details. She sketched a picture of the unfairness of the property market being the decisive factor in their downfall. However, there were days when Ellie's strength ebbed and she just went to weep at her mother's table. Ma didn't blame or lecture; she just mopped up and cooked plates of egg and fried potatoes, slipped Ellie the odd tenner despite her own short rations.

Ellie picked her way down the brashy slope to her cutting garden. There was plenty of weeding to be done after her weeks away. She'd not expected the task to be done well by her gardener; well, gardener was a rather inflated title. He shuffled up from the next village a couple of hours per week and his main joy was digging; mounding up great clods of earth, unsullied by plants — except maybe the odd leek or winter cabbage. So the task of carefully hand weeding around her flowers, without destroying greenery that was meant to be there, like bupleurum or euphorbia, was not one that enthused him. On her return home yesterday she'd ventured into the garden with a mix of joy and anxiety in her heart. She'd prayed that there would be no disasters like last spring.

'You need some more soil under those trees,' he'd said. Distractedly she'd agreed only to find, on her return from an extended shopping trip, that a lorry load of the weediest topsoil in the world was now smothering her carefully nurtured ground-cover plants. The most difficult thing about the whole situation was that it would have been unreasonable to be angry. The deed was done with the best possible motives. And so it was with Andrew really. He'd only wanted to provide the best for the family. The trouble was he'd been seduced by the company he kept.

When they'd moved to Derbyshire he'd undergone a creeping metamorphosis through his flirtations with the gentry. They'd made him feel that he was one of them but when push came to shove, commoners were just commoners, stranded without the safety net of family money. Andrew's entrepreneurial streak had got the better of him. No, to be honest his pride had got the better of him. His titled buddies built him up to be infallible and he was enticed into development schemes that appealed to his idealistic nature. Ecological green-oak barns proved to be his undoing. It seemed ironic that such a flexible material should have been the stumbling block.

Ellie had to remind herself of the background of the times though; everyone seemed to be rushing forward on a tide of fiscal fantasy. Andrew was not alone there. The American owners pulled out of the estate. So at the point he was left with massive debts his job as land agent also disappeared. It was almost a relief to move away from the scene of the crime. As an act of kindness, her old boss wangled Andrew a job with a firm of surveyors in Oxford. That was five years ago. Actually, from her vantage point now, when the sword of Damocles fell it hadn't been such a bad thing. It put a full stop to the fear that everything would come crashing down; when it did crash Ellie found she was good at picking up the pieces. It had hit the children hardest. Their trust had been scattered by the crash and they protected themselves by putting distance between themselves and their parents. She still felt that slight removal even today.

Ellie stooped to look at the green shoots of the sweet peas winding their way upward. Perversely the tendrils were not connecting with the helpful metal mesh she'd erected. They were choosing, so it seemed to her, to twine around the stems of adjacent plants. Well, where did we all look for our support? Generally from the soft and not the hard; the living, not the dead. She shuddered and inwardly berated herself. Why had she even begun to get involved with Max? She felt like she was plunging down in a lift that had been severed from its cables. Straightening up, her breath constricted, she tried to fill her lungs with air. How wrong she was to think Max couldn't touch her, that she'd forgiven him. Like Salvatore had said, she would have to do it all over again.

In her garden, listening to a rattle of wind in the ash heralding the onset of a shower, she thought of the day at Castello and the days that followed before her return home. That evening she'd talked to Salvatore in the olive groves, he had opened the way for her to tell him about Max's assault but she didn't. What would have been the point? She now doubted that Max had even remembered his actions that night and she wasn't going to be the one to remind him. And if she had told Salvatore it would have put him in an impossible position. Ellie knew he would be bound to make Max leave; it was the way Salvatore would have to behave. And so where would that leave everyone? Max spiteful, Salvatore possibly short of much needed course fees and, in the consequential gossip, Ellie labelled a tease or a victim; neither a stereotype she wanted.

It took her a long time to come to terms with the intensity of the emotions she'd experienced. In a few short days in Tuscany they'd poured down on to her; attraction, arousal, fear, disgust — and then a struggle for peace. But there had also been confidence, born from the possibility of new friendship, at being found attractive again. It was as though, when she had dared to step outside her usual boundaries, life with a capital L rushed in. And she had not been consumed. Indeed, she had lived on for two long weeks in Max's company. The overall feeling she brought home with her was one of strength. But how was she meant to use it? From where she stood now she saw a life that would satisfy many. After all, she had her children, her students to teach, her cottage, her garden. She just could not see her way ahead. Did forgiving mean forgetting and burying her rage at Andrew, at Max? As much as she wanted their actions to have no effect on her life, she couldn't make it true.

She had no peace. No peace, no purpose. The certainty that she had experienced standing in front of *Primavera*: where had it gone? She stood in her garden and prayed that God might do with her life what he would. Could she truly believe that would change things? Was it only in books, where life could be shaped and edited, that change seemed to happen immediately and consequentially? In real life change seeped up in unexpected places like a spring. It was the scent of water making the dry ground into a musky seedbed.

She bent down and rubbed spikes of rosemary between her fingers. She'd brought it back from Tuscany, crammed into hand baggage, hoping she wasn't flouting some agricultural law. It was a prostrate kind; low and spreading but possessed of the most pungent scent she'd ever known. The freshening breeze blew the volatile oil into her face. What did they say? *Rosemary for remembrance.* Salvatore, Nerine and strangely, Jonathan — for whom she hadn't had any time when she first met him — had been her supports in the final days in Tuscany. They were friendships she'd not expected to find in this part of her life.

★ ★ ★

Nerine came to stay at the cottage in July. Ellie met her from the train and she stepped down from the carriage like Isadora Duncan, scarf trailing, wide-brimmed hat clutched to her head. She looked like sorbet in her pastel colours. Ellie realised how much she'd missed her in those few weeks. Nerine was the kind of person who made you feel interesting — for how could you not be if someone as wonderful as Nerine chose to be friends with you? Sitting in the cottage garden like a lyre-bird she made Ellie's life less mundane. Helping herself to raspberries from the canes by the hedge she wouldn't talk until her mouth was empty.

'Delicious.' She stood like a prim ballet teacher and fingered another fruit. 'Looks just like a Tiller Girl's nipple don't you think?'

They laughed and seemed to go on laughing most of the afternoon. Nerine and she picnicked outside, the sun shining benignly upon them, talking over Italy.

'It was quite a revelation for me being with people, being a group for such a long time. I realise how much time I've spent on my own in my life,' said Ellie.

Nerine looked puzzled. 'But you teach . . .'

'Yes, but I go in, do what I do, then escape back to my own society. I've always worked in isolation really. Sometimes I wish I was part of some team — working together for some common purpose.'

Nerine snorted. 'Nice in theory darling, but I think the reality is, in most workplaces, that every individual has their own agenda.'

'You sound very cynical, Nerine!' Ellie rested back on her arms on the rug and looked up at Nerine sitting neatly on the swing seat. 'When you and Duggie were out in Ceylon didn't you feel as though you were really part of something, making a difference?'

'I suppose so. I mean I like to think we weren't the same as the average owner, but you know dear, I think I was too young to recognise it as anything worthy.' She paused and rolled her collection of fine silver bracelets up and down her bony arm. 'We did have fun though. Talking of group-living, I went to an ayurvedic treatment centre for a week once. That, my dear, was an experience!'

Ellie topped up Nerine's glass and waited. 'I mean they were terribly keen on using oils *everywhere*. A bit like the French medics always sticking things up your bum. We had these — *vasti* I think they were called. If anyone came out of the treatment room walking like a cross between a duck and a geisha — ' Nerine tipped herself off the seat and demonstrated, 'we'd all say 'Ay, ay, vasti was it?' '

Encouraged by Ellie's laughter Nerine went on, her face straight but her eyes flickering as if in response to the remembered scenes. 'And then there was this head treatment. They'd take about an hour to build a dam out of chick pea paste, rather like a sweatband, and then they'd bolt this upturned megaphone on your head and pour warm oil into it. You looked like a moronic Martian.'

Ellie was breathless with laughter, conjuring up Nerine in this parody of regal headgear.

'And the doctor said,' Nerine delivered this in deadpan Indian English, ' 'it's very good for headaches'. Well darling, I said, can't you just take an aspirin, for heaven's sake?'

'I missed all that.'

Nerine didn't see the connection.

'I mean, I didn't have time to travel and have fun. I went straight into a marriage so young.' Ellie was glad that Nerine didn't burst in with the usual comment about the compensation of children. 'Andrew did all that. Actually, Nerine, I realised that day you were talking to Jonathan that Andrew was probably working in the same part of the island where you lived. A good few years later, mind you.'

Nerine laughed. 'Small world, isn't it?'

Ellie smiled. 'I like the idea of all our lives nearly touching, but not actually meeting until the time is right.'

Nerine patted Ellie and then began to rock briskly on the swing. This back and forth seemed to echo the rhythm of the afternoon. They went between fun and philosophy; introducing bits of history to share and savouring joint memories. Italy gave them that.

'And those garden-ladies ... they can't have been as old as me but I thought they had one foot in the grave. That Vera, she was so ... ' Nerine cast around for the words, 'hand-knitted.'

'Well, she can't help not having your style, Nerine.'

Nerine broadened her eyes. 'Don't give me that! 'You're a suck' — as my god-grandson would say.'

Ellie smiled and changed the subject. 'Did I tell you that Jonathan had rung me?'

Nerine shook her head.

'It was a really nice chatty call. He said he'd been to a do at Benfield and the Porthams were really interested that he'd seen me. He said the one who was most keen for all my news was their son.'

Nerine looked quizzical.

'You remember, the one he called 'the banker chappie'. Jonathan said he wanted to know how I was coping and where I was living. I think that's because he has a weekend place around here. Jonathan said it quite surprised him as he hadn't put him down as a caring type at all.'

'Well, you never can tell by outward appearances. I mean, look how unpromising Jonathan seemed to be when we first met him, but in the end he turned out to be a dear.'

Nerine looked into the middle distance and vaguely detached herself from the conversation.

'And what, in the end, did you think of Jane?' Ellie slipped in.

'Ambitious but unhappy. Did you see the pile of cosmetics and creams she had in her room — enough to start up a franchise for Helena Rubenstein.'

Ellie didn't ask how Nerine found her way into Jane's room, and anyway she couldn't get a word in.

'She was just too cool for my tastes. All surface. I mean darling, could you imagine turning to her if you had some emotional crisis and needed consoling? She'd be wiping your tears off her Nicole Fahri and telling you not to cry too loud in case somebody heard.'

Ellie hadn't wanted to say this herself but was rather delighted by the way Nerine snipped to the heart of people. What she did know was that if Jane had wanted to cry on Nerine she'd have offered her crepe-de-chine shoulder willingly.

Nerine picked her teeth elegantly and went on. 'I felt sorry for her really, the poor dear, all buttoned up. She's the sort who'd sneer at country music. Too much unsophisticated feeling out in the open for her taste.'

She continued after a few sips of her drink. 'Which reminds me, what happens if you play a country music record backwards?'

Ellie looked at her, startled by the change of tack. 'I don't know — you hear satanic messages?' she ventured.

'No!' Nerine giggled. 'You get your horse back, your dog back and your lover back!'

When she'd stopped laughing Ellie said, 'Nerine, you're wasted — you ought to put this vaudeville act to good use.'

'Funny you should say that. Just before Italy I sent a few photos of passing celebs with a little 'think-piece',' she raised her eyebrows here 'to *Hello!* and — ' she paused for effect, 'they accepted them.'

'Wow. My friend the gossip columnist. That's brilliant, Nerine!'

'I'll say it is. The money has just about kept me afloat after the Italian overspend.'

They toasted Nerine's new career together and she explained how, when she'd got back, she'd been encouraged by her success and had planned to send in her picture of Max in Italy because she thought the name Penman-White would be a good draw.

It had turned out to be better than she thought. She'd been leafing through the financial pages of the *Telegraph* and seen a small item about Max; it was one of those very upbeat pieces that nevertheless left you with the distinct feeling that Max wasn't exactly having it all his own way on the board of Penman-White's.

Ellie willed herself to feel sympathy, to love her neighbour as herself, but all she could feel was *schadenfreude*.

While Nerine popped cherries into her mouth she eyed up Ellie. Spitting pips tidily into her hand she said, 'I know. Good, isn't it?' and they both smiled and moved on.

'Have you heard from Salvatore?'

Nerine shook her head at Ellie's question.

'He wrote saying he was coming to Oxford in September and if he had time he might call me,' said Ellie.

'Lovely man. Now there's a person with depth.' Nerine reached down to stroke Ellie's hair. 'More your style, I should say.'

'And happily married!' Ellie added cheerfully.

Nerine made the faintest of nods and smiled sweetly. Ellie remembered the sweetness for a long, long time.

★ ★ ★

Salvatore did visit Ellie at the cottage in the autumn. It was one of those September days when the sun was strong but low; its light split to leave only the oranges of the spectrum. Everything, all skin, was touched with warmth. Salvatore seemed to shine from the inside. He came for tea. He'd been making his annual visit to the Oggs, as he called them; not a troglodytic sect but Oxford Garden History Society, who had been a long-time link. They'd loyally furnished him with course participants for many years. Ellie thought those were his exact words. She loved his approach to English — the kind of formalism that reminded her of topiary. Although she loved it she wondered where, under all the refining, was the truth of the natural structure.

They sat in the garden as she and Nerine had done, but the conversation had a classical cadence, the bridges between themes were smooth, the tempo gentler. She asked, politely, how his family were, especially Maria. Salvatore, equally politely, answered her with a list of his wife's business achievements. She saw his hands cross in front of his body as he told her how they both disliked the long separations. She couldn't stop herself from saying that they both might really regret these partings — who knew how much time one had together? Salvatore looked at her then, looked into her eyes — she couldn't stop the tears gathering — and nodded.

As they talked it became clear that they shared some common ground in their faith. Salvatore said how his had grown in latter years. Ellie felt a muscular relaxation in being able to use the word God without being viewed as some odd anti-realist. They differed in their approaches; Salvatore was more ritualist and saw God as a disciplinarian, but always working for the good of the human soul, of course. Her God was a dependable friend before any of his other roles. As they talked on Salvatore was at ease, charming and charmed. Parted from his professional role he also seemed freer — to laugh at himself, to profess ignorance. He loved her garden — she knew the appreciation was sincere — and he sat and sipped tea, rubbing grass flowers between his long fingers and gathering in new topics of conversation. That afternoon an image came to mind of a restorer gently removing layers of grime from a painting; they now talked at a different level. Later, as the evening chill came stealing into the garden, Ellie marvelled that she could share her thoughts about Andrew with Salvatore. They took a step on from the evening in the olive groves, so many months ago. She was open, describing in detail her feelings of betrayal. Today, as they talked, it had become clear that these feelings could co-exist alongside an enduring love for her husband. Salvatore led her through the maze. She was free and immensely grateful.

Alone in bed that night she surprised herself by recalling the conversation with Max about paintings; the vehemence with which she'd renounced the values of new art. She didn't understand or accept such work and she rejected it with anger. As she drifted into sleep she began to understand how she might begin to assimilate and integrate that which gave her pain.

As the December days closed in and vital repairs against the winter continued on Palazzo Michele, Salvatore reflected on his autumn visit to Oxford. It had been very useful from the business point of view; old friends in the city had introduced some valuable links to a few of the colleges. He could see a way to attract year-round students. He'd also spent quite a large part of his stay in North Oxford socialising; being splendidly charming to women of a certain age who wanted a creative outlet. He really enjoyed it. Even the prickly matriarchs had a certain attraction for him. As a result, the courses were by no means entirely subscribed but they were well on the way to being so. This year it looked as though the teaching would do better, as an income generator, than his design practice. He'd thought before that he should be using the Palazzo more efficiently and perhaps run another summer course alongside his. He would run out of residential spaces but he had many friends who ran *agriturismi* so accommodation wouldn't be a problem. Then again he could have a day course that attracted more local clientele.

Salvatore leant back in his chair, eyes

upturned to the ceiling, and smoothed his hands along the rosewood arms that had felt the touch of generations of his family. As he pondered the plasterwork that was under threat from rain seeping in through the failing roof, he felt the weight of that family. Pride in his lineage came along with his mother's milk. Actually the *Marchesa* had never fed him herself but the image felt right. As he breathed he told himself again that the point of his existence was to steward the Palazzo for future generations. Did he believe that now? His children were gone, making lives for themselves, his eldest son didn't even live in Italy. And Maria. He couldn't believe any longer in the fable he had told himself for over a year. She stayed away more and more and when she came back it was though she existed alongside him rather than lived. They were cordial with each other but she had a way of half-engaging that almost brought him to anger. He hadn't dared to ask the right questions; he'd feared her reply. He'd never thought of himself as a moral coward because he'd been unafraid to express his views to his own children when he felt their behaviour had not been good for them; it didn't stop him loving them when they turned their faces against his advice.

But now he knew, because she had told

him so, Maria was unhappy with this marriage. If she wanted to leave surely he would be unable to give her what she wanted. The faith he had grown up in, the way in which he lived his life would be under threat. Marriage was sacred, for ever. How could it be the right thing to let her go? How could he throw away that which gave him peace — along with all the codes he believed in? His study door nudged open under pressure from a rising breeze and admitted a laser line of sunlight that traversed the centre of his body. For a fraction of a moment his mind was split by the thought that love might mean letting her walk away. He put his hand to his eyes and winced with the pain. What was the point of history if you lived it on your own?

When he got up to close the door Ellie was there at the forefront of his mind. He wasn't certain of his motives for visiting her when he was in Oxford. On the actual day he'd had no commitments and the sun was shining and he had the use of a car. He'd been adept at convincing himself it was only a pleasant interlude, but if she had not been there, or uninterested in seeing him, he wondered now how he would have reacted. And once more she began to talk to him on a different level. In the last years he could hardly remember talking to anyone else this way — certainly not to Maria.

Salvatore tried to appraise his wife objectively; his parents had been more than a little judgmental of Maria when Salvatore had brought her home all those years ago. Her background was less illustrious and his parents couldn't recognise the social circles in which her family moved. She'd come from a family where hard work was the ethic; her father was a self-made man. Salvatore was besotted with this woman who wasn't impressed by his background, who knew what she wanted and was active in her pursuit of it. She'd poured scorn on traditions and they had horrified his parents by marrying in a registry office alone. Maria wanted it that way and, in his youth, Salvatore loved this energetic iconoclast. But as the years had gone by he found himself reaching more and more into the resources of his faith. He would have loved to have had their marriage blessed in church but she had laughed off the suggestion, saying they only needed to be sure of each other. One thing was certain, her radical approach and ingenuity had saved the Palazzo. Now Salvatore sat and pondered — for what reason had it been saved?

Salvatore had listened, as he sat in the warmth of the cottage garden, to Ellie trying to make sense of her life. She'd tried to put in order the parts that had gone before, almost fashioning them into a tower on which she could stand and from there view her future; if he did the same what would he be looking at ahead of him? He'd always had a sense of purpose, the knowledge that he fitted his particular niche and it was thus ordained. As yet, nothing had actually changed for him but he sensed the imminence of a bend in the road. When you are young, he thought, it is easy. You see a hole in the universe that fits you. You are encouraged to make your dreams happen. If they don't, you have the energy to try again.

He thought back to his student days in Oxford and the reason for them. His parents had believed in an education commensurate to his future. In a family that had a pedigree establishing their right to a continuation of privilege, that future should surely be as the heir to a fine home and the natural respect that came with it. Salvatore stacked up the papers on his desk briskly, aligning all their ends by rapping them on the wood. His parents didn't foresee a changed world when the aristocracy were metamorphosed into another service industry. For all his privilege Salvatore was just as much a tradesman as the grocer down the road — except that he was selling dreams and aspirations. And to be truthful, the grocer was probably a better businessman. Salvatore sighed at the sheets of calculations in front of him, knowing that he would be lucky to balance the books again this month. Maria was the one who was good at that.

As he watched the December rain dribbling down the window-pane he heard Francesca's footsteps and the office door opened. She was pink-cheeked, smiling.

'We have a visitor who'd like to stay.'

Salvatore was confused by her need to bring this request to him and the glow in her face.

'He'd like to see you.'

When Salvatore entered the hall he saw it was Max. It was a bit of shock to see his bristling presence; more of a shock when, in that instant, he recognised the same aspirational energy that emanated from Maria. Who was he to judge as his parents had judged? But why had Max come?

'I'm here to source holly trees, would you believe?' Max grinned. 'Not my usual side of the business but we've got a manager off sick and a supplier gone AWOL. So, here I am. The first contact was bloody useless so, I said, I'll go and see my friend Salvatore. Dream a few dreams of Italian gardens.'

Salvatore smiled, trying to achieve the balance of grace and warmth that still did not appear too encouraging.

'Is business going well, Max?' he'd asked as he offered him a glass of wine in the library. He watched the hesitation as Max unpeeled from his leather jacket and threw it across the sofa.

'Actually no, not for me anyway.'

It wasn't the reply Salvatore would have expected. 'Oh?'

'There's this new design director. A real bitch.' Max swallowed his drink in Shakespearian draughts. 'Just came in and rubbished a lot of my pitch. The new broom. Oh, the board love her at the moment.' He looked into the middle distance with an expression of loathing. 'I've just got to sit and wait for her to sweep herself out of favour, that's all.' He looked back at Salvatore. 'Why is it that when I come up with an idea no one hears, but when she says exactly the same thing, everyone treats her like a guru? Hey Salvatore, what d'you reckon?'

Salvatore shrugged.

'Eyes like frozen peas. Cold cow. Knows exactly what she's doing to me.' Max held out his glass for more and Salvatore filled it, but just a little below its capacity. As if that will stop Max getting drunk if he wants to, thought Salvatore; never mind, it was a gesture.

'Women. They can be a devious bunch. Say one thing and do another.' Max was muttering to himself. 'Not a lot of people out there you can trust, eh Salvatore?' He looked up with a broad smile and while Salvatore was replying that he thought that was a somewhat sweeping statement, Max changed tack. 'So, have you seen anything of the rest of our Merry Band since the spring?'

'As it happens, I had to be in Oxford in September and I called in on Ellie.' Salvatore found his eyes fixed by Max, his attention sharp.

'Oh, in the Cotswolds, you mean?' Salvatore nodded. 'How was she?'

'Fine, fine. Lovely garden she has there. Quite a talent.' Salvatore wanted to keep the tone light. He wasn't going to share with Max the empathy he'd felt, the rightness of being in Ellie's company.

'I suppose she's got a nice cosy life. Kids off on their own, picture book cottage, roses round the door. The romantic life of an artist.'

Did Salvatore detect an edge in Max's voice? It was baffling, this slight bitterness; almost jealousy. Max must have been passed over by women many times; why had Ellie got to him? Salvatore began his defence.

'Well, she has been through some difficult times — ' But he reined himself in; he wasn't going to share Ellie's past problems with Max. He respected her privacy. 'I'm pleased she has some kind of peace.'

Max's head came up suddenly. He snorted.

'Hah! Peace. What's that? Just a cork in a bottle to stop the demons escaping!'

Salvatore let the remark go by but was uncomfortable. He tried to lighten the atmosphere. 'Well, all I know is that I'd have some peace if I could get my wretched accounts in order.'

Max laughed. 'If that was my only problem, I'd be a contented man.' He shifted on the sofa, quiet for a moment. 'Perhaps we can do each other a favour. For a bit of your expertise on the plants I'd be happy to help you with the figures, Salvatore. After all, it's what I do.'

Salvatore was more than tempted. Despite his suspicions about Max's moral life, he didn't doubt his credentials as an accountant. What harm would it do to have a bit of help from Max? After all, he was only going to ask him for fiscal, not ethical advice.

'That sounds like a fine business agreement,' was what he said.

11

April

'Mum!' The shout jolted Ellie into the present. She'd been gazing out of the window at yet another April shower, thinking of this time last year in Italy.

'For God's sake let me in!'

Ellie opened the front door of the cottage to a soused Sadie.

'Darling, why didn't you let me know you were coming?'

Ellie pulled her daughter in and hugged her. Trust a mother to start things with an accusatory question.

'Wouldn't have been a surprise then, would it?'

Sadie widened her eyes and wagged a parental finger at Ellie causing both of them to laugh. It was a surprise; Ellie didn't see her children much these days. They had stepped decisively into their own lives when they'd seen that their parents were unable to give them what they wanted. Ellie often wondered what it was they thought they wanted.

'I've got a long weekend, just finished a

213

project and the boss felt we deserved it, so I thought I'd come and say hello and be cooked for!'

'That's lovely. As long as you don't mind more company. Nerine, you remember, the lady I met in Italy — is coming down for tomorrow night.'

'Of course not.' The riposte was fractionally late, the smile altogether too bright. Even in her twenties Sadie didn't like to share.

'Well we've got tonight for a good girlie gossip.'

Ellie flipped a warm towel off the Rayburn and set about rubbing Sadie's wet hair. She'd walked over a mile from the bus to preserve the surprise; independent girl. But now, with the strands of hair sliding between the rough fabric, Ellie could only feel Sadie as the girl who'd had her hopes wrung out of her.

'I feel like your baby when you do that.'

Sadie looked softened, vulnerable; Ellie knew it would be all right to hold her. Tears itched their way upwards and she was glad that her face was pressed close to Sadie's cheek, away from view. They stood like that for over a minute, rocking and patting, then broke away half gasping, half laughing. Ellie snatched up the kettle busying herself. She was brave, brisk; 'You'll always be my baby!'

The hug, like the first wash on a

watercolour, set the tone for what followed. Conversation ran smoothly, each absorbing the other's words and building on the layers. Ellie hadn't been told much of her daughter's life of late; recently there had been a politeness between them. She'd heard that her career was going well and that seemed correct. Sadie's by-line often appeared in the newspapers and she sent her mother postcards from the exotic places she visited. She'd just come back from Kerala where she'd been co-researching a travel guide, one of those guides that told you everything — often more than you wanted to know. Ellie remembered reading one that began with all the diseases you were likely to contract; she didn't get as far as the section on the delights as she'd been so scared off. She admired Sadie's lack of fear; that came from her father's genes.

'Travel's easy, if a bit irritating at times. You've got to keep your wits about you though. It's not things like that that frighten me.'

'What does then?'

Sadie sat on the question, probably wondering if her answer might destroy the picture they were building up between them. 'Trusting.'

Ellie waited. Sadie didn't cry but she

looked as if her whole body had been attacked by gravity. When she raised her head she began to tell a story. An old, old story about being in love with a married man. It became clear to Ellie that this was the weekend of the ultimatum.

'I've told him he has to leave her. There are all sorts of good reasons why it hasn't happened up till now and when I'm with him I believe them, every one . . . ' She let the sentence hang and Ellie didn't rush in with encouraging platitudes; she'd been too recently on the other end of them. Sadie cupped her hands round her mug of tea as though she wanted to compress her thoughts within it. 'Oh I don't know mum, it's not just Paul. I wonder if I'll trust any man. I don't go in much for all that childhood shit but I wonder if it hasn't something to do with being around dad and all those ideas that never came to anything.'

Ellie wanted to speak to Sadie of things that have a beginning, a middle and an end but she was finding it impossible to order things so.

'Whatever your father did, he did it thinking it was the best for us. You know he was ever the optimist and couldn't believe that anything would have the wrong ending. He took risks I admit, and the stakes were too

216

high, but all he wanted was to give us a good life.' It was her script, the one she had rehearsed many times.

'Depends what you call a good life.'

Sadie stirred the sugar aimlessly, it clodded together with the drops of tea left on the spoon.

'I'll admit I was bloody mad when all the material things were taken away from us, but actually when I realised I was having a pretty good time without them — *and you too* mum, you really found a role when you had to go teaching — I thought I just wanted to tell dad to Give It Up!'

Ellie reflected on the years that had eaten Andrew up. The years the locust had eaten.

Sadie was trembling. 'I wish he'd thought about what he was doing. What effect his actions would have on us all.' She looked directly into Ellie's smarting eyes. 'All I ever wanted was for him to say I'm sorry that this has happened, life will just have to be different now, but we can all sort this out together.' Now she was crying. 'And then he died on us. Died still thinking *he* was sorting it all out — no room for anyone else.'

Ellie was somehow purged. She sat in wonderment at her daughter's articulation of the theme that had been running through her own mind for years. Salvatore's words came to her then. What she eventually said was, 'And you know what we have to do about that?' She answered the question in Sadie's eyes. 'We have to forgive him. It's hurting us and we can't move. Forgiveness is an act of will Sadie; if we wait to feel forgiveness it will never happen. And don't expect to have to forgive only once, it needs to be done over and over again.'

They sat in the kitchen, the afternoon light catching ordinary objects. Ellie measured her words, reluctant to press her beliefs on Sadie like another weight. 'I suppose I make sense of all the difficulties in my life by believing there is a divine purpose in everything — even the crap. The difficulty is seeing it at the time. Who said *we live our life forward but understand it backwards?*'

Sadie sat, head down, unresponsive. After moments of silence, when they let go of each other's hands, Ellie spoke again; she made sure her voice was light.

'I know what to do. What we need is ritual. I'll sacrifice the fatted calf and we'll have a 'forgiving supper'!'

Sadie wiped her eyes on her teeshirt sleeve and nodded. Their words, while they chopped and pared, sliced and peeled, seemed superficial but the communication was in the work. The meal became more craft than cooking. The meat was lamb, which Ellie felt to be apt. They took the food into the tiny dining room which, with its minute window, encouraged its occupants to look inward. Having fed well, they sat, all colour drained from the place by the coming of the summer night, and each lit a candle to forgive. Light restored, they both hardly dared believe in the power it gave them.

★　★　★

Leaving Sadie asleep, the next morning Ellie went to collect Nerine from the train. She'd enthused about the ease of the journey from satanic London when she'd visited the cottage last summer. It was about twenty minutes' drive to the station, a stone's throw for country dwellers, though sometimes Ellie was tired by the distances; her nearest shops were about as far away. Self sufficiency got you so far but she'd yet to learn how to grow her own loo rolls. Her car was old; a battered Volvo that was a relic of family life. She'd kept it because it kept going, and now it remained useful for its carrying space. At this moment the back was strewn with parapher-nalia from her painting classes; boards and paints that rattled at every pothole. She always felt guilty that she did not empty her car after each lesson and appear more organised. Somehow she liked the fact that the means of her expression was always available, always in transit. She didn't really like things to conclude, she liked the idea that they were there to be resumed; perhaps that was why she'd always left the lights on as a child or never switched the radio off now. It had been known for her to have three going in different rooms at the same time.

As she drove into the station car park Ellie was excited; perhaps there was some childhood memory of arrivals that fuelled the feeling, but Nerine always made her feel that way. Sadie would love her. Ellie's imaginings of the encounter made her smile. It had been months since they'd seen each other and there would be plenty to say. What she wasn't prepared for was the picture of Nerine's appearance as she tried to step down from the carriage; another passenger ran forward to help her while Ellie looked on from behind a padlocked picket gate. The frailty that Ellie had noted on their first meeting in Italy was now pronounced; her skin seemed to be dusted with a grey bloom like a Giacometti figurine. When they finally embraced her body swayed beside Ellie like a flagpole; her voice weak as she spoke.

'I know, I know. Don't try to spare my

feelings dear Ellie. I do not look good.' Nerine tipped up her face, looking from under a surreal hat, to capture Ellie's with a broad smile. 'But I feel fine, being here with you!'

As they'd begun their return journey, Nerine looked settled in the car; she'd firmly kicked aside rolling jars in the footwell and, as Ellie always expected of her, she'd come immediately to the point. 'I have just accepted that I must number my days.'

Ellie tried to drive perfectly straight and make the best possible gear changes. She didn't know how else to respond.

'But what I want most is to live my life with enjoyment while I have those days left.' Nerine's hand fluttered out and rested like crumpled paper on Ellie's knee. 'I'm sorry to give you such a shock, dearest girl, but can you please concentrate on my present *with* you, rather than your future *without* me?'

It was almost all she said on the subject until much later. And it was a lot later before Ellie fully appreciated Nerine's supernatural talent for banishing guilt. The weekend never laboured and watching Nerine's acceptance of her illness was a positive experience. But she wasn't 'being brave'; at times she did express regrets for the things that would pass away from her — she who immersed herself in life. It made Ellie aware of her own tiptoeing. The three of them sat in the garden, ate in the garden, played music in the garden. Nerine compared things from her last visit; wondered why the cottage was still overhung with its climbers.

'Scaredy-cat, you said you were going to give it an awesome pruning!'

Sadie laughed at the vocabulary, at the sight of her mother being admonished.

And Ellie had indeed said so. She had thought too much and acted too little. And there is only so much time in life to act. She watched Nerine, eating tiny mouthfuls like a bird but relishing each one, jiggling on her bony bottom and singing, and knew all was well. Nerine probably had no intention of inspiring anyone by her visit — inspirational people rarely do, thought Ellie — but she and Sadie both felt a kind of certainty when she was around; something they were loath to part from. By the end of Sunday morning it was decided that Ellie would drive Sadie and Nerine back to London.

'It's only sensible. And I haven't even been to see Sadie's new flat yet. Gives me a chance for a maternal inspection.'

Never mind that Nerine was in West London and Sadie was worlds apart in the

East End. Nerine knew that too, having quizzed Sadie.

'Oh my darling, you live just down the road from that marvellous house.' Nerine wind-milled her hand in the air, searching her memory.

'You mean 18, Folgate Street?' said Sadie.

Nerine nodded and Ellie begged enlighten-ment; within a matter of minutes a plan was hatched. By late afternoon they were on their way back to London.

'Are you sure you feel up to this?' Ellie watched Nerine with concern as she shifted in the front seat of the car.

'Of course!' Nerine bit back. 'I've always wanted to see the place and this was perfect happenstance; can't stop events now!' She smiled at Ellie and patted her knee.

With Sadie on A to Z duty, between them they negotiated the City Road and found their way to Spitalfields. Rain had followed them most of the way down the M40 and now the city streets were slicked black and the thunder clouds brought an early dusk.

Nerine had first heard of 18, Folgate Street by reading a review of a book about it in the *Daily Telegraph*. Reading the *Telegraph* seemed the only remnant of Nerine's background. She'd abandoned the other signs of being 'a person with breeding' although

Nerine somehow managed to subvert reading the *Telegraph* into radical behaviour. That afternoon, as she'd explained the house to Ellie, her face had become animated.

'It belonged to this marvellous artist, Dennis Severs. There's no doubt he was a passionate man, you could tell by the way he wrote about the place.'

Nerine could respond to passion. Her own sentences came thickly, falling over one another, as she described the man's years of collecting, the way he'd come from California in the seventies and bought a 1700's house in a deeply unfashionable area and set about infusing it with life. Now he was dead, too early, but his creation lived on. 'He invented this family that lives in the house and — ' Nerine had stopped short. 'No. I'm not going to tell you more about it. I think we should experience it.' Then she'd taken up her teacup and sent Ellie to the telephone to book a visit.

★ ★ ★

And now they were knocking on the front door; a door softened by layer upon layer of black paint. A gas lantern hissed above them and the thud of the knocker boomed into the hollow space behind the door. It was opened by a small, neat man who led the three of them into the narrow hall. Crammed in, they felt like schoolchildren as they listened to instructions; no speaking — the house is meant to be received in silence; no touching — but keep the rest of your senses awake. And so, untethered, they set off to travel the house. The wooden window shutters barred the outside world; inside it felt like another time altogether. There were sounds of horse-drawn carriages, muffled conversations and a baby crying distantly; scents of cooking, coal fires and clove pomanders. And in every room artefacts that told a story; the broken teacup on the drawing room carpet — a strange discord in a candlelit haven where the peal of church bells spoke of peace.

And every room took you somewhere new in time; Ellie watched Nerine reading the visual story in front of her, her face softened by shadows cast by flames from candles and coal fire. It was as though people had literally gone from the room before them; a powdered wig hung on the chair back, a white linen napkin had been abandoned on the table top. There on its polished surface, reflecting warmly, was a half pomegranate, its cut surface lying at an angle to the wood, the seeds reflecting pinpoints of candlelight. Nerine caught Ellie's eye and smiled. She didn't even seem tempted to talk whereas Ellie wanted to verbalise all her discoveries; why was there a bottle of supermarket sauce in the mahogany corner cupboard?

The drawing room was a delight. It was only later when Ellie read the book that she realised why that was so. The room was the quintessence of Harmony; *nothing too much, nothing too little . . . rich and yet uncluttered, with any ornament carefully balanced by equal amounts of plain space . . .* It was, as he wrote, a place to withdraw from the real world above and below. Sadie was silently regarding the forest green walls and fluted pillars. She seemed to be standing straighter, on her best behaviour, whereas Nerine just looked as though she had come home.

There were decorations; swags of walnuts and beechnuts tied with bows festooned the plain panelling and made it feel like Christmas to Ellie. She realised with some shock that her heart was captured by this femininity of ornament but her intellect wanted to reject it. Was it too many years living with a man who had imposed his sense of style on her? Wherever they had lived Andrew's masculinity had been stamped on the way they lived. Ellie remembered again Andrew's discomfort at moving to the rented house, where he was forced to live within another person's boundaries. He simplified the rooms by stripping them of their clutter and she was glad of that. But one thing he did not touch was the garden. That was up to Ellie. Perhaps in their last few years together Andrew and she had achieved some kind of balance in the way they lived. Having to rebuild their ruined finances together gave Ellie a confidence she would have found no other way. Ellie looked over to Nerine and wondered if she too was being taken into her own past by the spell the house cast. She was standing very still, looking into the flames of the coal fire. If you could personify equilibrium, thought Ellie, it would be Nerine at this moment.

★ ★ ★

It was the second of August when Ellie moved to Nerine's flat in town. The air had a thickness; no breeze to relieve the heat. Ellie tried not to inhale as hot dust rolled up from under the passing buses as she walked down Oxford Gardens. It was one of the last times that Nerine was able to answer her own front door. Ellie understood that she'd waited for her to come; held on to her small physical abilities until she arrived. She was gracious in her letting go. When Ellie had offered to come and look after her, for what would be her last months, she had accepted the offer with no demurral; never protesting that it was a favour she could not receive. Within the space of a week she could barely walk, so with a laborious concentration, Ellie supported Nerine into her small garden and settled her on the old steamer chair, its driftwood greyness marrying Nerine's silvery complexion. While her concentration was still sharp she watched the birds coming in and out and the ants trailing through the grass. Friends and neighbours came to talk to her and read to her. A raft of goddaughters and godsons floated in on the warm days and evenings, bringing into the place the smell and sound of life. Sadie came often in the time before she had to take up her bags and begin travelling again. The doctor visited regularly to manage her pain relief. The late summer heat remained steady and unrelenting but, while it oppressed Ellie at times, to Nerine it seemed to be just another factor to be accepted.

While the friends stayed Ellie was able to arrange practical issues. She shopped and cooked, taking forays into Ladbroke Grove and Portobello. There she found a whirling electric fan — like gold dust as the city dwellers had seized almost every means of cooling themselves — to put in Nerine's bedroom. The pulse of its working was a soothing constant day and night. The time went by; Ellie giving of it freely. She made arrangements for her own cottage to be cared for on an ad hoc basis and surprisingly help had come in the form of her son. He'd been working on a short term IT contract and was at a loose end for a month so he'd offered to house-sit. He'd moved in only a few days after she left. She'd gone back briefly over one weekend at the end of August when the heat was fever pitch. Nerine, then still very much in charge, had banished her to the country.

'I have a doctor and a goddaughter and very good neighbours. Go on, sort out your family and your bills and things. I shan't die 'til you get back!'

And so she went. It had been good to see Dominic and she'd been surprised at how well he'd been caring for the place. Neatly stacked washing and watered rows of vegetables met her. After Andrew's death he'd resisted the mantle of man of the house and sped off to live a pleasant, irresponsible life at university. Then he seemed to be punishing her for Andrew's death, but now she saw it differently. Perhaps Dominic feared being tainted with too much sadness if he came close to Ellie.

★ ★ ★

After six weeks Nerine no longer moved to the garden but stayed in her boat bed, ready to travel further. Ellie arranged the room so it was as calm and cool as possible, but she also adorned one wall with Nerine's collection of hats and turbans. Ellie loved to look at them and she saw the pleasure that Nerine had in surveying herself through these wonderful confections. Each had its own expressiveness that told the viewer something about Nerine; they moved from the surreal and anarchic, through the humorous to the not quite restrained. The centrepiece was a collation of pink and yellow feathers that recalled a demented bird of paradise or some extraordinary tropical fish. Yes, the fish was a better analogy; Nerine always swam willingly in the stream of life.

'I've always loved those paintings of annunciations,' said Nerine one morning, although by then morning and night were just academic distinctions to her. Ellie waited for her to go on. 'I think those Renaissance ones are as close to my vision of heaven as ever I will get.'

Ellie closed her eyes to see the Fra Angelico at San Marco. Nerine continued. 'There's something very secure about the way the scene is placed so firmly in a real place. Usually there's a garden, a flower or two . . . ' she paused, forming the thoughts behind her eyes, 'and the architecture is simple, so solid and regular, while, within those confines, Mary is experiencing the most amazing confrontation of her life.'

Ellie nodded. 'I know. It took me a while to see that. The fact that, in amongst the ordinary, was a meeting of the human and the divine.'

Nerine sighed and sank back into her pillows. 'Of course my dear, it probably is totally obvious to you because of your faith. But it speaks to me too.' She cleared her throat and shifted in the bed. 'Or rather — doesn't speak.'

Ellie waited for her explanation.

'In all those paintings, what I see is a silence between the angel and the woman.' The air in the room turned. 'A knowledge deeper than words. Mary just knows.'

Nerine fractionally turned her stiff body towards Ellie and looked in her eyes. 'Everyone has those times when they have that meeting with something supernal. After all my living, I simply believe that there has to

231

be something beyond or above or some-where.' She grinned, in a poignant mimicry of her more rumbustuous self. 'How all those different faiths end up sorting everything out I can't say I understand — but a great creator has to have a bigger mind than us created.'

'So you do believe there's a God, Nerine?'

The faded street noises provided a comfort blanket of sound in the silence of the room. The breeze from the fan lifted a white hair or two on Nerine's forehead.

'No, I don't believe. I know.' She lay with her eyes closed for a little while. Ellie thought she had slipped into sleep when she suddenly opened them and said, 'You know, the more I ponder religion or the absence of it, the more I think the most important thing any person can have is integrity.' A smile moved on her face like an incoming tide as she reached out her hand to touch Ellie. 'Alongside love,' she added. 'Read me something from the Bible, dear. I like to hear its language, especially read by someone who believes it!'

Ellie was momentarily off guard. Her faith was so feeble she was touched that Nerine might count her as a true disciple. She was certainly no evangelist and struggled in her memory to remember some reference; verses applicable to the comfort of the dying.

'Well, um, I don't know what. Is there

anything you'd like to hear?'

Nerine sensed the difficulty and laughed, an echo of times past. 'Doesn't matter, just open the book and read.'

As Ellie walked to the sitting room to find her own Bible she prayed a please God don't let me down prayer. When she'd settled back on the corner of Nerine's bed she simply opened the book as though she was cutting cards. Job. Oh no, she thought, a load of misery and judgment, and was nearly tempted to seek a soothing psalm. Nerine was watching her expectantly. On one page she had marked some verses and so she began reading.

'*At least there is hope for a tree: If it is cut down, it will sprout again, and its new shoots will not fail. Its roots may grow old in the ground and its stump die in the soil, yet at the scent of water it will bud and put forth shoots like a plant.*'

Nerine raised her hand to halt the reading. Ellie just stared at the words and wondered; like Mary she pondered them in her heart.

*   *   *

Nerine asked Ellie to write out the words for her. She spent two evenings, after the nurse had arrived for the night shift, painting them on card. Using some watercolours she found in the flat, she illuminated the text with curling Byzantine foliage and impossibly large fruits springing from a stump on a parched ground. As the water soaked the card she breathed in the dampness and thought of Andrew. If she really did believe in her God then she had to believe that he had come to claim Andrew as now she saw him claiming Nerine. Whatever Nerine had meant to express by it, the word she used, integrity, was totally accurate. For Ellie it was now clear — it meant an integration with God; and who knew how and when God came to show himself to any of us. God was outside time. In the seconds of Andrew's death there could have been an eternity of understanding. A long time ago a Catholic friend had said to her that the ministry of the dying was very powerful; it meant absolutely nothing to Ellie when she said it but now it was as clear as water. She wanted to tell Nerine how much she'd learned from her.

* * *

It was August and Salvatore was back in the Palazzo and running another course to support the weight of his past. This group was made up of perfectly pleasant people but they did not operate as a unit. Suppers were

234

politely subdued; each one melted back to his or her room when the eating was finished. It meant that Salvatore could have early nights but this was a dubious blessing. He had more time to study his single state. He would not admit it, and told no one. Months had gone by since he'd received the first paperwork on the divorce. The word battered Salvatore. It was the wolf to be kept from the door; it was taboo.

There had not been a divorce in all the years the family lived in the Palazzo. Admittedly there had been some less than perfect marriages but, in this building, there had always been room for separate lives to be built while the family structure lived on. It was probably so for his own parents. He reflected on their middle years when they had very different orbits and yet, in the end, in their old age, they found a gracious re-convening which sustained them to death. It would be painful to watch Maria going her own way but he would wait patiently until she returned to him. He would not respond. God had given Maria to him and they were ordained to be together. Marriage was for ever.

The post today had brought another letter. Ellie had been writing regularly since his visit to her last September and especially since she had moved into Nerine's apartment. She said she welcomed the hours she had to fill, sitting in Nerine's small drawing room after the chores were done. He could imagine her there; she had described the place in detail with her artist's eye. She found it a pleasure to write her letters or dabble with paints knowing that she was doing it merely for herself. Such a small island of selfishness in a vast ocean of altruism, thought Salvatore. They were letters full of small revelations; her reactions to the present and her memories from the past. But she also wrote a great deal about Nerine, quoting her reminiscences in detail over that summer. For Salvatore it brought the old lady's spirit to him, wonderfully alive. The words also illuminated Ellie's own tenderness. It was a tenderness that had gone from his marriage. Caring for those small details depended on having a true knowledge of the other.

There was a knock on the door of his study.

'I'm sorry, I forgot to bring this with the rest.' It was Francesca with a bulky envelope. 'Looks like Max's writing. Is he coming out again?'

Salvatore shook his head. 'There's no need at the moment. He's helped a lot. But there's no need.' Salvatore tailed off, reading the disappointment in her face. As she left he pondered the relationship; he'd not meant Max to be more than useful. He certainly didn't want him to be involved with his family. But insidiously Max was becoming part of his life. Ever since the end of last year, when he'd accepted the offer of help with the accounts, there had been periodic visits. He sensed that Max valued getting away from England but was baffled by his adoption as confidant. Perhaps confidant was too strong a word; Max was good at relating all the external dissatisfactions but Salvatore suspected that he never gave away what was truly eating at him.

On the last occasion barely a month ago, aided no doubt by the wine, he'd come about as close to revelatory as he was ever likely to get. They'd sat on the terrace in the steamy July night. Salvatore had thanked him again for his help and Max countered.

'It's actually good for me. Your problem is one I can solve. Nice, tidy rows of figures all coming neatly to heel. Beats the shit at work and home.' Max didn't need any encouragement to continue. 'I don't know what's going on. I just feel, like, what's it all about? This lot on the board, it's like they're out to wreck the business; sell the birthright, you know?' Max sucked at his glass. 'Stupid bastards want to get rid of some property assets, but it's crap timing. If they had the balls they'd hang on in there; things are going to turn. And Tim, I just can't get through to him, he's not listening.'

'Your stepfather?' asked Salvatore.

Max nodded. 'He just makes these noises; pats me on the back and doesn't want to know. It's like everything I've done doesn't count. He's lost the plot I reckon.' Max was quiet for a moment or two. 'And you know, it makes me think, what have I got if that goes pear-shaped? The business, the family, the social life — it's all one.' He laughed, a hard little cough of a laugh. 'I had a teacher once. Good bloke. When I was going through a particularly shitty patch with exams and stuff he said *You know, Max, you mustn't confuse your work with your life.* And here I am, twenty years on, no life to speak of! Can't even get into the secretaries' knickers any more.'

Salvatore made no comment.

'Sorry, Salvatore, I've shocked you.' His air of brave self-derision subsided. 'I just sometimes wonder about blood being thicker than water; would I be here now if I'd had a real father around?'

Salvatore's opinion of Max was on the verge of softening. He was struggling to find words to help when Max hardened again.

'But that's all bollocks. You play with the hand life deals you eh, Salvatore? What's the point of dwelling in the past? Claw your way into the future I say!'

And the moment was over. Max was into his plans, probably to leave Penman-White's far behind and find a nice country retreat where Salvatore could design that garden.

'I rather fancy something in the Cotswolds. I've actually got my eye on a particular somewhere. Could we get away with olives do you think? This place has a south facing slope and terraces.'

Salvatore had remembered being encouraging; talking of hardy varieties had meant not having to struggle with tender feelings. Max's remarks about dwelling in the past had jarred.

★   ★   ★

In the bleakness of winter Salvatore had gone to Locarno, determined to find his wife again. Not long after the first time Max had turned up unannounced at the Palazzo Maria had sent him an email. She couldn't even lift the phone and talk to him. In it she had warned him that she needed to be alone and wanted them to spend Christmas separately. When he insisted on seeing her she had cleared a space for him in her apartment and her life, but really, Salvatore knew, he was outside of it now. He couldn't say that the days with her were unpleasant. In fact, she had been sweet to him. In retrospect it was the sweetness of dripping honey that could cloy and suffocate if inhaled. He'd met with her circle of fashionista friends; they tolerated him because he was Maria's husband but more than that, because he was the owner of a fine Palazzo and a useful pedigree. They were *tutti tirati* — so impeccable — these people who stitched labels on to everything in the world. But now he could see it — so did his wife.

On their last evening Salvatore would have preferred to be alone with Maria, but she insisted on taking him to a party given by the owner of a garment manufacturing business. It would be good for networking, she said. Salvatore had given in but only after negotiation; they would leave after a decent interval and have a quiet last supper somewhere together. They'd arrived in the private lift to be greeted by Karl, small and wide with flesh like putty; his hand pale and damp as he grasped Salvatore warmly.

'Ah, Maria's husband. She's told us a lot about you.'

Always a difficult first line to counter,

thought Salvatore, especially when Maria had not returned the favour and given him any information on his host.

'All good, I hope,' was his standard reply as Karl's wife fussed around him at chest level, offering drinks, smiling up at him through her gold-capped teeth. He looked down into her ample cleavage and felt like one of the towers of San Gimignano; erect and aloof from the curving landscape below him. He watched Karl's hand connect with the bare flesh on Maria's back and saw him hook a fleshy thumb through her dress strap as he guided her towards the other guests. Was it only afterwards that he recognised this as a small intimacy beyond the norm, or had he read it clearly then? For most of the evening Salvatore had been apart from his wife. He conversed with fashion editors, photographers, models. Someone asked him if they might do a shoot at the Palazzo, possibly?

'You can make a lot of money for just a few days of madness and mayhem.' She had laughed like a breaking wineglass. 'I'm surprised Maria hasn't thought to ask you about that.'

He was certain then, thinking on these words and watching his wife in the crowd, that Maria no longer wished her two worlds to connect.

They left the party far later than Salvatore would have wished and she led him to a chic *trattoria*. 'Home from home' she called it. They slipped in from the curdled atmosphere of the back street.

'That was such fun.' Maria was glowing as she slid herself into a corner seat. An obsequious waiter shimmied around her, flourishing the starched napkin. Salvatore was seated opposite, irritated by the candles and flowers that came between them.

'I could see you enjoyed it.' All the way here, Salvatore's thoughts had been bent upon his first words; they were not to sound reproachful or full of self-pity, but now they were uttered, he knew they had been just that. Maria raised her hands behind her head. Salvatore watched her beautiful breasts rising, watched the body language of one untouched by his words, by his presence.

'Yes, Salvatore, I did.' She stretched back further, her throat taut. 'When I'm here, with these people, appreciated for my talents,' did she really think he didn't appreciate her talents? 'I feel very alive. I feel as if I'm moving forward.' She looked at him directly then.

'Moving further and further away from me, Maria.' Salvatore pushed his hand across the table, offering it. She floated her hands down from her head, outlining her waist with them, smoothing the napkin on her lap.

'I suppose that's true,' she said, head bowed slightly as if receiving the scent from an invisible flower.

'And will you consider coming back?' He waited and watched.

She looked up. It was barely there but it was a shake of her head and then the word, 'No.'

He said nothing, just listened. As the plates came and went from the table she talked. Salvatore saw the bowl of *seppie* in front of him, fixed his eyes on the small rings of squid floating in the black ink and the blackness seemed right. He forced the fishy pieces to his mouth but they burned in his throat. The food was taken from him nearly untouched; Maria's plate was clean and white, he saw. She had eaten, no savoured, the *orecchiette* while she told him they had no future together, nothing to bind them any more.

When the heavy platters of wild boar appeared his appetite was gone, his stomach closed down. As he toyed with the dense meat, he asked, 'Have you found someone else?'

Another shake of the head, then she was adamant in her denial. Salvatore was unconvinced, conjuring the sticky-fingered

Karl into Maria's bed. She persevered and in the end he had to believe. Perhaps she was trying to be kind to him, denying he had a rival, but to Salvatore this was worse. It was a rejection of everything he had ever been.

She must have read his face, for she put down her knife and said, 'Oh Salva, it's not you, it's me. I want different things now; a different way of living that would mean asking you to give up everything you love.'

'You could have at least asked!' His voice was loud in his own ears. He wanted the courtesy of being treated as equal.

She sat back, the dark eyes wide. 'I think I have, over these last years, but you haven't wanted to listen.'

'Very well, but I am listening now.'

She shook her head again, for the third time. Salvatore's full portion of meat, glistening in its cold sauce, was taken away from in front of him. Maria called for the *conto*, the meal was at an end.

Back at her apartment they had talked long into the night. He had put before her the weight of their past together: she had countered with the lightness of her spirit without him. When they parted to go to bed in the ghost of the dawn, for a few moments he wanted to make her be his wife; held her by the shoulders, buried his head in her neck.

She was stiff and unrepentant. Salvatore turned away. He wanted to fight, to recapture her, but how could you trap a shadow?

★ ★ ★

Salvatore pushed himself up from his desk and went to open a window. Even this early the August air was limpid. Where had the months gone? What had he been doing? No, he wouldn't blame himself. It was not as though he hadn't tried. For some time after that week together he had flown uninvited to see her wherever she was, Locarno or Milan, sometimes for just a few hours at a time. He'd tried to understand her life. But he had to admit that she had turned into a character offstage; there was so little he knew about her life in the wings . . . on the wing. He picked up Ellie's letter from the desk and turned it in his hand, playing with it as he played with the words in English. Ellie. When had she become this important to him? It was disproportionate to their time together. A year had gone by since she had first come to the Palazzo; the next April came and went. That month stayed in his memory as being the last time he had flown to Locarno to see his wife. His reception then was devastating; Maria answering her door in the afternoon, half-clothed and waiting for him to leave.

Then Ellie's letters had come more and more frequently. He saw now how dependent he'd become upon their presence. Ellie was resistant to computers and so email wasn't an option for her. At first Salvatore had been impatient with such archaic communication, but soon he enjoyed the very process of each letter's arrival; the fact that every one was written on heavy cream paper and that this weight sat palpably in his hand when the *postino* gave him the envelope. Then there was her writing; large, with deep descending strokes, the blue-black ink pooled in places and threaded out in others. He began to be able to tell her mood even before he read any words, from the style and force of her characters.

He folded the letter sharply and rushed it back into its envelope. How could he be contemplating this woman when he had to be the resolute one in his marriage?

12

As August ended Ellie had planned another couple of days back at the cottage. Dom was no longer caretaking and her sweet neighbour was on holiday, so she needed to check up on things. The last time she'd been away from Nerine it had worked out well; Nerine was looked after and Ellie returned with peace of mind about the cottage. Without that distraction she nursed Nerine single-mindedly.

As she drove back down the M40 the landscape opened up. The day was sunny, with a clarity of light specific to September. Machinery was combing blond fields. Harvest seemed to come earlier and earlier these days. The poor raped land, immediately ploughed, fertilised and replanted. When was there a time to lie fallow for fields or humans? Her time with Nerine was something like it. The world had contracted to within the confines of the flat and its small garden. Life came to them. Mornings and evenings saw visits from the qualified, drugs reassessed, dressings changed. Ellie's place was as domestic angel; washing, shopping and cooking, although the latter dwindled with Nerine's appetite. She did find moments for herself, but in no way did she resent giving her time to Nerine. She thought of her prayer of over a year ago when she had asked for her life to change, for there to be a purpose to her existence and marvelled at the answer. Nerine's death would not have been a request, that was certain, but she could not be angry. What was there to be angry about? Nerine had lived a full and loving life and was dying with acceptance.

The car almost found its own way to the gravelled forecourt of the cottage. Long spires of purple veronica and burgundy orach, heavy with seeds, had shot up through the chippings. Nature wasted no time in asserting its dominion. Ellie crumbled some of the seeds in her fingers.

'*Atriplex hortensis*,' she said aloud. The Latin name gave her comfort; it was like reciting some natural liturgy. *Hortensis* meant 'of the garden'; little had she suspected how the plant would take over her garden so rampantly.

When Ellie pushed the front door it resisted; a pile of post impeded its opening. Gathering up the bundle she inhaled the cottage's familiar smell of sweet damp and wood smoke. She walked through to her small kitchen with the envelopes and dropped them on the counter. Her priorities were a cup of tea and a walk in the garden. When the kettle was on the hob she gave the back door a friendly kick to open it — it always stuck — and went to assess the changes. She could see immediately that the heat of August had had its effect. The lawn had caramelised with only a hint of green where it found shade. No need for cutting; that had probably saved her a few pounds in Jack's charges she thought. The long grasses on the boundary were moving with the wind; a river of limed gold. She walked towards them, noting in her progress the damage wrought by the drought. There were gaps in her flowerbed where she had lost the thirsty feeders but equally there were surprises. Plants that thrived in the dry were taking over. It was redolent of a Tuscan wayside. Were her gardens in sympathy with the gardens of Palazzo Michele, she wondered? The rudbeckias were soft pink, like the faded terracotta of an Italian wall. The heleniums were rich bronze and orange. The colours looked perfect against the ochre and olive tones of the garden.

And the wild blackberries were ripe, even if they were not swelled with juice. She still found a few of her cultivated raspberries in the kitchen garden but the majority of the crops were desiccated parodies of their true selves. Dom had done such a good job of watering earlier in the summer and it was sad to see his efforts wiped out. Still, there was always another year. She'd begin again in spring. As she pondered, just beginning to wonder why Jack hadn't lavished his usual care on these poor burnt creatures, she remembered the kettle. Her wild sprint back to the kitchen got her there just in time to hear the ominous hiss of a nearly dry vessel and early enough to prevent disaster.

Settled at the kitchen table with her tea Ellie began sifting through the post. She lobbed the junk mail into the bin, most unopened in its tacky plastic wrapping except for one rather appealing brochure on Italian holidays. She scanned several bills; they hadn't been waiting too long. Dear Nerine had insisted on giving her something to help with her finances. To stay with Nerine Ellie had given up a course she taught in the summer and so she accepted the payment gratefully. She was feeling the virtue of financial balance when she came across a letter in a heavy envelope. She opened it with a vague curiosity. It took her several attempts to assimilate it; each time the fear grasping her more fully. The tea at her elbow became stone cold as she struggled with the letter's contents.

Dear Mrs Brinkmayer,
REF: Debt Recovery 5567990/008/SH/mm
We last had reason to correspond with you and your husband, the late Andrew Graeme Brinkmayer, when you made settlement of part of a substantial debt (see enclosed copies of correspondence.) At this time Michigan Mutual Bank accepted you were in no position to discharge the remaining sum owing.

However, the debt remains extant until December of this year. Following a review of your situation the Bank's advisors find that you now have substantial assets and would be capable of paying the sum still owed. The terms of the original loan agreement require you to inform us of any relevant change of circumstances and your clear breach of this requirement may incur serious additional penalties. With interest the sum now payable amounts to substantially more than the original debt. Please see the enclosed statements of calculations.

We would advise that you acknowledge this letter, and set out the steps you intend to make to facilitate repayment, within seven days. Failure to do this will result in *commencement of further proceedings to recover the amount outstanding.*

If you would like to discuss this matter please call me on my direct line.

Yours faithfully,

Seymour Hopper

Solicitor, Debt recovery dept, Michigan Mutual Bank, Grand Cayman.

It was not entirely unexpected; Ellie had braced herself for this moment for nearly three years but it was still hard to believe that these few words had such power. What had finally spurred the bank into taking this action? How did they know about her inheritance? A rock settled in her guts. Senses evaporated as she seemed to become all mind, a mind that raced in whirring concentricity. Of course she prayed, it was her reflex, but it was whining, panic stricken, survival prayer. The date on the letter was nearly a week ago and so the machinery would be well in motion now. Ellie wished she had a cigarette, she badly wanted a familiar ritual to displace the chaos. Instead she began to sing, quietly like a moan at first, later with bravado; her voice wavering when she pitched in the wrong key. She sat down, she stood up, she paced the small kitchen, threw her tea down the sink and washed and dried her cup. She tidied and wiped, lining up mugs and plates, stacking saucers, polishing knives. As she did it she knew it was futile; it did not restore one degree of calm.

Strangely, she noted in an almost detached fashion, there was really no anger left in her. It was just another disappointment, just another way in which Andrew had let her down. What she felt was an overwhelming loneliness. Who could she share this with? Not Nerine. Her grasp on the outer world and its problems was loosening daily. Ellie couldn't disturb that gauzy fading. Not her children, not yet. Not her friends; none of them would have money like this to offer. She thought how weary they must be of Ellie and her problems; she was weary enough of them herself. She walked outside again; as she sat in her garden she was grateful that she had spent the first few minutes of her arrival out here, untainted by the sense of impending loss. It would be hard for her to look at it again in the same way. A garden should be a place of hope and faith in the future; the seeds of autumn that germinated in spring to bring a flourishing summer. She, however, was still reaping the effects of Andrew's miscast sowing.

★　★　★

Just an hour later, when the cold panic had subsided, she went to get pencil and paper then sat in the sun and made lists. It was clear to her that the only way she could find such a huge sum of money was to sell the cottage; so she should prepare if she was to lose this home too. It was how she could discharge the debt and have money left over. This was her moment to act.

This last hour it had finally 'come together'; she had finally assimilated the chain of events that had brought her here and she was ready to take responsibility for this outcome. Nearly six years ago when Andrew had been riding the wave he had persuaded her to act as guarantor on a property scheme of his. She couldn't even tell herself that she didn't know what she was doing; after all she'd been warned quite clearly that their home would be forfeit should the debt not be repaid. But it was a bit like those small print postscripts on the loan adverts; there to be ignored. She'd done what Andrew asked of her without much thought; after all, you trust your husband, don't you? And then she'd tried to close her ears and eyes when everything came tumbling down. Even now as she tried to think herself back to that moment she felt an overwhelming shame that she wanted to run from.

Ellie had left it to Andrew to mop up. They'd sold the house and he'd dealt with all the debt repayment. She remembered how she sought his assurance and made him promise that 'they' wouldn't be able to touch them again.

'Don't worry,' he had said with a smile for a child; hugging her to him and making her believe it was all all right. 'They've taken everything we have, there's no more that they can take!'

And it was the truth at the time. What he had continued to conceal from her was that there was still a huge outstanding debt that the Bank would not discharge. She had discovered that only after his death. Strangely then the feelings of betrayal mixed in with the grief of loss were almost helpful; she had somewhere to direct her anger. At that time she had truly raged; but when she calmed down she began to look at things from his perspective. After all, he was only trying to protect her and spare her pain. Today she reprocessed the thoughts through her head endlessly; no doubt Andrew thought that the term of the debt would be long expired before they had real assets again. He probably planned for them to sit in their rented house with just enough to live on for six years, after which time the Bank couldn't come after them for money. What he hadn't planned was his death. What he hadn't foreseen was Ellie inheriting her mother's cottage.

After Ellie took over the cottage nearly three years ago, she had talked with the solicitor who was dealing with probate on her mother's estate. He was a bumbling but kindly man who wished to see her cared for. His avuncular advice was to sit tight.

'The Bank has not made any moves to recover this money for three years and it's unlikely they will now. After six years they can't come after you any more. I would advise you Ellie, just to carry on living your life and taking care of your children.'

Ellie's conscience had worried her. She now had assets which meant she could repay the debt and to her that was probably the right thing to do.

The solicitor had glossed over the morality. 'Look, Ellie. Off the record, they're a big offshore concern that writes off debts thousands of times bigger than that every year. You need that money more than they do and really you got into this situation through no fault of your own.' He'd put an arm around her shoulder. 'Don't worry about it.'

Ellie had been persuaded then. And now, she could hear the advice in her head already;

friends and advisers would urge her to try the law, to plead her case. If she failed she could always try to take out a loan against the property. But Ellie was certain now that this would not be the route she would follow. This time she could choose exactly how she would deal with this situation. Last time she had been a passenger on Andrew's ship. Compared to him she was a financial baby but she had a simple sense of right and wrong and she kept within the boundaries of her knowledge. This time she would have the courage of her convictions.

But how had the Bank realised she had assets? Ellie puzzled over the way they'd found out and as a thought struck her, her body sagged like a deflated tyre.

'The break in,' she said out loud to herself. The smart car parked in the lane. It had to belong to a snooping banker. Well, more likely the hired hand; she couldn't see Seymour Hopper wasting time to seek her out. But that was months ago; why the delay? She sat with her head in her hands again trying to force her brain down new pathways. Suddenly she laughed out loud.

'Jonathan! Oh my dear Jonathan. What a cosmic joke!'

Of course she hadn't been found out by some romantic, cloak-and-dagger agent, she'd been betrayed by gossip. She could see it all now; Jonathan's cosy chats with the caring 'banker chappie' up at Benfield. That's the way things would have been linked. Ellie wailed — a proper physical response that comforted. She was tired; the anxiety wrung from her. At least now there would be a finish to this episode; an ending that accorded with her own sense of justice. Ellie felt a certain peace in knowing exactly where she was headed. She was going to cut off this painful limb as speedily as possible. First she called Nerine and her carers and told them she had to sort out some urgent plumbing problems for another day or two and then she called Mr Hopper at the bank. In the end the man sounded like a mere cipher, not the devouring monster she had feared. He informed her that they wanted an appointed agent to value her assets. They simply wanted swift repayment of the debt, which could, as a bottom line, mean appropriation of her property. When Ellie made it clear she intended to sell he said that of course she was free to market it with any agent she wished.

★ ★ ★

Two mornings later she opened the cottage door to a familiar face. However, if the face was familiar, the name eluded her. He stepped into the breach.

'Mrs Brinkmayer.'

No one had called her that for years. She was so busy hearing this name that she lost his.

'We met a long time ago. I knew your husband professionally when we were both in London but we met at your house in Derbyshire.'

'Yes. Do come in.'

Ellie felt the leaves of her memory stirring; prompted not by words but visual signals. He was wearing the country estate agent's uniform of a dun coloured jacket, made shapeless by the plunging of surveyors' measuring tapes into the pockets. His trousers were of a colour between porridge and Cotswold stone, made of a stretchy kind of material. He ducked forward under the low lintel, offering his hand and his card.

She read, 'Robert Carlisle-Brown. Partner.'

She looked at him uncomprehendingly for a second. He had been Bob Brown in his last incarnation. 'I didn't recognise the name. I didn't know you were double-barrelled,' she said, watching for the explanation. After some hesitation he laughed awkwardly.

'Ah yes, well, Lucinda and I added our names together.' He coughed and recovered himself. 'Looks good on a card don't you think?'

Ellie smiled. Lucinda. She'd been plain old Lucy back then. She couldn't help liking Robert for his awkwardness about this bit of game playing. If a new name helped his career who was she to judge? Names were strange constructs. Given by your parents, it was remarkable how few people rejected them. She'd never taken Andrew's name for herself. It seemed a needlessly totemic thing to have done now.

'Well. I'm still Ellie,' she said as she led him into the sitting room, 'although sometimes I wonder if that doesn't sound a bit girlish for me now.'

Robert chortled politely.

'But I call myself by my maiden name. I can't remember, was I down on the legal documents as Mrs Brinkmayer?'

Robert sat on the low, lumpy sofa. His long legs stuck up at an uncomfortable angle and his clipboard slithered down to his lap.

'Um, yes actually — as the wife, but if you'd prefer me to call you Carroll on any paperwork?'

Ellie waved her hand in dismissal. No. Best to have this finished in the name of Brinkmayer, she thought. Robert looked pained as he stumbled over his words.

'Can I just say — er, Ellie — that I'm really sorry to be the one who does this?'

She'd been through this all before, years ago. Then she watched Andrew fight to fend off the humiliation. He couldn't bear to be seen to fail so he wouldn't declare himself bankrupt. Ellie was surprised at her detachment. It was just a pity, she thought, that Andrew hadn't faced things then. If he had, she wouldn't be inheriting the legacy of his actions now.

'It's OK, Robert. Actually I'm glad. I hope that you'll just do your best for me.'

He nodded. He assured her that their history would help him in his efforts.

★ ★ ★

After Robert had calculated and jotted, drunk her tea and gone, Ellie sat and measured her state of mind. It was surprisingly peaceful. The sound of a welcome shower of rain lent a background rhythm to her thoughts. She may have had her hand forced but from now on she was in control. She wasn't stupid. She would market this cottage to get herself the best price and she certainly would take advice on the amount of interest the Bank expected her to repay. Conversations with Dom and Sadie hadn't been totally plain sailing but, when she made it clear that this was the best way to find a resolution, they had come onside — well, maybe she still had some work to do with Sadie. Her children must know that she would never disadvantage them.

Ellie felt tired but she didn't have the will for anger any more. She resigned herself to saying goodbye to another home. The visit to Folgate Street came to mind; identity bound up between the walls of a house. Folgate Street had told two stories; the imaginary one that Dennis Severs wanted to tell but also the truth of his life and occupation of the place. It was the small intrusions of present life, like supermarket sauce, and the decisions he'd made about the story, that laid a paper trail to his door every bit as much as the things he collected passionately. Ellie realised now she had never been fooled, not been truly engaged with his imaginary family. She was far more interested in its creator.

She would have to create herself some-where else, in some other context. The one thing she couldn't experience in her daily life, continuity, she was finally learning to experience inside herself. She was not her house, not her work, not even her body. She was a living creation and creation is constantly changing. The thought was a break in the clouds. Ellie got up and opened the

French window to the garden. The scent of dampened grass floated in and she almost collided with a bee. The insect brought her focus back to the rose around the doorway. Bee and flowers were at the zenith of their productivity; some flowers just young buds, zipped tightly into green jackets, others fatly unfurling and with the greatest intensity of colour. But today the ones that seemed to her the most beautiful were the open blooms, their centres receptive to the comings and goings of the bees. It was a last chance; they would not remain this lovely for much longer. She let out a breath, only then conscious that she had been holding it inside her.

Ellie stepped back into the room. All these bereavements. She knew she was finally accepting them. She felt like she was crossing the stepping-stones of the universe; propelled in each move by a hugely benevolent power. She had really loved Andrew. She'd loved him precisely because he was not like her. Ellie didn't fool herself that she had ever known him completely. She hadn't wanted to. She had been the open flower, he the bee. It was just the way it was. Since his death, however, she'd learned a lot about different ways of being. Immediately after Max's assault she'd wanted to turn back time and become the closed bud. Now, she had no inclination to armour herself against the world.

After all these months she wondered about Max; she wished she'd been brave enough to face him with his actions; ask him 'why?' A momentary thought that she might try to find him soon passed, for he'd not shown any signs of remembering what he'd done; if it was buried that deep within him what hope had she of exhuming it? Max just felt, *What you don't know can't hurt you.* Never mind those around you, thought Ellie. There was nothing she could do to make Max see that responsibility came with every action. She'd missed the moment. All she could do was pray that he would learn. It was a prayer that she had prayed with Nerine. Sweet Nerine. Ellie didn't know if Nerine was praying with her to keep her happy. But it did seem to give Nerine comfort too. Together they had trawled through the parts of their lives that were painful or joyful or unfinished and they sent them off to be dealt with. 'Your God's laundry!' Nerine had called it. Often when Ellie prayed she felt desperate or futile, it was a last resort, but in those hours with Nerine she felt a sense of expectation.

★　★　★

Both letters had come on a Friday; traditionally a day of woe. Salvatore read Ellie's first. He wondered at the restraint of someone who had such urgent needs. She committed them to a piece of writing that would not reach its audience for days. No phone call, simply a continuation of her habitual process. He studied his reactions minutely; what was it that he wanted? It was a homecoming for Salvatore; this relationship through words. Words of a language that now came to him as easily as his mother tongue. He felt a little sad that she wrote as if to a distant mirror, wanting reflections. He wanted her to step through the frame and need him.

Dearest Salvatore,
    I have to tell you how things have moved on again for me.

Ellie described the way the debt had arisen, the letter from the bank and how she proposed to deal with the matter.

I don't think I need to tell you what kind of terror that brought, the ripping away of what we deem our security, it engenders fear in us weak humans. But Salvatore, I couldn't believe how quick was the process between the wound being inflicted and the healing beginning. It reminded me of those times when Superman hears the cry, descends and, with fingers moving too fast to discern, reconstitutes whatever disaster has occurred into its former self. Except that I am not my former self. I am better than that!

You know, Salvatore, that I would have prayed when I got that letter, and believe me it was a desperate prayer, screamed out from rock bottom, full of desolation. But within almost minutes of that agony I began to take decisions for myself; decisions that are taking me forwards and not backwards for the first time in years.

Miraculously, within days I seem to have a buyer offering me the asking price. The selling agent thinks it is a more than fair amount and he's offered me a very special percentage for his services — after all I haven't needed to advertise. It's a property company that has made the offer. That did give me a few worries but the agent reassured me that the planning restrictions here are such that no one could make a massive change. Anyway, the agent also believes that the company director actually wants the cottage for his personal use. I would like to think he'll love it as I do although I'm able to be detached about giving it up now, even my beautiful garden. I expect I'll need strength to cope when I actually have to leave.

Salvatore could sense a pause in the letter. The writing resumed at a subtly different angle and pressure.

The property company is called Ramband, a strange name but Dom tells me it's probably an 'off the shelf' company. Apparently somewhere there are people just coupling together strange words and registering them as company names to sell on. I quite like the idea of doing that as a living, don't you?

As to how I shall actually live I'm not sure. I shall have a little capital from the sale and perhaps I'll rent for a while. I've always got my teaching but at the level I do it at the moment I don't know how much of a mortgage it would support. They've been very good at the college, allowing me to take time away. I doubt if now I could get a 'proper job', I'm not qualified enough and I'm too old. I find that quite funny; I hardly feel as though I've got started!

I suppose I've enjoyed my work on the whole. Sometimes I go into the chill school rooms — do you know how bleak they feel when the school is emptied of children on a winter evening — and wrestle to move the furniture and set up for the prospect of maybe only three people turning up and then I wonder why I'm doing it. It's hardly a job with kudos is it? Not like a doctor or a lawyer. How do other people view it? Essentially as a manual skill; teaching people who have time on their hands, old ladies who want to dabble in watercolour. But it's not like that at all, Salvatore. I like to help people find things inside themselves, to express things outside words, to feel that totally brilliant moment when they create something out of nothing, out of a nowhere with infinite possibility.

Does this sound a deal of high-minded rubbish? No. I shouldn't say that to you, Salvatore. I think you understand. Anyway, as for the old ladies, they're brilliant. I taught one who had cared for her handicapped son for fifty years and was still doing it and another who turned out to be a Nobel Prize winning scientist!

Nerine could win my Nobel Prize. She's continuing to face her death with such dignity and peace, Salvatore. I wish you could see how easy she makes it look. She is draining away from us bit by bit: she sleeps a great deal, but there are moments of availability to this world. Sometimes she sits up in bed and demands full make-up and to wear one of her favourite hats!

She's made me do little paintings of her like this — you must see them — she says no photographs now, she wants to be seen subjectively only. I find it impossible not to respond to her joy. There's no other word for it.

Do you see, Salvatore, how I can hardly be cast down by the loss of a house when I watch Nerine losing her life so gracefully? I don't suppose it can be too long now. For some time Nerine has been planning her own memorial service, she knows exactly what sort of effect she wants from the music and readings. What surprised me was that she wants it to be in Oxford. Apparently the choirmaster at Keble is an old friend and she has a cache of elderly relatives around Banbury. She said it seems more sensible, patted me on the hand and said 'and much more convenient for you.' It was all I could do not to cry.

Salvatore put down the letter. Ellie was almost by his side; he could nearly touch her. There were other pieces of paper on the desk. One was a solicitor's note; short, formal, to the point and accompanying court papers for the further stage of Maria's divorce petition, filed in Switzerland. She'd thought of everything as usual. The flat and the business in Locarno had given her a way to short circuit the drawn out procedure of Italian divorce; with his agreement she could be out of this marriage in a few weeks.

The other paper on the desk was a photocopied sheet; he must have made it himself some years ago. Marsilio's words; *In Isaiah, God speaks thus: 'He taketh the wise in their own craftiness' and again 'The Lord knoweth the thoughts of the wise that they are in vain.'*

It should therefore be enough for man to know that the beautiful working of the single universe is governed by the wise architect, on whom it depends. From goodness only goodness can spring. And what proceeds from that can only be ordered well. Therefore everything should be accepted for the best.

So simple to read the words, so difficult to enact. What advice could he give Ellie? None. He admired the simplicity of her thought and action and her faith that doing the right thing would bring the right results. He vaguely wondered how Dominic and Sadie had felt about the decision; whether they even knew of it. Doing the right thing often had a fallout that didn't seem well ordered at the time. How hard to act well when it meant loss — Salvatore was not entirely sure he would be able to do it. Was it wrong to refuse Maria what she wanted?

★   ★   ★

Saturday morning dawned and with it the exodus of another group. As they went, so Max arrived. Salvatore had tried to dissuade him, saying that the accounts were really in good shape and that his visit wasn't necessary. Max wouldn't have it; he said he'd just come for a break then, it had been over a month since the last time and he could do with a weekend away. Sometimes Salvatore felt the price of Max's help was too high.

'It's good to be here. The only place with a bit of peace,' Max had said as he'd swung his case into the hall. Francesca had poked her head out from behind the library door and her face had lit up when she saw him. Salvatore felt uneasy at the scene.

'Mia cara, Francesca, how ravishingly beautiful you look today.' Max had stepped forward to enfold her in a bear hug. Francesca had blushed into his cashmere and asked what he needed.

'No more than your divine presence!'

Salvatore knew he was brisk with Francesca; asking her to do some chore that could have been done at any time.

'You'll have to forgive us Max, if we can't spend as much time with you this weekend as we'd like, but we need to prepare for another influx.'

Salvatore smiled gently. Max wasn't fooled, he knew.

'Shame. I'll just have to ration my portion of the delicious Francesca,' he said to her retreating form.

Salvatore watched as she looked back over her shoulder and smiled coquettishly; an innocent *putto*.

'But will you be able to talk to me about this garden of mine? It has the real possibility of happening.'

'You don't let the grass grow under your feet, do you Max? Yes, of course. Some time after dinner suit you?'

★   ★   ★

They sat outside in the warm night, Max's face hardly readable in the darkness. It took him some time to get to the point over a post dinner brandy. There were minutes reminiscing about the 'Merry Band' as he'd always

272

dubbed his fellows on the course.

'You know, Salvatore, I really look back on those few weeks with quite a fondness. I liked being with a set of people feeling like you were all after the same thing.'

'What was that, Max?'

'A bit of cultural enlightenment. To go home having learnt a bit more about art, life, the whole damn thing!' He laughed. 'I wonder how everyone's lives have moved on. Don't you, Salvatore?' Max searched his face. 'But then perhaps you know? Do you keep in touch with everyone else?'

'Now and again.' He was guarded.

'That Nerine was a character, wasn't she? You know she wrote a piece about me for a magazine. Wasn't entirely flattering I have to say, but funny enough to forgive her. I'm sorry the old bird is dying.'

'How do you know that? Are you in touch with her?'

Max was hesitant. 'No . . . uh, I think you mentioned it last time I was here, didn't you?'

In July, when Max was last here, Nerine was hardly diagnosed. He couldn't have told Max. Salvatore was unsettled but let it pass.

'Now you're thinking of this place in the Cotswolds what about looking up Ellie, Max? Is it anywhere near? She could give you a lot of help on plantings.'

'Mmm. It's near all right.' Max tucked his shirt tail further into his waistband. 'I doubt that she'd want to help me out though.'

Salvatore guessed this remark came from injured pride. He was probably still smarting over Ellie's rejection. Salvatore was relieved; only then did he realise that suggesting that Max get in touch with Ellie had been a sort of test, for Max and for himself. As much as he'd tried not to judge Max, he still didn't want him too near the woman he cared about.

'Look, actually, what's the point of discussing this garden of mine until I've actually completed on the property?' Max said. 'It's just nice to be relaxing somewhere where I'm not arguing with everyone.'

'Fine. Arguments at work?'

Max shook his head. 'No. This is family. And this one's a real bowl of manure. I shan't go into it but let's just say it was a blood-letting that should have happened a long time ago.' He shrugged. 'Families eh, Salvatore?'

Yes. Families. Or the lack of them. Salvatore had learned a few things about Maria recently that confirmed his suspicions about her affair. They made him want to argue; to not go quietly. He wasn't sure that he could agree with Ficino that all things were for the best.

13

When Ellie returned to London the temperatures were declining and so was Nerine's hold on physical life. But as the mists of late September rose it seemed that she was living more through her spirit. What did they call it in literature — the pathetic fallacy? That had always seemed a cruel phrase to Ellie, probably because of the modern overtones of the words; when had anything exciting pity or sadness, anything emotional, become associated with moral weakness? And why should any link between a natural universe and a human soul be deemed misleading or a delusion?

Towards the very end Sadie came to stay too. Ellie was grateful for her representation of the real world, for at times she felt that she was travelling too closely with Nerine, being sucked into the vortex of another existence. Sadie's presence was like a metaphorical pinch for she brought with her the grit of everyday. Nerine slept more and more and she and Sadie talked of shopping and blocked drains and emotional dilemmas in her presence.

'Sweetheart, you know that I'm very grateful that you're here.'

Sadie looked up from her breakfast newspaper reading, smiled and nodded. They were very close to each other in the tiny kitchen. 'I wanted to be with you just now.' Sadie's face was taking on the formlessness that precedes a cataract of emotion.

'Whatever's the matter?' Ellie extended her arms towards her daughter but was barred by Sadie putting up her hands and turning her face away.

As it contorted she gasped out, 'It's Paul. His wife's pregnant.'

'Oh my love.'

Ellie sat down close beside her, trying to balance on the small folding chair, and waited.

'It should be easy shouldn't it? End of story. Woman betrayed. Woman goes off to find new life. Good comes out of adversity.' She let go and sobbed, her words propelled out with each jolt of air. 'But I love him. I'm in so deep that I can't lose this part of my life. No, it's not part — it's my whole life!'

'What does he say?' Ellie proffered the kitchen roll.

'He's shocked. He says he wished he'd left sooner but now — ' Sadie wiped the slime from her nose and looked up at Ellie, 'but now, he doesn't know what to do.'

Ellie tried hard not to fit everything neatly into a box of her making. She didn't even know Paul. She only knew her daughter loved him blindingly. But her heart was aching for Sadie, getting ready to brace her for the inevitable end to this not very original story. She knew enough not to say anything but just to hold her, now that such a gesture was allowed. They talked through all the possible pathways, Ellie breaking off regularly to make cups of tea and watch over Nerine. There were to be no conclusions and so when Nerine awoke, Sadie washed her face and sat and read to her. Nerine, who would have been so perceptive, was now unaware of the turmoil in Sadie's life as she gradually released her grasp on externals. Although she was concerned for Sadie, Ellie had to admit to herself that she felt relief when she left for a short trip to Ireland. The rhythm of life in the flat continued on peacefully; Ellie was surprised how easy it felt to take care of Nerine and how she neither resented the time with her nor worried about the progress of the sale of the cottage. Things were taking their course. At times it seemed the lawyers conspired to make it a grindingly slow one but she trusted that the conclusion would be right. Her solicitor was trying to negotiate an extended completion in order to give her time to sort out her next move. On her better days Ellie decided it was unproductive to worry about it; she had put stuff in storage before, she could do it again. The solicitor was also bargaining for lower interest payments on the debt. It all took time. Being used to measuring the hours by Nerine's presence, Ellie didn't want to hasten the passing of time but hold on to every minute.

So here she was, watching September conceding to October and waiting for Nerine to die; except that she didn't see it like that. Nerine spent time planning her own memorial; not proscribing every moment but she wanted 'beauty and emotion'.

'I'm not one of those who'll say don't cry,' she said, 'I think you should have a good cry at a funeral. Cry copiously but don't be sad for me. I've had a wonderful life. I've been present at every day of it and don't even regret the bad and the sad moments.'

Ellie wondered if she'd be able to say the same as she came to the end of her life.

She really enjoyed living out these days with Nerine, especially the moments when she could talk to her, and even the parts where she slipped in and out of lucidity. It was like that on the last morning. At around eleven they were talking quite rationally about some plants in the garden when Nerine sat forward and her eyes fixed on a distant point.

'There's a boat coming. Where's it going, dear?'

Ellie was briefly thrown; in her desire to supply a suitably fitting answer she simply blurted out, 'Heaven.'

It seemed to be the right answer because Nerine lay back, murmured, 'Ah, that's right,' and closed her eyes. Within the hour she was dead.

$\star \quad \star \quad \star$

It was the evening when Sadie called from Ireland to be given the news.

'I knew, Mum,' was what she said.

'What do you mean? How did you know?'

'I was in this church in Kerry and, you'd be pleased, I thought I'd try a prayer for Nerine.'

Ellie just listened.

'Well, I can't say it sounded very convincing but then I opened my eyes and looked up at the stained glass window. It was a picture of Jesus in a boat, that story about stilling the storm I suppose. And I knew just then that Nerine had gone sailing off.'

If the moment had been a painting it would have been a very bad one, possibly done on black velvet with a large orange sunset and baby deer.

'Mum, did you hear me?'

'Yes. What time were you in the church?'

'About mid-morning. Would that be right?'

Ellie was crying. Leaking massive amounts of water. She was crying to flood the desert. 'Oh yes, that's really right!'

★   ★   ★

Nerine's cremation service had been brief; attended by just a few of those who cared for her in her last days. A plain rite conducted by a parson who hadn't known her. At the end, a plastic jar of ash that Nerine had asked her goddaughter to take to Florence and scatter in the Arno. By comparison the memorial service at Keble had been unreal; almost an act of theatre. It was strange to Ellie to be surrounded by unfamiliar people — an audience there for the performance. Sadie had come for Nerine's sake and Dom had come just in order to support her. Apart from her children she could only say she knew Salvatore; her relationships with some of Nerine's godchildren and friends were sketchy, although now bound by her death.

All the words in Ellie's eulogy were heartfelt but, although they seemed to help others connect with their grief, they did not bring about the same melancholy in Ellie. She was sad that she had lost such a friend; sad that she'd only been able to know her such a short time. But she was happy that Nerine's death had been as exemplary as her life. It had been a privilege to be asked to share that. Ellie listened raptly to descriptions by those who'd known her longer and been not a little surprised to discover other facets of Nerine. They were parts of her life that she hadn't shared with Ellie. At first she felt almost betrayed by the revelation of these 'secrets'; then she began to appreciate Nerine's talent for living in the present and sharing it so completely that there was little time to introduce the past.

One elderly gent had rung Ellie on reading the notice in the *Telegraph* (where else?) and begged to be allowed to say a few words. Watching him shuffle painfully to the lectern she was nervous about his peroration. She need not have been; he surprised most of those who'd known Nerine by revealing that they'd been on the same music-hall bill back in the 1930s — he as a stand-up and she as a sweet singing ingénue. At eighty-six he hadn't lost any of his timing and the gathering loved him, most of all for loving her. In a faltering voice he described a woman who'd kept this friendship alive for so many years. The tributes made Ellie feel as though she'd merely dipped a toe in the water compared to Nerine. Knowing someone who lived life with such a light hand on the past and a fearless attitude to the future must help Ellie to cope with her present.

At the end of the service, Ellie was glad to be temporarily alone among the crowds filling the sunken courtyard. She wandered along the side of the chapel looking at all the flowers, pleased that Nerine had not put a prohibition on them. Many were sweet hand-gathered posies, plenty of them from her god-grandchildren. There was just one that looked like it was the product of lavish budget. She turned the card; 'I'll miss you, you lively old bird. Love Max.' It was a bit of a shock but she couldn't fault him for the thought, just the ostentation.

When most of the mourners were gone, the cakes put away and the wine glasses packed up by the caterers, Salvatore remained. He put his hand gently on her arm.

'Ellie, that was beautiful. I'm sure Nerine enjoyed every moment.'

Ellie imagined Nerine's reactions to all that had gone on that afternoon and it was then that she felt bereft. Her too-expressive face betrayed it, she knew. Salvatore gathered her up and her tears dampened his jacket. She was so grateful for his comfort. There was an empty space, once filled by Nerine. How strange was the state of 'ceasing to be'. The cottage remained silently waiting for her to return but it was no longer a restful haven, it was in a kind of dynamic restlessness as though every atom of it was swirling about itself. She could no longer view it as truly hers; for her, it too would soon cease to be. When everything threatened to pass away from you where could you find a place to stand firm? Salvatore held her at arm's length, took out a fine linen handkerchief, dabbed her eyes and suggested it was time to leave.

It took half an hour to drive back to the cottage. Ellie had insisted that Salvatore should stay with her; Sadie too, but she had had to go back to London to prepare for a trip. It was Salvatore who opened the door for her and put on the kettle to make tea. Ellie gave way to these small acts of proprietorship and began to imagine another owner under this ancient roof. As tears threatened she made her escape upstairs to her room, pleading a need to freshen up. Ellie sat before the mirror of her dressing table and watched her eyes redden and her face sag into a mask of unhappiness. She'd watched it in others over and over during the day. But she found it almost unbearable to watch this woman, her youth and energy faded, crumpling before her and to accept it was herself.

Ellie straightened up and briskly cleansed her face. She reapplied lipstick, willing herself not to look in her own welling eyes. She needed to think in another timescale. When you are young you see things as lasting for ever. The passage of time is interminable, sometimes unbearable in its slowness. But nothing does stay the same. She remembered her father comforting her when she was going through difficult times. 'Everything passes', he would say. Not only the bad but the good too; Ellie had to face again the end of another part of her life. Her bravery of the last few weeks slipped away from her. Had she really prayed for change? Not this way, please God, not another forced upheaval. As she sat she wondered how many times this would need to happen to her before she learnt, like Nerine, to hold life lightly. She wanted to be able to pass through events without allowing them to tether her to the ground. If she could look upon this new loss as a release she would be free to gather up her tent and move on.

★　★　★

'Come and drink your tea, Ellie.'

Salvatore called her into the sitting room where he was assembling a fire. The chill of the September afternoon was settling. As the sun sank it was diffused through a mist that rose from the fields.

'Do you mind if we take a walk around the garden before the light goes?'

'Of course not, but would you rather be alone?'

Salvatore was looking at her, waiting to judge if her answer was just a dissembling.

'No,' she said, and meant it.

They went, in silence at first. She had a familiar inventory in her head while Salvatore just looked and accepted things as they were. Ellie began by regarding the garden as imperfect. It had grown away from her while she had been apart from it. She'd discovered that Jack hadn't been coming because he was laid up with a bad back and now Nature's reign and rule was asserting itself. Scores of bullying evening primrose had sprung up amongst the herbaceous. She regarded them as interlopers while Salvatore commented on how beautifully they glowed in the fading light. The nettles were allowed to grow in order to encourage butterflies, but she confined them to a small corner. Now they had marched with colonising triumph into her flowers. She had an almost physical sensation of the wiry rhizomes snaking under the soil, making their insidious progress.

Mid-way down the garden the tall skeletons of foxtail lilies stood above what should have been bright clumps of heleniums. It was obvious the rabbits had been in, probably some time ago. The stunted plants were vainly trying to flower close to the ground.

'Oh the bloody bastards!' She couldn't help herself. The words came out as unexpectedly vehement and charged with real anger.

Salvatore looked at her; Ellie saw the question in his eyes but also the beginning of a smile at the corner of his mouth.

'I'm sorry.' She laughed. 'It's just that, let's say, I have a rather interesting relationship with those rabbits. We spend a lot of time trying to outwit each other.'

'And you thought they'd do the decent thing and cease trench warfare whilst you were away, did you?' Salvatore smiled and put his arm around Ellie. She felt the bracing of the previous weeks and years falling away. The last time she'd begun to let go like this was with Max. Ellie scrabbled mentally to replace her emotional scaffolding.

'And look!' she said brightly, walking out of his reach, 'if it's not the rabbits, it's the moles or the slugs.'

The small area of grass, too humble to be a lawn, was traversed by neat mounds. The soil looked beautifully worked, like the 'fine tilth' they always exhorted you to prepare in the instructions on the back of seed packets. It was just that it was in the wrong place. Ellie stood still, staring at the tiny hills. She was trying to let go of the way she thought things ought to be and really appreciate the mole's work.

'No. Can't do it.' She kicked at the earth and walked away, aware of Salvatore standing behind her, probably watching with the same wry amusement.

When she looked back she saw him, head bent, concentrating on making a roll-up. Ellie hadn't smoked for months, certainly not in all her time with Nerine, and she suddenly felt a craving to be holding the poisonous stick; to be pulling the smoke deep into her lungs. Salvatore raised his head and looked at her as he licked the length of the gummed paper. She took note of the brown irises and the whites, almost luminous against the deep tone of his skin in the fading light. Salvatore proffered her the cigarette.

'Want it?' he asked.

Ellie just nodded and took the few steps back to him. Yes, she did want it. She waited while Salvatore rolled another for himself and then lit both of them. The smoke hit the back of her throat, the acrid taste undimmed by any filter. She held it down inside her until she couldn't do anything but let go. After just this first puff her head was light and she felt distinctly out of control. For Ellie, the anticipation of smoking was so much better than the event itself; after a couple more puffs she tried not to let Salvatore see that she had more or less abandoned his handiwork, letting it smoulder between her fingers.

'It's OK Ellie, you can get rid of it if you want.'

She looked at him lamely. 'But it's such a waste . . . ' she tailed off.

'No, what I think is a waste is you being unhappy.'

Ellie waited, shivering slightly in the cool, damp air.

'In the second half of our lives there's not enough time to squander on the state of unhappiness. Ellie, you've had to go through so much pain in a few years, I think you should live by your heart. Cut off from the bad and look for the good that's going to come in the future.'

In Ellie's head the question 'how' mingled with some scripture. *I know the plans I have for you, says the Lord; plans to give you hope and a future.* Ellie thought, I wish he'd damn well let me in on those plans, as she spoke back to Salvatore.

'That's rather easier said than done. I suppose to you it's just an intellectual exercise to sever yourself from the past.' Ellie flung the cigarette butt into a morass of mildewed Michaelmas daisies. 'But what I desperately need now are some practical solutions.' She hugged herself.

'You're cold. Come inside and we'll discuss it.'

It was warm in the sitting room; Salvatore's fire had taken a good hold. While he went off to make fresh tea Ellie sat and stared into the flames. Now and again they flared up; tiny spits of blue and green flame amongst the yellow declared the release of some stray mineral. What did she learn about at school? Latent energy? The idea had captured her imagination when not a lot else in science lessons had. The idea that a seemingly inert log or lump of coal was a storehouse of power. It only needed ignition to produce overwhelming energy. She gazed again at the crackling wood; what seemed like destruction was in fact only transformation. The heat and the light were miraculous; more able to enhance life than insentient timber. Salvatore came back with two mugs.

As Ellie sipped he said, 'I do want to give

you some practical solutions, Ellie. If you'll let me.'

★ ★ ★

It was strange how all these lives had collided in his home in Italy. No, strange was not the word at all. Ordained. As Salvatore sat in Keble College Chapel listening to the power of the Rachmaninov he reflected on the times he had sat here before. He would cycle from his digs in Longwall Street, a matter of a few minutes, to attend services. He could see with the perspective of years why Keble had drawn him with its amalgamation of Victorian and Byzantine decoration. He was the outsider then; Italian, religious, reserved. They said the English were reserved, the Italians effusive. He was a walking refutation.

How right that events should turn full circle after nearly forty years and he should be sitting in Keble feeling so at home, almost integrated into its fabric. Nerine had known of his Oxford days but she'd not spoken of her connection with Keble. That was Nerine; she had no necessity to impress. Salvatore silently thanked God for her life to the strains of the Znameny chant 'Thou didst destroy the condemnation of death.'

The choir sat, settling with a sound like

muted thunder in the echoing space, to leave a silence like thick honey. The tap-tapping of shoe beats sounded on the tiled floor. Salvatore watched Ellie, made small by the building, walk for what seemed like for ever to the dais under the apse. He scrutinised her from a distance; this woman who had begun to infiltrate his senses. She had her own style; certainly not conforming to high fashion but individual and comfortable. In an extraordinary act of sharing she had revealed to him how self-doubting she was, but her exterior belied that. The sculptural roundness of her body reminded him of a Picasso painting, of a jug actually. It was a good simile for Ellie; pouring out generously. Her solidity, the hair that dropped across her eyes, the floating clothes — all presented an image of calm to the world.

She began to speak, the huge presence of the mosaic Jesus towering over her. They were words with which she expressed gratitude for having known Nerine and humility that she should be able to speak of her before all those who had known her for much longer. Salvatore thought, 'But probably not much better.' It was not always time that brought the deepest relationships, it was a coalescing of spirits. After tributes to her talents, especially that of living life to the full every day, Ellie described a conversation with Nerine in her last weeks. She talked of a painting of the Annunciation and Salvatore conjured up the faces of Mary and the Angel. Ellie described Nerine's response to the picture; how she was touched by such an awe-inspiring happening, taking place within ordinary domestic walls. To Ellie this was a perfect metaphor for Nerine, a woman who transformed the commonplace of every day and always saw the beauty; saw the angel offering his lily rather than the restrictions of her surroundings. Ellie visualised Nerine's death as the time when she held out her hand, took the flower with its perfect form and scent and said a resounding yes to the angel. It was a fitting image with which to end her words.

Salvatore watched the reactions of the congregation as she stepped back to her seat. Some had heads bowed, others gazed fixedly ahead; most seemed to be quietly contemplating the picture in their minds. Everyone would learn more about Nerine within that hour. Bizarrely, Salvatore had an image of a perfect English hamper, probably from Fortnum and Mason, being opened up on the banks of the Isis. As the river flowed by Nerine's life was unpacked, each good treat there to be enjoyed. It was a wildly random selection of contents; a colleague from the Homeless Shelter describing her faithful service whilst a godson told of the night, not so long ago, when he had begged Nerine to leave a jazz club because he was tired. The choirmaster, her link to Keble, had a difficult time choosing which anecdote to tell, he said. Eventually he chose to describe the time when Nerine found accommodation in London for a choir of one hundred when their arrangements suddenly collapsed. She had personally found room for ten in her small flat; ten who had reported the best time of their lives. He cited this as a wonderful testament to her generosity to people, her gift of hospitality and her ability to embrace change. The last words resonated for Salvatore. Nerine didn't cower under the wave of change; she jumped in and moved along with it. She was a content woman. Salvatore stood to sing, watching the light sparking the colours in the stained glass. He ordered his thoughts into an elegant phrase, 'the only way to eradicate pain is to accept change.'

After the service there had been champagne for those who wanted it or tea for those who did not. There were sweetmeats, nothing practically sustaining, simply delightful little treats. Sadie found him in the crowd and offered him some truffles from a dish.

'Nerine would have loved these, wouldn't she? She had a real sweet tooth.'

Salvatore nodded as he took one. 'Yes. I noticed that. Francesca, my niece who helps me in Italy, was always complaining how she had to clear away half-finished plates of her excellent pasta and yet got sweet-talked into bringing second helpings of dessert.' Salvatore corrected himself while Sadie laughed. 'I don't mean she complained really, you couldn't complain about Nerine.'

'No. You couldn't.' Shifting the plate, Sadie offered her hand. 'Pleased to meet you, Salvatore. I'm Sadie, Ellie's daughter.'

He knew. As he'd watched her pale and sharp profile in the chapel he thought how unlike Ellie she looked; only some mannerisms seemed to link them. He tried to conjure up Andrew from this female reflection. Another history; a whole part of Ellie's life that he wanted to explore.

'Mum obviously loved her time on your course.'

The conversation was polite. Sadie was playing her part well; the self-sufficient child. He barely managed ten minutes talking to her but he felt a warmth for this daughter of Ellie's; he was not necessarily drawn to other people's children, generally finding them to be incoherent splinters of their parents and thus inconvenient barriers to the main relationship. Sadie he liked immediately. Maybe he was wrong to respond to instinct, but his insight told him she had a real loyalty and love for her mother. He would have to tell Ellie how much her daughter loved her; probably she'd be surprised for the signs were not obvious. They were buried under a brittle and independent exterior.

Salvatore circulated amongst the mourners eliciting their stories of Nerine. Someone should write her biography, he thought; the story was too rich and varied to die with her. How different his history; written mainly in one place, around one home. His life had been invested in the Palazzo. It was unthinkable that he should ever be severed from the place, or the ghosts of his family that peopled it. He thought of Ellie having to give up her home for a second time and it produced a physical pain in him.

'Do you feel OK, Salvatore?'

The question came from Sadie. He nodded at her, joining in her game of façade. As he'd sat and listened to the synopses of Nerine's life he had been struck by how many times she'd walked in, run in, to action. He compared himself to her; his life was filled with thought and reflection. How many times had passed when he could have done something and yet he hadn't until his hand was forced? Perhaps it was like that with Maria. He had seen the signs for years if he was honest; she had tried to talk to him about leaving the Palazzo but his heritage, his reason for existence, was totally non-negotiable. So she left, bit by bit; gradually withdrawing her life from his. It was clear; he could now admit it; he had chosen a building above his wife. The past above the future.

*   *   *

As he drove her back to the cottage, Ellie was quiet.

'I think that went well.'

'At least it's one hurdle over,' she had replied. 'It's very good of you to have come to the service, Salvatore. Lucky you had some business here at the same time.'

He watched her, huddled in the seat beside him, and wanted to say that he would have come just for her but he didn't. Things needed to be said; not here, not now, but he *would* say them later.

14

She heard Salvatore taking a breath in. 'Come and live and work at the Palazzo. Your skills are a perfect complement to mine and I've been thinking for a long while of running more courses.'

The newly brewed tea was in danger of cooling once more as Ellie sat by the fire and listened to Salvatore's plans. They had obviously been a while in the formulation for he seemed to have thought through every detail; which rooms she would occupy, how she could teach and also help with planning and administration, how they would draw up an agreement allowing them both the possibility of bailing out.

'Why would you offer me this?' Ellie at this moment was inclined to unbelief. 'Why would you take a risk like this? Working and living in the same place. You don't know what I'm capable of or what I'm like!'

'I think I've got to know you rather well through your letters, through your history. Enough to make this a serious offer. Are you going to take a risk too?'

Salvatore pushed the abandoned tea

towards Ellie. 'It's a lot to think about. I know the English need tea in times of crisis,' he laughed gently at her, 'so drink up and let the idea settle in your mind.'

Ellie felt his steady gaze upon her. She sat rubbing her eyes and pushing her hair back in a ritual that she hoped implied thought.

'In fact,' he said, 'I think you could do with some sleep. Why don't you go to bed now?'

It was barely seven p.m. but Ellie was overcome by such weariness that she didn't resist. 'Thanks. I will. You'll be OK? Help yourself to anything.'

Salvatore nodded and ushered her towards the stairs with an elegant mime of dismissal. As she regarded his tall figure, clad in black, she recalled a Renaissance portrait of a Doge; the aquiline profile, the hands raised in a blessing on his flock.

Once in bed, under the goose down, Ellie struggled to get her thoughts in order before sleep could overwhelm her. It should be a breeze — easy to accept; instant home, new job, new life. What about her family? At pushing fifty could she translate to a new culture? What about Salvatore and Maria? What exactly was he expecting of her? There were no pathways left in her mind capable of making the necessary computations. Ellie gave in and slept. She dreamed of her lost friend in vast marble halls, conducting massed heavenly choirs. Nerine was good-humoured but totally insistent on perfection, stopping every few bars to correct and encourage. 'If we are singing a new song it has to be with heart,' she repeated over and over. Ellie so wanted to talk to her. As she watched, the choir became discernible. Ellie searched the rows of faces for some she recognised. Her parents were there, arms upraised in wild alleluias. Her mother looked happy; Ellie, in the midst of the dream, knew that this was important. Andrew was there too; he had his arms folded across his chest and was looking straight at her with an expression of amused irony. Below him was Maria, exchanging kisses and hugs with her neighbours on all sides. Then she reached up to Andrew who responded with passion. Ellie couldn't continue to look. She was glad when Salvatore appeared by her side and led her away.

Ellie awoke, feverish, at about five a.m. In those first few moments of consciousness when her intellect was not truly in control, she felt a stimulation of appetites; not only was her stomach rumbling with hunger but she also felt needy of physical connection, and it was Salvatore she wanted. As she returned to the outer world she began to quell her responses with the words in her mind. 'This is a business arrangement. If you can't see it like that then don't even entertain the idea of going to Italy.' Language gained the ascendant; sensations began to fade. However, there remained the merest pinprick of illumination and warmth that lodged in Ellie's heart.

Finches were haranguing each other in the eaves and muffled thuds and snorts filtered into Ellie's consciousness; it was a tractor negotiating the lane outside her window. There was barely a pinch of light, too early to say if the day was to be blue or grey. She was awake but not able to move; a state she'd always found interesting. She imagined the voice of a figure in a white coat, slightly raised to reach into the deep. 'It's all right, Eleanor.' Who called her Eleanor? Her parents. 'You'll be able to move soon, you are in the process of what we call waking up.'

And she knew she would, in a few minutes, be on her feet. It was miraculous really; the way the will preceded the act. As she lay inert, pieces of the world came back to her. Things that were here and things that were not. No Nerine. Her throat constricted and her belly tightened, her body trying to man the barricades, but it was unequal to her need to cry. Her will to cry. The tears were blessed;

they rolled on and on, unstoppering her; lubricating and disinfecting. They came for a while unconnected to conscious thoughts and then ceased. The lull was temporary. The cycles of tears and peace felt like birth pangs, contraction and usurping energy punctured by pregnant inertia. Her mind fuelled each wave, thoughts brought tears. She cried for Nerine, for Andrew, for her mother, her father, for the departure of the old life. All is well, she thought, I am allowed to do this. With everything falling away she could give herself the gift of mourning and time to say goodbye. No longer parented, she alone had to go forward.

When she finally got up, the pillow was damp from pressing her face to it and smothering the sound of her sobs. She would rather Salvatore did not hear. It was not from pride and there was no reason to believe he would not be caring and sympathetic, but Ellie just wanted to keep this moment for herself. There could be too much talking. She tried to move quietly to the bathroom but the floors groaned. She tried to turn on the taps without noise but they squealed and hissed. It was as though the house was responding to her movement in it with complaint. Lying in her bath she tried not to think, concentrating on the enclosure of the warm water and the slime of the soap. She scrubbed vigorously at her feet and knees, replacing mental activity with physical action. She tuned into the world outside coming to life, a motorcycle ripping through the village, wind shaking the remnants of leaves in the ash tree. Rain blew against the window. She could hear the sound of each tiny drop; a shower then, not a deluge.

★ ★ ★

It was when she was in the kitchen and could hear Salvatore moving about that she brought herself to think about his offer, to be prepared with an answer. What could it be? She couldn't make another decision now. It was as though the muscles for making them were weak, unused to too much exercise and she needed time for rest and recuperation.

'Good morning, Ellie. Did you sleep well?' She noted again that the English language suited Salvatore; it seemed tailored for him.

He bent to kiss her cheek.

'Yes. I was out like a light.' It was all that was required, this politeness.

They made breakfast together and sat in the kitchen to eat. Salvatore seemed to fill the small space. His knees barely fitted under the table. Ellie stole looks at him as he buttered his toast. He was still slim, perhaps

302

the smallest hint of a stomach under his black turtle neck sweater, but not the excesses she had. She would be embarrassed to show her body to him. The random thought brought a blush to her cheeks and she rose in confusion.

'Excuse me, it feels rather hot in here.' She tugged at the back door and it stuck. Salvatore got up studiedly, wiping his mouth and placing his napkin carefully before he came to help. They were very close as he pulled and when the door released they fell against each other. He apologised, she laughed and the moment was over. Ellie needed to be careful. It was her neediness that had misled her before. She was not about to mistake friendship for anything else.

Over the tea and toast Salvatore repeated the straightforward reasons for his offer. And for the first time he told her that Maria had left him. But he said it in a way that gave her the impression that the door, for him, was certainly not closed.

'Look Ellie, I don't want to be a source of added pressure. I just want to lighten your load and mine too.'

He looked tired, she thought; his eyelids drooped and the dark eyes were dulled. Perhaps he really was asking her because he needed help.

'Whatever you decide about my long term offer, a break would do you good. You've been caring for Nerine for months. At least let Francesca and me care for you for a week.'

It was tempting. What she had here was not appealing, being alone for the first time in a long while. When Ellie came back to the cottage she expected to feel a sense of rightness of place; she'd always loved to come home after time away. But it was different this time. Perhaps it was like when you died; she'd watched the dying begin to will a detachment from things.

'But I've so much to arrange here. Packing up. Storage. I really need to get the garden into better shape. And there's the small matter of where I'm going to live.'

Salvatore shook his head. 'The garden is not your responsibility now. Introduce the new owner to Jack.'

Just the fact that he remembered the name of her gardener was almost enough to persuade her. Salvatore went back to sipping his coffee. He was casual, he didn't look her in the face as he said he had arranged three days of business in Oxford; while he was there she would have time to make some calls and set things up. He didn't want to advise her on her financial affairs but if she had enough to pay for professionals to deal with packing up and moving she should do it. He was right of course. In the past she'd done it both ways and now she wanted impersonal efficiency to accompany her departure.

'You have nearly two months before completion. You can surely take just a week of that time to think about things. Until you decide if living in Italy is not for you there is no point in looking for anywhere to live in England.'

When he left — his cheek was warm and scented as he kissed her — she wandered around the cottage. Had she panicked? How could she have decided so quickly to sell? A sense of guilt came over her. Her mother had — what was a good word? — *stewarded* this place for nearly twenty years and she had managed barely three. Ellie had to remind herself again that she was living her own life.

'It's OK to make your own decisions and your own mistakes.' She said it aloud into the blank room but wasn't entirely convinced by her own words. She felt like some self-help junkie and laughed remembering the times when she'd pasted such stirring sentiments on her bathroom mirror. *Affirmations* was the terminology, she remembered. Was she looking to Salvatore to affirm her? Perhaps she was.

The day had turned out grey and not blue.

The rain continued on and off. When she stepped outside to survey the garden there was a chill wind, the first bitter northerly of the year. October in the Cotswolds was a time when there were intimations of winter. It was too soon; she wanted to postpone the cheerless days. She tried to bring back the Palazzo in her imagination. It was all there, intact. She shut her eyes and could feel her feet upon the stone floors and her hand upon the warm rosewood of the doors. The feelings were vivid. She opened her eyes to bring herself back from the last images that had welled up; a bed, a dark room, an endless night. Perhaps, Ellie thought, she needed to go if only to banish some ghosts.

Ellie moved from room to room in the cottage. When she had first returned from London there were a few moments, no more, when she saw her home as an outsider would. Even the scent of it had been unfamiliar to her. Now she was back, a spider in her web. Walking the familiar routes and pausing to touch familiar possessions. For the children this place had been a thread of continuity in their disrupted lives. Ellie had spent three years making this a place for her family and twenty years knowing it as her mother's home. Her mother was so much better at giving things away than Ellie; she would not have put conditions on her gift. Ellie stood in the middle of the room like an emotional weathervane; her senses strained to monitor exactly what her feelings were. She should feel bound by her attachment to the cottage; leaving this place should give her serious difficulty, real pain. But the expected feelings were just not there. Instead there was, she hardly dared to describe it as such, a lightness and a peace.

She dropped to the sofa, looking about her. The way she had created this space pleased her. On a tiny budget she had harmonised the room; warm grey, coral, grey-green; she had balanced the colours like a three-dimensional painting. She had also absorbed some of her mother's antique furniture into the design, still managing to keep the room spacious and uncluttered. That was Andrew's influence upon her she thought, smiling to herself. It took her a moment to realise that she recalled him neutrally, without heaviness. White was his favoured colour and he had loved to keep every surface bare: not for him the memorabilia that Ellie liked to keep around her. Even his closets were tidy; he was not ashamed to let anyone open their doors.

It had taken Ellie years to allow herself the luxury of her own choices. Was she really contemplating going to Italy and moving wholesale into Salvatore's life? The answer wasn't clear. All she knew was that the alternative was not staying here. Once more she felt the certainty washing over her; it was a resolution born of the road to Damascus school of decision making. It was not hasty or intemperate or emotion led, she was too peaceful for it to be any of those things. The Ignatians called such a feeling *consolation*. Everything, said Ignatius, should be taken to God in prayer. For Ellie that was the easy bit, natural as breathing. If 'normal' people knew the extent of her inner conversations she would probably be labelled schizophrenic, except that Ellie never heard the voice of God. She just believed that exactly when she needed them, people or circumstances appeared that gently guided her along the right path. Andrew was sceptical of course, but even he sometimes declined to pass judgment on her 'godincidences', as she called them.

Ignatius said that a decision should be lived with as if it were already resolved, for a day, a week, a month, however long it takes. During that time reactions should be noted; if prevailing feelings are joy and peace then this *consolation* is a confirmation that the decision accords with God's will. If restlessness and unease manifest themselves then this *desolation* is a sure sign that the wrong path, away from God, is being followed. Andrew always used to ask why there was any need for God in this equation. He said all that was being described was human conscience. He was exasperated when Ellie said she believed the conscience was the way God broke into human lives and that everything good came ultimately from God. She smiled now to think of his fulminations and to realise how sure she was of her own ground. She'd always thought of herself as deferring to Andrew.

Still, she had a pressing decision to make now. The time was short and she would have to make good use of the days Salvatore was away.

'I am going to Italy to work with Salvatore.' She said it out loud. She said it knowing that what she truly meant was, *I am going to Italy with Salvatore to work out if that is where I will spend my life.* There was no thunderbolt as yet. Ellie spied a cobweb stretched across the corner of the inglenook and got up to sweep it away. It set her off with a desire to sweep and polish and make the place as lovely as possible. As she worked she calculated what she needed to pack and what to store, and there was still no fear. For the first time in years she felt as if she was being truthful.

She wasn't tossed like a leaf in autumn wind; she was a tree growing to an authorised pattern.

★ ★ ★

Ellie had lived for a day with the prospect of going to Italy when she turned things around and imagined not making that decision. It was on the third day, Saturday, when she expected a call from Salvatore, that she tried to assess her reactions. All the reasons why it was an impractical proposition had flown up but she had batted them away like a kitten with a wasp. She couldn't say there was an obvious depression when she imagined Salvatore leaving alone: she simply struggled to remain detached from the situation, trying hard to believe that staying at home would be just as good. It was this forced-ness, this sense of a not-right-fit that persuaded her. If it was all right with Dom and Sadie she would go away for a week and get another perspective on things. In fact, if it wasn't all right she'd go anyway.

It was liberating, this permission to behave unexpectedly. Ellie inhaled deeply and almost fancied she could smell rosemary and warm dust. The scent that did reach her conscious was a gentle dampness — the legacy of days of steady rain. Ellie looked at her watch; eleven a.m. Before Salvatore rang she wanted to speak to the children and tell them she was going. Dom's answer machine was on but Sadie was there. She sounded as though she'd been woken by the phone, her reactions slow. Ellie's news seemed to bring her back to sharp thinking.

'Mum, I'm sure you could do with a break and . . .' she hesitated, 'why should I tell you what to do?'

And Ellie thought now she will, how strange when your children begin to direct your life.

'But have you thought how much you've got to do if you're moving, let alone the little matter of finding somewhere to live?' She drew breath. 'All these rapid decisions, you're a bit hard to keep up with.'

Ellie read between the lines. *If you're moving.* Sadie was still clinging on to the hope that she would relent and fight to save the cottage. She had discussed this decision with both her children and had fondly imagined she had their wholehearted backing to slip out of this particular noose.

'Sweetheart, I know it all feels like a landslide. But I'm not making any of these decisions on a whim, you know. I think and pray hard.'

Ellie recognised the starchy silence as Sadie's recoil from the word pray. She needed to highlight the rational and practical for her daughter.

'And I have been busy these last few days, sorting out people to do removals and storage and beginning to pack a few things.'

The sound Sadie made had an encouraging timbre.

'There are nearly two months to completion. Plenty of time when I get back to decide where to go. The agent says there's a decent amount of rental property around and that's probably what I'll do to start with.' As she spoke she began to relish the freedom; she had a picture of a hermit in a cave, unburdened by paraphernalia. As to her thoughts on living in Italy, she couldn't share those baldly over the phone. Maybe it wasn't quite honest but Ellie didn't want to stir up Sadie without cause. After all she might come back from her week quite determined to be in England. 'I don't suppose you've got a chance to come home before I go tomorrow?' Ellie asked.

'Sorry, no can do.' Sadie was brisk. 'But strangely I'll be out in Italy just about the time you'll be getting back.' She had to update some accommodation entries in Rome. 'So make sure you give me Salvatore's email before you go. I quite enjoyed talking to him at the service.'

The call ended cordially; it was a relief to Ellie that Sadie hadn't been more censorious. She tried to place herself in her daughter's shoes; all the landmarks were shifting. The family home being irresponsibly cast aside by a mother who esteemed her own moral values above her children's inheritance. That was Sadie's unspoken subtext. Ellie was sorry if that was her view, but she held firm to the sense of rightness. Her children were important to Ellie and they would have everything that was hers to give. She felt certain Dom understood that. He, more than Sadie could probably see Ellie's need to free herself from a past governed by Andrew's way of doing things. That was probably because his life was moving forward; he had a job, a flat, a sweet girlfriend and a life in a settled community. Sadie was less rooted with all her travelling. Ellie winced; she'd been so caught up with herself that she hadn't asked Sadie about Paul. It was unlikely she would have had an answer, but she should have asked. The silence of late suggested to Ellie an unresolved stalemate; the wife pregnant; Paul unable to break away from either woman and Sadie allowing the tide to flow over her. No wonder she had heard bitterness in her daughter's voice. Sadie needed her mother simply to be available and yet here she was, about to set off for Italy.

★ ★ ★

If Salvatore was honest he had not expected Ellie's agreement. The evening of the memorial service, Ellie had asked him why he wanted to take such a risk and he had evaded the answer; packed her off to bed. Sitting in her small kitchen at breakfast he had been able to give her a clear response. Maria had left him. She no longer contributed financially or practically towards the Palazzo and Salvatore needed to earn more revenue and find another pair of hands. Ellie was the perfect choice; she had skills and need of a home. The fit was serendipitous. Whether it was the whole truth, Salvatore concealed even from himself.

The few days he stayed in Oxford he made sure were totally occupied organising and networking. He disciplined himself not to phone her until the Sunday night; he had returned from evening Mass where his prayers had been earnest, although frankly without proper expectation, to call her. When she said yes he was more than thankful, he recognised a spark that had been absent for years. What he said to her, however, was moderate, calm, almost paternal. She needed to hear only the message that he was concerned for her welfare and motivated by altruism.

* * *

When they were back once more at the Palazzo Salvatore became unsure of what level of company Ellie sought.

'I suppose being at Nerine's was a bit like a retreat, especially towards the end,' she said to him on their first evening back in his home. They were sitting in the library drinking *limoncello* after dinner. 'And although I still need some of that solitude I do crave a return to real life.'

Salvatore waited for her to go on.

'I spent a lot of time thinking about my life in comparison to hers. And I wasn't envious but I was humbled and inspired by her lack of regret.'

Salvatore nodded. 'And from what you tell me she seems to have had the marvellous ability to move forward and do the next thing.'

Ellie looked up at him and he felt they were connected; her whole body assented as she spoke. 'Yes, but she seemed never to be rash

315

in her decisions, they were taken from a firm base. And when she decided on a course she didn't look back.'

'No man having put his hand to the plough, and looking back, is worthy of reward.' Salvatore quoted.

'That's good, where did that come from?'

'It's a paraphrase by Marsilio Ficino of something in the Bible.'

'The philosopher who inspired Botticelli?'

'Yes, that's right.' Salvatore was pleased his teaching had remained with her. 'There are volumes of his letters here in the library. Worth reading sometime.' He really wanted her to enjoy what he enjoyed.

Ellie smiled. She looked slightly detached as though following a different line of thought. 'Salvatore, do you know what I'd really like to do this week?'

He waited for her request, watching her words bringing new animation to her features.

'I'd like to look up from my books and my paintings and march back outside into the world. Can we go out walking or window-shopping? Can we eat out, meet your friends and family?'

Salvatore hadn't expected this. It collided with his imaginings. Until she asked he hadn't realised how much he had wanted to cocoon Ellie here and keep her to himself. How would he introduce her to people, to family; what exactly was she to him? Looking at her face he decided it didn't matter. He was happy to give her what she wanted.

★ ★ ★

The light of October was low, as it had been in the April of Ellie's first visit. The symmetry appealed to Salvatore. The autumn light was clear but without the same piercing edge of spring sunshine. It was mellower; it had more mercy. They took walks, a fine English tradition, among the vineyards where the leaves were now yellowing and dropping. Their boots gathered up sticky clods from the damp earth. Salvatore made a point of stopping and talking to neighbours, where he might have avoided it, and introducing Ellie. He watched her sometimes struggling to understand but always intent and eager to tune into the person.

As life faded from the landscape, bringing everything down to tones of brown and earth, Salvatore found the opposite within himself. Being with Ellie kindled feelings long atrophied. By being there she made him acknowledge the half-life he led with Maria; reflected back in his wife's eyes he had become conservative, unchanging, maybe even rigid. Ellie saw the possibilities in him; her picture was far from the one Maria saw. Salvatore felt like one of those children's hologram cards; hold it one way and the man cries, angle it to the light the other way and the man laughs.

With Ellie there was laughter. Together they twisted words into puns and played with their sense and nonsense. With two languages the possibilities were endless. It was a joy to be with someone who loved words and enjoyed fitting them to the time, the place and the mood. They used English for the difficult ideas, perhaps when Ellie wanted to discuss philosophy, because her vocabulary would not always stretch over the concepts. Italian came more naturally to express feeling; sometimes what she said surprised him, it was so straightforward. Perhaps she didn't have enough Italian words to introduce nuance or subtlety into her statements but he was glad. Maybe the fulsome language was unintended but he didn't want to correct her when she said she 'adored' his straight back or was 'drowned' by his knowledge. And when there were no words the silences were natural. Beneath the surface the stream ran on, circling rocks and weed, but at its interface with the air the surface was unrippled.

Walking the third day, their conversation was punctuated by shots. Salvatore watched the bird hunt through Ellie's eyes. On his own he would have passed by the groups of hunters gathered in the fields, with pick-up trucks and dogs, without much thought. She wanted to linger. It wasn't for the novelty, similar sights were familiar in the Cotswolds, she said, but she wanted to absorb the differences. She watched for some minutes without comment then said, laughing, 'Much more talk!'

'Do you go out with the hunters, Salvatore?' Ellie asked.

'No, not now. It was part of my landscape when I was a child. My father encouraged it, probably more as a social skill than anything else.'

They walked on, Salvatore describing the camaraderie of the shoots. To him the soft corpses were by-products. He may have come home with tangible results from his day's labours but it was the sense of community that lasted in his memory.

'But I have other responsibilities, so those days are over for me. No time or money for such leisure now!' he laughed.

'Is that how you see your future, working to keep up the Palazzo?'

It was a hard question from gentle Ellie. Although Salvatore's steps continued through the field, his thoughts were faced with a closed gate. He hesitated. 'I'm prepared to do that for my family.'

He saw Ellie watching him. Her face was soft; she didn't speak but her whole body was asking him questions. He imagined her saying 'Do they want that?' but she said nothing. In the silence Salvatore recognised the deconstruction of his life. Shots rang out, a loud and insistent volley that echoed the disparate confusions. Divorce. Integrity. Inheritance. Purpose. Future. Salvatore saw himself attempting to remain on the tramlines and wondered why he had drawn Ellie into his problems. But he couldn't speak of it to her. Instead he said, 'Look, if we walk down this way it will take us into the village. There's a market there this morning.'

Ellie allowed the unasked and unanswered question to pass and smiled and took his hand for a moment, pulling him along the new path.

Down in the village the warmth of the enfeebled October sun was concentrated in the square. Tables were laid out under trees that still had their leaves but were fading from green to yellow. This amalgamation gave the place a golden glow and Salvatore infused the sight through Ellie's eyes. She hovered at table after table.

'What are these?' was her refrain time after time. Salvatore explained, enjoying his role as her teacher. She sighed at the price of the truffles and marvelled at the different ways to use a chestnut.

'It's a pity you aren't staying a little longer. I could take you to the chestnut festival in Piancastagnaio next week.' Ellie was sorry too but she wanted to know more and he told her.

'Gathering the chestnuts is very much a communal affair. There are, I suppose you could call them elders, who watch the crop of chestnuts to see when they are ready — they split when they are ripe. And after this happens they call on everyone to help harvest the crop. Villages work as cooperatives. I've been 'volunteered' to help on a few occasions!'

'It sounds very romantic, the fruitful harvest and all that,' murmured Ellie.

'And very hard work. That's why we need a festival after, to wind down in style!' Salvatore was tempted to tell her of the petty inter-family squabbles that could arise too but he didn't want to lift the veil of romance from her eyes. He wanted her to love everything about this place so that she would want to be here. Besides, seeing the place he had known all his life through her eyes was renewing his perspective.

'Perhaps we could walk tomorrow where they are gathering the chestnuts. It's quite interesting.' Salvatore watched Ellie's head nodding in enthusiastic agreement. Salvatore liked that. He liked her engagement with just the small things in life. The way she picked out the bread and cheese and olives for lunch. The way she was delighted by the fact that a woman offered her windfall apples free of charge. She was impressed by the heart of things, not by their material.

They walked back up the hill, past houses with fading geraniums in their front gardens, and off the road into fields once more. When they had found some smooth stones to sit on, they shared their food. At times she chewed slowly, her face up to the weak sun, her eyes closed. She asked him questions and listened carefully to his answers. They bantered and they recollected memories of their shared history, but she wanted to know more about his long life before and between these times. He should have been alerted by a diffidence in Ellie's face as she questioned him.

'I'm sorry to have to ask, but what about Maria? What does she want? And does she know about your plans with me?'

'Of course you must ask. I've invited you to share a future here and you must know everything.' Salvatore brushed some crumbs from his thigh with an overzealous attention. He looked away from Ellie, at stalks of brown and brittle corn that were still standing, unharvested and ready to be ploughed in.

'Maria has been very straightforward. Although it is not what I want, she is intent on divorcing me.' He had at last admitted it. 'However, she proposes to leave everything behind. She says she knows how much the Palazzo means to me, so as long as I make no claim on her money she will make no claim on Palazzo Michele. What she does want is for both of us to make provision for our children.' He looked to Ellie for signs of the pity he feared, but she simply nodded.

'And I have told her that, since she is not around, I need to employ someone to help with the business and that you are here this week to consider the offer. That's correct isn't it, Ellie?'

She nodded again. Salvatore read a kind of relief, or was it gratitude? on her face.

All she said was, 'Thank you Salvatore. I think you probably know how much I appreciate the truth.'

They gathered up their rubbish, straightened up and continued on their way upwards.

As they did Salvatore wondered on his version of the truth. He'd said that Ellie was there only to take Maria's place in the business. Was that entirely true? Ellie said she appreciated the truth; perhaps he should tell her that he didn't truly know what exactly he wanted of her. It was a kind of schizophrenia; the whole way he had lived his life — did live his life — meant there could be no room for anything other than a friendly business relationship with Ellie. Even being forced into a divorce from Maria he would still remain spiritually married to her for ever. And yet he was getting closer to Ellie all the time. Why was he subjecting them both to a situation that could not end well? He formalised his words.

'I can't promise you that every detail and question will be answered in the short time you have here, Ellie, but I'm hoping you will have gathered enough information to make a decision about living and working at the Palazzo.'

He didn't even have enough courage to say living and working with me. He watched Ellie. She was breathing hard from the stiff climb they'd made up to a ridge. A vineyard fell away below them on a southerly slope.

She stopped to catch her breath. 'Well, if it's all right by you I think I'd like to extend my stay for another week or so to gather more 'information'.' She stressed the last word; her tone was lightly ironic and Salvatore couldn't quite follow her meaning. But his bewilderment couldn't suppress an uprising of joy.

'Of course it's all right. And Francesca will be delighted to have more of your company. Being locked away with an uncommunicative male most of the time isn't much fun for her.'

'And maybe I can make myself useful. She tells me that you have a lot of bed and breakfasters turning up over the next ten days.'

Salvatore nodded and told her of course she was not expected to help but then again she would be able to see first hand what exactly was involved in running the bread and butter side of the business.

'Then no one can say we just sold you the romance of the place!'

They crested the hill and began to walk the slope down. The Palazzo was in the distance. A few yards ahead a neighbour was picking the last of the red grapes. The mature plants were stocky and gnarled, firmly trained on to their wire cordons. They watched as he tossed the ripe fruit into baskets ready for their transformation into new wine. No one spoke except for a formulaic 'Ciao' but Salvatore felt the metaphor hung between them.

15

After the first week the days were beginning to be ordinary. It was what Ellie wanted; to be just part of the fabric of the Palazzo. The romance of the strange was falling away but she was happy, even when grappling with Italian bureaucracy; years in education had equipped her for endless form filling. Learning more about the place, and Salvatore, was not a chore. She was slipping into a new relationship with both. Salvatore and she even began to resume the more honest conversations they'd had in the past. There were moments when it felt like more than just friendship but then Salvatore seemed to draw back once more. Ellie reined in her imagination and believed she felt peaceful with the way things were.

The days had been busy with the bed and breakfast brigade but now there was an air of winding down. Yellowed chestnut leaves lay on the courtyard like warm hands. The sun rose later but still had heat in the hours around lunchtime. That was when Salvatore had left to go into Siena. He'd gone to pick up some building materials and she'd expected him back late afternoon. Then she'd missed his phone call. Francesca had let Ellie know that Salvatore intended to stay out for supper with his elderly uncle; they'd met by chance in the Campo. Salvatore said he'd be back around ten.

The sun had just gone down and the cool of an October evening descended into the cavernous rooms of the Palazzo. Ellie anticipated retreating to the warmth of her own sitting room with a drink, content in the knowledge that they had no guests booked in that evening. As she filled her glass from the bar, the buzzer sounded on the outer door. Ellie hoped it would be Salvatore, back early but without his key, rather than some random traveller in search of a room. She was tired; not up to hospitality this evening.

The dark stopped her from seeing clearly. It was not until she had opened the door and was leaning out towards the figure, that she saw who it was. 'Max,' she said and immediately pulled back.

The light of the hallway spilled onto his face; casting half of it in deep shadow.

'We meet again!' His style was bright and breezy, unsurprised. 'How are you, Ellie?'

She knew her face betrayed her and her body blocked his efforts to plant a kiss on her cheek. It was a shock, this unilateral decision by her physical self, to reject Max. She'd hoped it was over, consigned to the past, forgiven; but it was not. 'I didn't know you were expected. Did Salvatore know you were coming?'

'No.' He walked past her through the door and let his case drop heavily on the marble floor. She looked at the four-squareness of it and read the message 'I intend to stay'.

'Well, aren't you going to ask me how I am?'

'Oh yes . . . sorry . . . how are you, Max?' It was without conviction.

'Fine, fine.' He was scanning the hallway as he replied. 'Nobody else around?'

Ellie shook her head but instantly qualified the gesture. 'Francesca's about somewhere and Salvatore won't be too long.'

Max didn't seem to be listening. 'It's funny isn't it, you and me, drawn back to this place all the time?'

Ellie didn't know how to answer or even really what the question was. She must have looked blank because Max asked her another.

'Don't you know that I come and occasionally help old Salvatore with his accounts?'

She didn't, and briefly wondered why Salvatore hadn't told her, but that wasn't something Max had to know. 'Yes. He did mention something about help with the administration.'

Max smiled, no doubt reading the dissemblance as the lie it was. 'Have you been enjoying your week here?'

Ellie nodded, annoyance rising; if Salvatore doesn't tell me about Max, why does he tell Max about me? 'So, you've been speaking to Salvatore this week, have you?'

Max avoided the question by spinning on his heel and scrutinising the hallway again. 'When I first came back last December, this place seemed somehow smaller, a bit seedier, maybe even less romantic.' He laughed. 'A definite whiff of damp about it. What do you think about the place, coming back?'

'I like it. I like that edge of reality. It's more like home.' Ellie looked at him directly but he still didn't want to engage. 'So, have you come to help with the figures again?'

Then he did look at her and said quietly, 'No. Actually I've come to see you.' There was a momentary silence before his tone returned to self-confident. 'So, howsabout you find me a room and later I can tell you why.'

Ellie's heart was chilled; she had the same reaction when Nerine first told her in the car that she was dying. There was a need for normality in order to distance herself from the feeling. She paced decisively to the desk and, with it between her and Max, she metamorphosed into charming hostess. She smiled at him; became chatty.

'The room that's made up is the one I stayed in on our first visit. I'm sure you'll like it.' She walked him along the hall and turned the key in the door. As she lifted the latch the click echoed into the space beyond, as it had that night. She was ahead of Max, closing the shutters and checking the towels in the bathroom, then laying the key in his hand.

'Shall we meet for a drink in the drawing room in about an hour?'

Max checked his Rolex and agreed. Then she made her escape.

★ ★ ★

She had been waiting in the drawing room for over twenty minutes. She couldn't think what had possessed Max to come here. He said he'd come to see her. Why? Was he seeking to make amends? The body language hadn't exactly spoken of that. Whatever it was, his presence had disturbed her so that she could think of nothing better to do than buy time. For an hour she had alternately let her thoughts of their last meetings roll around her mind and then suppressed them. *Don't* be overtaken by the past, Ellie. It was a mantra she kept repeating to herself. Since she'd been here with Salvatore she hadn't needed to face those words. She had been gloriously living in the present, with an occasional glimpse of future thrown in. In less than two weeks her past was displaced and neatly tidied away into a hiding place in another country entirely. All was peaceful. She, the woman who pretended a faith that hinged on forgiveness, had believed she had forgiven, that she herself was forgiven and that all things were new. It only needed Max to show up and destroy that superficial peace.

It was nearly seven-thirty and she didn't like the feeling of being in Max's power. Whatever his intentions, she wanted to know them now. Her equilibrium was deserting her. Ellie had been in two minds about ringing Salvatore for support, but was almost grateful when she'd got his voicemail. She knew it was necessary to face Max on her own; it would be a resolution of sorts. She'd made the choice not to talk about his assault on her to Salvatore and it was too late now. So she left no message. Now she had to face at least two, maybe three hours with Max. Not quite alone though; she'd asked Francesca to make them both a light supper and to be on hand that evening.

331

'And when you pour drinks, don't make them too generous.' Francesca had looked to her for the subtext. 'I could do with an early night and if I recall, Max with a drink in him is prone to rambling on'.

Ellie checked her watch again. Seven thirty-two. Her hands were idle and her mind in overdrive. She got up from the sofa and walked through to the library. She scanned Salvatore's collection. Needing some calm she reckoned a moment or two at the feet of Socrates or Hegel would help perhaps. In fact she pulled out a volume of letters by Marsilio Ficino; Salvatore had urged her to read them. She glanced at the letter headings.

'On the Wise and Fortunate Man'

'It is Better to Write Good Things than Many Things'

'On the Desire for Happiness'.

The words below were succinct. Complexities seemed to be simplified. It was just the balm Ellie needed but it was to be taken from her by Max's arrival.

She saw his mouth first; with an extended grin he stretched out the last 'e' of her name and then opened his arms expansively like a favourite uncle beseeching a three-year-old for a hug.

'Ellieeee! I'm so sorry if I've kept you waiting,' he proffered the back of his right hand to her, 'but I managed to scald myself with the hot water and it rather slowed things down.'

Ellie's defences moved from red to amber. Maybe, she thought, he hadn't been trying to manipulate her after all.

'Oh no. I'm so sorry. Can I get you anything for it?'

Ellie moved forward to look more closely but stopped short of touching Max. Words poured inconsequentially. 'It's just one of the vagaries of the hot water system. When the house is full the temperature evens out somewhat, I believe.'

Max waved his hand to decline any help but his eyes were so fixed on her that Ellie backstepped and sat down, gesturing to Max to do the same.

'You seem to be part of the furniture here, Ms Ellie. Quite settled in eh?' Max smiled down on her as though he were the elder. Ellie just raised an eyebrow, choosing to return the attention to Max.

'Shouldn't you tell me why you're here?'

Max nodded and Ellie waited. 'There's no easy way to say this.'

Ellie's breath seemed to fade from inside her and a pulse started up in her clenched thigh muscle. A soft knock on the door demanded disproportionate attention from them both. It was Francesca with glasses of *vin santo* and bowls of sweet almonds and *tozzetti*. Max stood up to take the tray and kiss her.

'Ah, the adorable Francesca. Still working you hard I see!'

She coloured up beautifully, casting down her eyes and responding easily to Max's flirting. She looks like fresh fruit, thought Ellie. Max seemed in no hurry to put an end to their banter. Francesca finally realised she had her cue to leave after five minutes, five minutes in which Ellie said nothing but sat silently cradling her drink.

When the door closed behind Francesca, Ellie said, 'Go on. You were finding it difficult to say something to me.'

Max was standing and pacing the edges of the Persian rug. He had his back to her at times but when he finally spoke he was looking down into her face.

'Ellie. I am Andrew's son.'

'What? Andrew who?'

'Your husband Andrew.'

'No, that's not possible.'

Ellie looked away from Max. She looked hard into her glass. This was the owl flying in the day; fruit ripened in frost. At first nothing would connect in her mind — but when it began to, it was more terrible than the blind panic. If she believed Max she would have to go back to the beginning, to rebuild the marriage, to make peace with Andrew all over again. More than that, it would make Max's assault bestial. She would not believe. Her hand was on her mouth, nausea rising. She threw back her head, feeling the strain in her throat.

'Oh my God, why are you allowing this? Protect me from this evil man and give me your peace.'

A small part of her was a spectator. Even in this desperation she felt she should preserve her dignity; but what dignity had she left to her, confronted by a man who assaulted her with the dishonesty of another she thought had cared for her? All she had left was her trust in a God who was meant to love her. Where the hell was he when she needed him? Ellie saw Max at her side watching like a wary crow. The expression on his face was unfamiliar. He appeared to be at a total loss. Sitting now with a bowed head he offered nothing but silence and Ellie was grateful, wanting no more information. They sat in that way for eternal seconds, the presence of ordinary life creeping back in with the passing of time. There was a fly that buzzed around their heads and landed on the soft velvet of the sofa; the noise of Francesca shutting a door somewhere far off; the sticky warmth of the glass still in her hands. That was the way it was with the most painful times in your life, thought Ellie; the small things that continued on around you served as jabbing counterpoints. She remembered how the sun shone and the postman whistled on the day that Andrew died.

'How? When did you know?' She struggled with her thoughts. 'You said your father died when you were a child. It's rubbish. It's rubbish,' she repeated, wrapping herself tightly in her own arms as though the less surface she presented to the world, the less pain she would feel.

'You never had any idea he'd got another child?' Max was strangely still as he asked the question.

She looked at him, at the hardness in his jaw, and the puzzle coalesced; the intimations of Andrew; the dead body that would not sink. She had to believe it.

'Oh my God, no, no, I didn't,' she sobbed. And in that moment she was given insight. 'Did you think I knew, Max?'

He was silent, looking away.

'What kind of person would that make me?' she asked.

'One I could hate more easily. One I could load all the blame onto.' He looked at her then. 'Except that it became harder when I met you.' He tailed off.

It was quiet, only the hiss of an ancient radiator covered the silence.

'But then I rejected you.' Ellie let the words hang. She got up, swilled the warm wine from her glass and refilled it. 'I think I need to know everything. And I promise, in return, I will be truthful.'

He told her some of the story then. He thought his mother had always told him the whole truth, admired her for honesty in fact, for she'd been open enough to show him his birth certificate with his dad's name on it; Andrew Graeme Brinkmayer. Ellie nodded. His mum had had an affair with 'Drew' out in Ceylon in the sixties when they were both doing VSO. Ellie put her hand to her mouth and held her breath. Andrew was mid-twenties, his mum just nineteen.

While Max was growing up his mother had always told him that she and Drew had planned to marry. She'd come home at the end of her placement to make all the arrangements while Drew finished off the last six months of his contract out there. It was then she found out she was pregnant; she said she was so happy about that. Max's face softened.

'I never thought my mother didn't love me.

There are a few pictures of me with her. I was this really sombre toddler; huge; there's one of me on her lap, pretty much obliterating this pretty, laughing girl.'

'I'm sure she does love you, Max.'

'Yes, but she lied to me, cut off a whole part of me.' After a pause he continued the story. His mum had told him that, just before Drew was due to return home, he had a second and fatal bout of Dengue fever.

'So, there we were; one lonely pining woman and a fatherless child, struggling along on our own in a rural slum for years, before Tim came along and she married him.'

'How did you discover the truth?'

'One of those stupid coincidences that aren't meant to happen outside of novels.'

Ellie listened while Max described sitting in his dentist's waiting room the February before the course and reading an old copy of *Country Life*. There was an article about an estate in Derbyshire and brief paragraph at the bottom, an obituary for Andrew Brinkmayer. Ellie nodded again, leaning her head into her hand. 'So, what did you do? Go and talk to your mother?'

'Actually no.' He found it hard to express himself then. He fought to put words in order. 'A whole lifetime of not speaking.' The phrases were staccato. 'It's like sitting on a

338

volcano.' The clichés seemed heartfelt. 'I couldn't. I had to keep it to myself, to work it out in me first.'

Ellie wanted to touch him then but she didn't. He seemed too raw. She could hardly believe that her own pain could be so diminished by his. But what she was nursing in her heart was a fear that Andrew *knew*; Andrew had yet more secrets; and moreover, Andrew had failed to be a father to the boy and damaged the man.

'I went to the Family Records Office and found his birth and death certificate. It all fitted.' Max looked at Ellie who was now able to face him steadily. 'And your marriage certificate and then the children's birth certificates.'

She waited, watching his body; could imagine the bile rising in his throat as it had in hers.

'And I was so *angry*. So angry that I hadn't had any of that — *stuff*.' He was shouting.

Francesca came to the drawing room door and leaned around it, quizzical, concerned. Ellie smiled and waved her away gently. Max went on, a little more calmly. 'I suppose I thought I'd just get more lies from my mum, so I planned to start at the other end.'

'What do you mean?' asked Ellie.

'Find you.'

It hadn't taken a great deal of detective work, Max explained, to track down Ellie's address. He'd come to see where she lived on a few occasions; walked the footpaths at the bottom of the garden. The view of the cottage was good before the leaves appeared on the trees.

'I remember what living in the country was like from those years with mum. No one locks their doors.'

Ellie started. 'It was you! I knew someone had been in the cottage.'

He nodded. He'd just wanted to get a sense of the person, the people, his father had lived amongst. He wasn't sure he wanted to know them but he wanted — how had he phrased it — 'the power of information'.

'There it was, on your desk, a bit of a gift really.'

'My booking for the Garden Course.' Ellie pushed her hair away from her eyes. 'So, you came to Italy to find *me*?'

Max looked at her as he spoke. 'What if my real father had known all about me? What if he'd chosen to forget me? He'd gone on to have this lovely wife and happy family . . . '

Ellie wanted so much to ask him then, '*did he know?*' but Max had his head buried in his hands and was mumbling, 'If I couldn't have him, perhaps I could at least have what he had.'

The sense of it didn't immediately come to Ellie but soon the coldness of Max's intentions crept over her; his interest in her, the kiss in the garden.

'Revenge, Max?' Ellie was at a loss.

'Not then. More like getting even,' he replied.

Now was her chance, this was the moment when Ellie could face him with just how far his need to get even had taken him. How poisoned he was that he had acted without consciousness, without compassion. He obviously had no recollection of his assault upon her. But she didn't speak. Later she wondered if it was just a failure of courage or had she stored up the news so that she might have power — and her own revenge? Instead, in that moment she asked him, 'What do you mean, not then?'

'I couldn't understand you, Ellie. We seemed to be getting on so well, and I truly began to like you. And then you dropped me like a piece of garbage.'

Say it now. 'But, Max, I have to tell you — '

Max put his fingers to his lips and wouldn't let her go on. 'No, Ellie, listen to me, maybe it shouldn't have hurt so much, but it did. It wasn't all acting, I really was attracted to you and I was beginning to trust you.' His body relaxed a little. 'Maybe I was on the verge of telling you all this then . . . As it was, I just got blocked once again from knowing the truth.'

When could Ellie tell him her part of the truth? Would it help anyone to inflict such damage on a broken man?

'So, if you didn't get it from me, what about your mother?'

Max breathed in hard. It was difficult he said, to walk into her life and just turn a world upside down. Especially difficult as he worked for his stepfather and wasn't sure how much he knew. Ellie sensed a fear. He reckoned, he said, that if a lid had been kept on things all these years, perhaps that's what he should do too. Ellie recalled the first time she'd met Max; the bravado of his words about *playing the hand that life deals you.*

'The problem was,' Max said, 'things got really messy in the business. It built up over the whole of last year. Got to rock bottom this summer and I could see my days at Penman-White's were numbered.' Max looked like a small child, perched on the edge of his seat. 'Turned against by my own family. It's not fair. A real father wouldn't have treated me like that. Blood is thicker than water, don't they say?' He bleated a laugh. 'I felt like saying to Tim, biology doesn't make bastards;

it takes a supreme act of free will to be that much of a shit!'

It was at that point Max had escaped to Italy and turned up at the Palazzo. They'd chatted about everyone on the course and Salvatore had told him about his visit to see Ellie.

'It all sounded so perfect, so cosy, so untroubled. It really got to me.' He hung his head. 'I'm sorry, Ellie.'

She was tense, waiting. Perhaps he did know what he'd done. Perhaps this was her chance to make peace with him. 'For what, Max?'

'I told the bank you'd inherited a cottage.'

★ ★ ★

Salvatore met his uncle in the campo. When he was still far off, he'd seen the back of the frail figure sitting at a café table and was touched by the smallness of humanity. The scale of Siena's buildings put people into perspective — little dots on the map of life going about their business in a beautiful world. There were still throngs of tourists even this late in the season, all balanced in the dish of the *campo*, but with space enough for everyone to enjoy the place; their bubbling anxiety to possess the memory of the city didn't oppress Salvatore. He walked the gentle slope of the cobbled arena and, reaching his uncle, touched him gently on the shoulder.

'*Zio Ercole, come va?*' The old man started slightly, the stiff neck wound up from attention to the small coffee in front of him. Salvatore was bathed by the old man's delight.

'*Caro Salva!* How good to see you, son.'

He was entitled to address him thus; Uncle Ercole had been another father to him but Salvatore had never told him how much he owed him for that relationship. He sat down beside him and they talked; Salvatore explaining his reasons to be in Siena, Ercole pleased at the chance meeting. The sun was lowering, slanting now across the *campo* and spearing its way through cracks between buildings.

'I know about Maria.'

Salvatore was off guard. 'Who told you?'

'My boy, it didn't take a man of mighty intellect to see which way things were headed. Business commitments don't part lovers for that long. Anyway, Francesca told me about the divorce papers.'

Of course, if Maria's talked to her other people must know, thought Salvatore; and there he was, imagining he was an island.

'Don't be too hard on her, she was just worried about you.'

Salvatore nodded.

'You know I am here to talk to.' Ercole put his dry palm on Salvatore's arm. His uncle's hand lay on his own dark and muscular body like a piece of driftwood. 'You always did keep things to yourself too much.'

'I don't know what to do.' Salvatore could hear his own voice, flat and weary, and recognised that he was asking a question. A waiter approached briskly and efficiently took Salvatore's order, unaware of the inner turmoil.

'What choices do you have?' His uncle's voice was steady. Yes, what choices did he have? Salvatore had been through them all but the wrong answers bobbed to the surface like corks in water. It was a while before he answered.

'If I'm honest, I can choose to let Maria go quickly and quietly or I can choose to make it a long and unpleasant process.' He leaned away as the waiter deposited coffee and water.

'No hope of reconciliation?' The tone was the same; not invested with the slightest accusatory tinge, for which Salvatore was grateful. He shook his head.

'I believe in the sanctity of marriage, you

345

know I do, and I think I've tried my best to keep this one together, Uncle.' Salvatore looked into the watery old eyes; faded but trained on his own face like a watching cat. 'What can I do if she is really intent on leaving me?' He stirred sugar into his coffee. 'If her will is that strong, I must let her go, and my beliefs tell me my future is to be alone.'

Salvatore felt his uncle's body shift on the small tin chair. The sun had gone now from their side of the *campo* and there was an edge to the air. 'Shall we get something to eat? Yes? I'll just call to let them know I'll be back at the Palazzo later.'

Within minutes they were in a favourite haunt and Salvatore's cheeks were being pinched by the motherly hands of the owner, Rosa. Time had blurred her exact relationship to Salvatore but she was some kind of family and he was feeling like a small boy again. Salvatore and his uncle were hustled into a favoured corner, Rosa's skirts swishing a way past startled tourist diners.

Ercole spoke first. 'I suppose you'll need help with the business. Francesca tells me you're thinking of employing an Englishwoman.'

Salvatore laughed and waited to hear what else Francesca had reported. Ercole continued. 'She likes her very much, this Ellie.'

Salvatore knew that. There was nothing not to like in Ellie. His uncle would like her too. 'Yes, she's a lovely woman. Been through a lot. Widowed, he left her in a financial mess. You should meet.'

Ercole nodded. 'You're helping out a lame duck, are you?'

Salvatore's body stiffened. 'Not in the least, she'd be a godsend to the business, very talented. She has lots of ideas and she's wonderful with people: I'd say she's helping me.' As Salvatore saw the slow smile on his uncle's face he replayed his defensive outburst and understood the cunning of Ercole's remark.

'Tell me more about how she's helping you.'

Rosa had brought wine and Salvatore filled glasses as he thought. He told Ercole how he laughed again with Ellie, how in this week particularly they shared the pleasure of planning the future. He told him about Nerine; the way Ellie had supported her, the correspondence that had flowed between them all that time. Salvatore talked through pasta and meat, through sips of wine and water, every now and then pushed on by his uncle's questions, like a canoe propelled by a smooth paddle.

When Ercole laid down his gravy-stained

napkin on the table, he simply said, 'And now you love this woman.'

It shouldn't have been that surprising but it was; to hear the words he had prevented himself from even thinking spoken by another. He didn't know how to respond immediately, then he said, 'I'm in no position to love her.'

'Oh Salva!' Ercole was laughing gently. 'My boy, you've been waiting all your life to be in the right position. It's about time you acted without an eye on being in the correct place.'

Salvatore didn't understand. His uncle's elbows rested on the table; he placed his palms together in front of him as in prayer. 'Things have always been expected of you, my dear Salvatore. And you've always tried hard to fill those expectations. Look at the way you've kept up that lumbering albatross of a Palazzo, look at your family!'

Both disintegrating, thought Salvatore.

'You have lived by the rule book and it has brought you thus far . . . '

'But . . . ' added Salvatore.

'But, it is time to change,' he said, the kindness in his eyes almost pushing Salvatore into a region of emotion he did not want. 'You have a few more years to live than I, God willing, and you need to live them with love.' He paused. 'Does she love you?'

348

Salvatore shrugged. Ercole's weak eyes were moist. 'Don't be afraid to find out, Salva. Take the risk. When we know we are truly loved we are able to give back — and not just to our lover — we're able to make a generous outpouring that enriches the rest of this tired old world.'

It was an eloquent speech from the old man. Heartfelt. But wasn't Salvatore supposed to believe that it was God who loved him so deeply, so unconditionally that he, Salvatore, was able to behave in this generous way? Human love was just a poor reflection, a second best. Was he meant to deny his beliefs just to gain second best?

His uncle knew him well. It felt as though he was tracing Salvatore's thoughts. 'You live in this world, in this moment, Salva. I don't think our Lord would deny you earthly love, it was what he preached. Ercole placed his hands flat on the table between them. 'What are you listening to, the rules in your head — or God? Go and pray, Salva.'

★　★　★

When they had parted Salvatore drove into the night, the car straining at hills, held back by its load of building materials. He turned into a dark lane leading to a vineyard and turned off the lights. Up above the stars came quietly into focus: millennia of time, dotted up there in the heavens. What time had he left to live here below? He sat, rolling his rosary between his fingers, the familiar words jumping from hand to brain. Then it was as though he had seen the beads anew; unwrapped, uninvested with meaning or mystery. Here he sat trying to conjure divinity from activity. The outward show was too important to him, he saw now. Being seen to do the right thing wasn't everything. It was relationship that mattered. Ellie saw that.

He thought back to her talking of the annunciation at Nerine's memorial. Before that day Salvatore had always seen the *event*; God tells Mary what to do, Mary does her duty, a necessary bridge to the bigger story. But Ellie had slipped into the heart of Mary; feeling her awe at His love, her humble relationship with God and her willing acceptance. There was only this time in which she could say yes. Now there was only this time in which Salvatore could begin another cycle. He sat in silent communion that took him beyond words. He was totally present to a moment of surrender and, under the dark sky, he felt bathed in light. If his God loved him, despite his transgressions, he could love Ellie.

When he at last looked ahead he saw the serried rows of vines, all trained into their productive shapes; giving what was demanded of them. At this time of year they were readying themselves for a time of rest, an unconscious sleep. Salvatore felt a reversal of seasons within him. He had had his sleep, his fallow time waiting for Maria's love to come back to him. His uncle was right, this autumn was a time to take a risk. What could he lose? If he talked to Ellie and she wanted no more than business or friendship between them, then he could be happy with that. If she too wanted more then they could take the risk together. Salvatore longed to be in the circle again, to give love and be loved back. As he turned the car the headlights lit up part of the wall of the vineyard; it was breached. Stones lay in a messy pile, but there was a way through.

16

It was finally too much, this accumulation of bad things. Stop, stop, stop. The lines Ellie had read to Nerine filled her head; she'd held fast to the hope, the trust, and this was her reward! The lines she hadn't read out loud thundered in her mind; *man dies and is laid low*. No, all Max's actions couldn't be forgiven, forgotten, fixed. Ellie put down her glass and walked to the window. The dark pane reflected a lamp in front of it. She saw her pale and weary face and rubbed at it with her fingers. Pulling the blind down to obliterate the image she turned back to Max.

'You told the Bank?' her tone was incredulous. 'Why do you want to go on torturing me? Maybe I hurt your pride but I hardly deserve this.' The power in her voice was climbing. 'Do you really take no responsibility for your actions, Max?' She moved very close to him, almost spitting the words into his face. Her hands were in the air and she was bellowing like a wounded animal. 'Do you not remember?'

Max shook his head and backed away from the pain of the sound. He looked at her; a palimpsest, almost an innocent. 'Remember what?'

Where all else had failed, Ellie's anger propelled her. 'That you tried to rape me. Last year. In the room where you're staying now.'

There was definitely recognition amongst the shock. It may have horrified him but she thought Max knew he was capable of such a thing. She watched him exhuming the shadow. Then he was wide-eyed, on his feet and with his hands clasped to his head. 'Christ no. Oh Ellie, Ellie. I'm sorry, I'm sorry.'

She winced at the blasphemy followed by regrets. Thoughtless. Too easy. She could not then say she forgave him, that would have to come later, but there was a kind of cautery in the moment. Perhaps it was hate that was sealed off, cut down. For Ellie there was certainly the relief of fear faced, maybe for Max too?

He had sat down again, stripped down like a skeletal leaf, when Francesca knocked at the door once more.

'I'm sorry to interrupt but there are people here wanting rooms and you ask me to tell you ... ' She tailed off as she read the stiffness between the two figures; looking to Ellie to ease her discomfort.

'Yes, of course. Thank you.' Ellie was quick

to rise and grateful to have something ordinary to attend to, leaving Max without apology.

The family were carrying bags into the hall. The sound of four voices pitched at different levels moved like music in the echoing space. As Ellie watched Francesca dealing with the paperwork it came to her how comfortable she was with her present and how she felt a part of this place. Ellie watched the family; the parents orchestrating the move from car to rooms; the children listening, taking their cues. There was an easy harmony between them. On this acquaintance they appeared the model family. That was maybe their bit of luck, their path to follow. It is different for so many of us, thought Ellie; I will have to learn a new way.

Ellie asked Francesca to set up a table in the corner of the library. The sweet girl had willingly volunteered to expand supper to feed the family as well and she made the latest change without demur. Ellie said they'd help themselves so Francesca could concentrate on the guests. As she sat across the table from Max she remembered the night he'd taken her to the restaurant. His demeanour was transformed tonight. He wasn't straddled back in his chair, exuding the confidence of the old Max. He sat tidily, one elbow on the table, his chin cupped in his hand. Ellie arranged her napkin on her lap. Swallowing would be difficult, she knew; thank goodness Francesca had made nursery food, a gentle risotto.

'Look, Ellie, I don't know how I can say anything to you . . . '

Ellie was measured, thankful for the new quietude within her. 'I just want to ask you some questions. Give me the respect of answering truthfully please, Max.'

He nodded.

'First, the Bank. Why did you tell them about my cottage? I can't see the point.'

Max shifted in his chair and pulled out a pack of cigarettes. He asked by sign if he might smoke.

Ellie shook her head. 'Salvatore has some rare volumes in here, and not only that, we might find ourselves soaked by the sprinkler system.'

It was a feeble effort to lighten the atmosphere and Max tried to smile as he moved to rolling his fork between forefinger and thumb. He watched it intently as he began to speak. The lamplight in the library made his face look soft, one eye merging into shadow, the other a sparkling, seawater blue. Andrew's eyes, she allowed herself to think.

'It's just that everything sort of exploded in

me this summer — the secrets, the lies, the job — my life crumbling basically. And there was no one I could hit quite as easily as you.' He made an attempt at a smile, 'I suppose I saw you as the bitch who had it all.'

Ellie's expression obviously gave her away.

'I know, I know, my perception was seriously skewed. You may not believe me, but I am truly sorry. Especially now, Ellie.' He scarred the white damask tablecloth with lines from the pressure of the fork. 'I was pretty obsessed with finding out about my father. What he was like, what he achieved and, I suppose, how I'd measured up.' Max looked up at her, more vulnerable than she had ever seen him. 'And it's not that hard, if you know where to look, to find out a financial history.'

Ellie listened as Max told her how he'd discovered the outstanding debt and then remembered their conversation in Italy about Seymour Hopper.

'It was such a brilliant image, the devouring locust, I couldn't forget it. And somehow, he grew in my imagination to be the *instrument of my vengeance*.' Max delivered the last phrase as though it was fresh from a boy's comic. Then he strafed his fingers through his hair. 'After one particularly bad day at work I simply sent an anonymous note to him, and the rest is history.'

Ellie tried to think in straight lines. She tried to recapture how she had felt before this news; she had relinquished the cottage, let it go. Was the manner in which it was wrested from her about to change that? The past was trying to take hold of her again and that needed resisting. But there was more she wanted to know.

'Is it you, buying my cottage?'

Max just gave the slightest nod of his head. Should this bit of news be irrelevant to her, or should it be the last stage in her destruction? What Ellie found, welling up from inside her, was not hysteria or stress, but a true belly laugh.

'You are Ramband! Oh Max, how funny.'

She watched his reaction. It was as though she was looking at the frames in one of those peep shows; his expression went from fear, to bemusement, to incredulity.

'You do realise your father never lived there?'

'Yes. It wasn't sentimentality, just pure revenge. I can see that now.'

'But if it was pure revenge why didn't you let me have it with both barrels the minute you walked in? Watch me squirm?'

'That's what I was intending when I came

tonight. If there'd been the slightest possibility that you knew Andrew had another child, I would have gone all out to destroy you, no doubt about it.' Max was animated, leaning towards her. 'Do you remember, Ellie, when Salvatore told us about those paintings? I think I rather saw myself as Mercury, messenger of secret knowledge. I had some power at last. Power to take your neat and tidy life away from under you. Power to make you feel as bad as me.'

It was salutary to be the target of such venom, but following her immediate anger Ellie was now strangely detached from its effects. She sat and tried to make sense of her emotions, aware of Max watching her. Too often she sidestepped and tried to hold her feelings in check, do what she felt was required of her. It was right to turn the other cheek, wasn't it? The answer she heard was, not with a spirit of resentment; that was no good. Anger had given her relief; she had had an honest reaction, she now realised. But the honesty and anger had had its moment. She felt somehow shielded from Max's ill will, as she saw its confused perpetrator in front of her. What she feared might still have power to undermine her would be Andrew's part in all this. She had to hear the truth and have the courage to deal with it.

'I need to know.' She faltered; it was hard for her to do this. 'I need to know if Andrew knew about you. Knew he had another son.'

The pause seemed interminable.

'No. Now I know for sure that he didn't.'

'How can you be so sure?'

Max began to tell her about the day he finally faced his mother.

'It was terrible. Watching her past catch up with her. I went to see her thinking I'd make her pay, but in the end I felt sorry for her.' Max began to fold his napkin in smaller and smaller squares, making the creases knife-sharp with his fingernail. 'She sort of took the wind out of my sails and I came away feeling cheated of the victory.' He looked at Ellie clearly. 'Maybe I thought you'd give me that satisfaction. No emotional attachment to you, you see?' Now there was not a trace of the conqueror in his eyes. 'Anyway, all the stuff she told me about coming home to make wedding arrangements was a pack of lies. She ran away from Andrew because he made her unhappy. But the one truth in all this is that she never told Andrew about me, Ellie. In fact you gave me that confirmation, I don't believe Andrew would have kept it a secret from you.'

Ellie breathed a deep breath; she wondered if Max was right. Wanting it to be the truth, she sat quietly while Max talked on. Ellie listened to a story of a young, vulnerable woman, far from home, who allowed herself to believe she was loved. The description of Andrew in his twenties, given by Max's mother, married very well with the Andrew she knew in his forties. Confident, knowing what he wanted, happy to receive love but unsure of how to give it back.

'There was stuff I really didn't want to hear. I think my mum was just desperate to let me know she hadn't deprived me of a father without good reason.' Max sighed, reliving the pain. 'She said he just sucked the life out of her; it was all just sex.'

Andrew was uncomfortable with tenderness right up until his death. It was the vital missing piece. Ellie stopped Max in his flow of words, just gestured for silence while she tried to think. He began to eat self-consciously while she sat quietly. Max's mother had made her choice. She must have believed she could not change Andrew and chose not to live without that tenderness. Ellie wondered what made her think she could do better; why had she volunteered for a lifetime of being the missing piece?

'Your mother was an insightful girl, I think. Your father,' the words caused her to stumble, 'your father was a very good man in many respects, but it's only now that I can face the fact that I spent much of my life being the compensatory part.' She could see Max looking to her for qualification and knew he wanted to hear nothing but good about Andrew, but it was about time some truth was told. 'I mean he tried to love materially, physically, but it was left to me to provide emotional and spiritual tenderness for the family.' Ellie moistened her lips. 'Max, if there's any reason at all for our lives to have collided in this way, I think it's partly for you to hear this.'

Max pushed his dark hair back from his face and breathed a juddering breath. 'I know,' was all he said and then, 'All the things we do, even unknowingly, have such fantastic effects, so far-reaching; there's no excuse for not thinking about the consequences.'

Ellie felt the weight rise from her; it was lifted and hurled away. The words were hardly audible because Max almost whispered to her.

'Please forgive me for everything.'

Ellie sat and watched Max as though from a great distance. His words were received by her ears that evening but not yet by her heart; she was too bruised to take that step. At best his plea occluded her turmoil, like an eclipse of the moon. As she rose to put an end to the deadlock, the only words she could find were, 'I don't know if I can, Max — but I will try.'

★ ★ ★

Salvatore's car turned gently into the gateway of the Palazzo at about ten-thirty, the headlights scattering some late-wandering geese. When he let himself in he found Ellie in the hallway and Max walking out of the library. It was not what he'd expected; his thoughts on the way home had been higher; hopeful. Max represented a too solid reality. Salvatore tried to greet him politely, feigning delight at his visit. He inwardly berated himself for this Janus face. He'd had such resolutions to speak plainly to Ellie and yet the first words he'd spoken turned out to be insincere. Max seemed unreactive to Salvatore's greeting. He looked tired, his eyes pink and his appearance dishevelled. It was a relief when he excused himself and went to bed.

Ellie linked her arm into Salvatore's and suggested a nightcap. A pleasant surprise when he'd expected her to follow suit and also make for her bed. They went to his private sitting room, Salvatore feeling blessed by her closeness. She sat beside him on the sofa, feet tucked up under her as she sipped a brandy.

'Did Max say why he's here?'

Ellie's reply seemed a long while coming. The silence alerted him. Salvatore had meant to start proceedings with an innocent question, no more than small talk really, but it seemed he had not.

'I don't know how to start this . . . '

Salvatore knew his face was a mask but underneath his eyes would be wide, his mouth open as he anticipated some horror. Was she in love with Max? Was she going to tell him she was leaving? Not before he could tell her, please God. That's your problem, Salvatore, you think too much and act too little. Truly stupid thoughts now, this minute. Anyway Max was too young for her, although that didn't stop women these days, did it? The chatter in his head only died down when he had to concentrate on Ellie's words.

He could see the words were hard for her to form with chronological accuracy. Sometimes she slipped back years, sometimes she was vividly describing the meaning of the present. There were so many elements shifting against each other; Max renamed as what? Stepson? His bizarre appropriation of her cottage, her trust in Andrew rearranged, her fears for her children — a family now metamorphosed. It was hard for Salvatore to adjust his understanding. Yet amongst this mound of fast-piling words he detected something about himself; he felt a fierce need to protect this woman that took him over. Intellect deserted him; the reaction was in his gut, and it was to reject Max's part in Ellie's life.

'What will this mean, Ellie? He'll want to see you, won't he? I imagine you will be seeing more of Max?'

Ellie looked blinded. She swung her head — not quite a yes, not quite a no. Her tone was almost terse. 'I don't know Salvatore, I'm just telling you what he's told me. I have no plans and I don't suppose he does either.'

'And I have to — '

'Please don't think that I — '

Their words clashed with each other, cancelling out any sense.

'Please go on.' Salvatore deferred.

Ellie looked at him, her body tensed like a hunting cat. 'I need to tell you one more thing. The hardest part. I wanted to tell you a long time ago, but I couldn't.'

And when she told him about Max coming to her room, he was able to forget his own stupid, superficial wounds, finally aware of the comfort she must need.

'Ellie, why bear this alone?' He groaned it into her hair as he held her close to him.

'I'm not alone now,' was all she was able to reply.

As he sat with her in his arms he felt anger and sorrow. It was anger that he'd thought he was beyond experiencing. It was overtly directed at Max but it was knotted and tangled with feelings for Maria's lover too. The sorrow was for the two women he cared about; with him they were both uneasy with the truth. What was it about him that did not invite the important confidences, where was he lacking? It was time to give in order to receive.

'Ellie, I want to tell you how much I care about you. How much I want you to be part of my future here.'

Ellie drew apart from him and tried to smooth her flying hair. She was watching his face minutely. 'What do you mean?'

What did he mean? How could he express this to her?

'I love you.'

Now it was Ellie's face that was gaping; he had rendered her speechless. He didn't want this, he never wanted to take anything away from her. React to me, Ellie, was all he could think. The passing seconds opened a chasm of doubt for him.

'Yes. But what does that mean, exactly?'

Another question and the future depended on his answer.

'It means I've run out of words, Ellie. It means I don't know how else to tell you that I want you to be part of me and me to be part of you. It means I want to take a risk and commit myself to you for the rest of my life.'

He could see the tears in her eyes. She was struggling with words; it was as though she'd used up her store of energy and coherence with the tale of Max.

'But . . . I don't see it. You can't. You're a Catholic. Is that what you really want?'

'You are what I really want, and if I have to give up things to achieve a life with you, then so be it.'

Ellie bent her head and wiped at her eyes. When she looked up she said, 'I can't expect you to give up your faith for me. I can't allow it. That wouldn't make us happy.'

Salvatore took her once more in his arms again; kissed her tears, kissed her lips, breathed her into him. 'Oh Ellie, believe me, I am not giving up my faith.' He gently pushed her hair back from her eyes and studied her face. 'But if we are to attempt this road together, the only thing I need to know is, do you love me, Ellie?'

She looked at him closely, clearly; there was a hesitation but when the answer came it was firm. 'Yes.'

It was enough.

He had led her to her own room then. In the early hours he bathed her face with cold water, kissed her chastely and left her sitting on her bed. Back in his apartment he went through his routines of washing and brushing his teeth as though he'd never experienced them before. His body reacted to water as though each nerve ending was separate. His body anticipated the pleasure to come; before long their appetites would be, could be satisfied. One thing he knew, his soul was full, having feasted. In his bed but no longer feeling alone, sleep was vagrant. He weighed the information he had been given that evening. It was as though he could only hear what Ellie had told him with the perspective of time, filtered through the knowledge that she loved him. She said how much her idea of forgiveness was being tested, how it was still beyond her reach. Yet Salvatore, viewing from the outside, could see how much she was moving towards it. How clearly she had shown him that the only loser was the one who would not forgive. He'd read it year after year, night after night in Ficino's letters but, not until the lesson was in real flesh and blood, had he really understood. If she could contemplate forgiving Max, who was he to be bound to Maria by wrongs not right? His resentment was a small dog he could sit and pet; it colluded with him loyally and reinforced his position day by day. From this night on, it would be off the leash.

Too awake, he settled to a few pages of his beloved philosopher. Ficino's words on the *triplex vita*; the man had written to Lorenzo de' Medici: *No reasonable being doubts that there are three kinds of life; the contemplative, the active and the pleasurable. And three roads to felicity have been chosen by men: wisdom, power and pleasure.*

To pursue any one of them at the expense of the others, according to Ficino, was wrong or even blasphemous. As he rocked in the sea between waking and sleeping Salvatore mused on the aphorism. Where was the balance of his life? Certainly he'd set himself on the path of wisdom and he'd applied himself to his duties. Tonight, however, he had felt the power, with its accompanying freedom and relief, of acting viscerally. Now, after so long, there was a real possibility of pleasure. The thought lay with him in bed.

17

Ellie had an image in her mind of endless doorframes, receding into the infinite distance. There was, however, no building, no structure around these frames. She could see through the next and the next and the next because each door was wide open. And it was she who had flung open the first with that 'yes' of hers. How did you know you loved anyone? It was a leap of faith; it was a response to the knowing rather than the understanding part of yourself.

As Ellie waited in bed for the sleep that would not come she tried to calculate and quantify. How good a risk would this relationship be? What were her terms for this new phase of her life? No lies. That was the solid rock. But to know what constituted a lie to another person you needed to know what they meant by the truth. Ellie drew up her knees and sat in thought under her sheet, the whiteness reflecting moonlight. Would Salvatore's version of the truth allow him to be free from Maria? Unless he had undergone some sea change how could he walk away from his marriage and become a part of Ellie's life? No answers came and Ellie had to walk around that particular doorframe and hover on the threshold of the next open door.

★ ★ ★

The morning came, mist-filled early, waking Ellie to a new reality. The weight of last night's revelations pressed down upon her; severance and conjunction in the space of a few hours. The pieces on the game board were moving too fast for her to appreciate her new position. As she washed and dressed she breathed slowly, willing herself to deal with each moment and not look too far ahead. Enough sorrows for today. But what to deal with first? It was tempting to dwell on the hurt. So, Andrew didn't know of Max's existence. In that case she couldn't blame him for anything. Ellie shook her head. It was a thread in Andrew's life, act first, pay later. Oblivious, he had created another sadly unaware human being; the cycle went on. Max continued, impulsive and unthinking. Ellie brushed her hair with vigour; the strokes were a physical balm. Perhaps Max had listened to her last night. That may have been a genuine remorse that she heard. She put down the brush as voices crowded into her head. *Make him pay. Make him give back the cottage.* Ellie flattened her palms against her ears. 'No.' She said it out loud. Studying her reflection she realised she had no wish to look back. Maybe some would call it avoidance, fear, but she felt that Salvatore's words of commitment had made the way clear. She recalled his hands wiping away her tears and her body unfurled. For too many years, long before Andrew's death, she'd sought such tenderness. There had been pain in the smallest, most prosaic absence; no one to put sun cream on her back, make her tea or to find the mote in her eye. Twenty times a day she had missed the touch of someone who cared about her. With Salvatore, she could imagine taking the risk of giving herself again.

The guest family were already at breakfast when Ellie came into the dining room. She was heartened to see that the children were arguing mildly; the voices comforting in their normality. Salvatore was sitting at a corner table with a coffee and a paper but stood as she crossed the room.

'Ellie.'

She saw his face searching hers hesitantly, almost waiting for a blow to fall.

'I'm fine.' She smiled and they sat across from each other at the small table, knees almost touching.

'Is that the truth?'

She nodded at him, saying 'Lot of it about at the moment. Truth, I mean.'

He laughed gently and reached to touch her hand.

'Look, Salvatore, before we talk about anything else I want to just say that I told you everything about Max because I want no secrets between us. But I really don't want you to think you have to fight my battles. I'm calling my own truce.'

Salvatore nodded. 'I respect that, but I really do want to be a proper part of your life. Do you believe what I said last night? I want us to have a future together, emotionally, physically and spiritually.'

It was an eloquent sentence to accompany coffee and conserves; straight to the heart of the matter. Ellie responded to this energy in Salvatore as she would to the crackle of static in the air. She could feel her defences breached.

'I know, I want it too, Salvatore. But I'm only just finding my way as my own person. Can you understand, before I join in on your life, that I need to be sure?' She watched him watching her, giving her all his attention, and the feeling was intoxicating. If she wasn't careful she could capitulate to everything he wanted. 'You know I love it here at the Palazzo. It's beautiful. And as long as it's viable I'd want us to be here. But . . . ' As she hesitated Salvatore finished her sentence

'We mustn't stay here at all costs.'

Ellie nodded. 'I know it's your history but history is meant to help us understand the present, isn't it? Please, Salvatore, I don't want to see you living life under a burden. But if giving up the Palazzo one day is too high a price to pay, you've got to let me know. Now.'

Salvatore gathered her hands into his, lifted them and kissed the palms.

'No. That's a small price.' He replaced her hands on the table and sat straight. His words were measured. 'We must set out a business plan with targets. Think about our financial future.' His face softened. 'I'm sorry, Ellie. I can't pretend it's my strong point. I'm more inclined to mysteries than money. I'll need your help.'

Ellie relaxed at his honesty; his need gave her confidence. 'Thanks, Salvatore.'

'For what?'

'For needing me. If indeed we are to be together, I want to share it all.'

'Are you doubtful about us being together?'

'Depends what you mean by that.'

'Oh Ellie, for me there is no other way except marriage. I know it can't be tomorrow, but it is what I want.'

Ellie watched his body move fractionally; the precursor to a larger movement towards her. It was as if the depth of his will spilled into this slight action.

'Is that what you want too, Ellie?'

Ellie closed her eyes, tried to shut out the clamour of externals and the din of conflicting thoughts. She was for a moment, both fractional and infinitesimal, a still, small centre. 'I don't understand, Salvatore. How can you have changed your position so radically? Your religion . . .' she faltered. 'You believe that you are married to Maria until death. How can you contemplate marriage to me?' Her voice was barely audible as she added, 'It makes me fear that this is some impulse out of grief,' she looked into his face, 'that I am a way of filling a vacuum.'

Salvatore's whole body expressed denial. 'No, no, Ellie, that is not the truth.' His face took on the transparency of a painted angel as he began to tell her of his moments in the vineyard. Here, he told her with the fervour of one recounting a dream, he had stepped from being under judgment into a relationship with a merciful God. 'I was prompted at last by my wise old Uncle Ercole.' He took her hands again, 'But you have been telling me the same things ever since I've known you.'

By his response Ellie knew her face must have betrayed her unbelief. She shook her head.

'Yes, Ellie. I don't mean you've always put it in words. It's the way you deal with the problems in your life that speaks.' He paused and smiled. 'But I do look forward to talking to you about things that matter.' He sat back again, still holding her hand across the table. 'I'm going to talk to Father Giovanni as soon as I can. I know I need all the wisdom I can get to find a way through this. It's true, if Maria had not left me I would never have parted from her. But I'm not blameless. I accept my part in her leaving and I have to ask forgiveness for that. Past mistakes can be washed away.'

As if by directorial design, as Salvatore finished his sentence one of the children sent a glass of water spinning from the table to crash on the tiled floor. Ellie caught the earthy scent as the liquid seeped across the surface, finding the channels between the tiles and running steadily along them. Ellie and Salvatore laughed. They saw heads turn suddenly towards them and the surprise on the faces of the family, who were now loudly chastising each other. Francesca was ready with dustpan, brush and cloth. There was every hope of peace restored. In the middle of the scraping chairs and raised voices and frantic activity, Salvatore raised Ellie's hand to his lips, kissed her ring finger and asked, 'Please, my dear Ellie, when it is possible, will you marry me?'

*   *   *

It was after Ellie had said a heartfelt 'yes' that Max appeared. He was bleary-eyed, a glowering spirit. But his presence no longer had the power to disturb. As he brought her past hurling towards her, Ellie was more sure than she had ever been that she had made the right reply to Salvatore. She felt his hand upon her arm as Max approached.

Salvatore rose. 'Shall I leave you both?'

'No.' Ellie heard her voice in unison with Max's.

'I'll get a chair and organise some more coffee then.' Salvatore slipped away as Max took his place opposite Ellie.

He rubbed his hand through his hair and blinked at her. 'Do you hate me?'

'No, Max, I don't.' She could see him waiting for her to say more but Ellie felt no compulsion to speak. She sipped her fruit juice. Salvatore came back and Max drank down a whole cup of coffee as if it was his last.

'You know, I can be out of here in an hour if you want.'

Salvatore and Ellie exchanged glances. 'It's not what I want and, no doubt, Salvatore would say the same.' She watched his face; Max was trying hard not to betray himself. After a while she said, 'We've got a real chance to put a full stop to everything that's gone before, Max. To start again.'

He nodded.

'Not that we can pretend all the deceit hasn't happened,' she added.

'I know. I've been thinking about all that.' Max tugged on his crumpled shirt. He looked as though he'd slept in it. His eyes were fixed ahead and he talked beyond her, beyond the window. 'I'd really like to meet my half-brother and sister.'

'Why?' Ellie was almost sharp. She felt Salvatore put his arm around the back of her chair. 'I mean, why now? Why the hurry?'

Max laughed. 'Not exactly a hurry after twenty-odd years, is it?'

Ellie smiled. 'I'm sorry. It's just that, well, I have to find a good time to tell them all this. I'd rather you didn't force the pace, I suppose.'

'Yes. Of course.' He looked clearly at her then. 'But, what you said about deceit — I want to, I need to be . . . ' He took a breath.

'I don't want to be a secret any more. And I want to make it right. Everything I did.'

Ellie didn't ask him how, just then, although she wanted to. In hindsight she was grateful for the interruption of the family who came over to say their thanks and goodbyes. The farewells seemed appropriate.

★   ★   ★

In the days that followed Ellie felt herself acclimatising. For several mornings she woke in her bed to the new-reality of her life and needed to spend time adjusting to the fit of it. Her old self wanted to see-saw from elation to despair. How much easier, her old self whispered, if there was no Max, no thorn in the side. You could just get on with being happy. Her new heart didn't accept these murmurings. Darkness was necessary for comprehending the light. She remembered reading somewhere that death was the dark backing a mirror needs if we are to see anything. For Ellie it was time the past was put to death. In the present, Ellie was happy alongside Salvatore. Each day built a common life. She gave herself permission to gradually fall in love with him, knowing that she already did love, had loved him. Where was that line, *The comfort they might have of one another?* Written for them. Together they had to deal with history and they needed time in which to do so.

The first opportunity came sooner than Ellie's natural pace might have dictated but it was timely. Francesca had called Ellie to the phone.

'Mum, it's Sadie.'

'Darling, what a lovely surprise. Everything's all right is it?'

'Yes, of course. Why shouldn't it be?' Ellie regretted her phrase; was suitably chastised for what Sadie had read as smothering. 'I'm in Rome finishing these guide entries and I thought, as you're still there, I might come up and stay for the weekend.'

Not entirely rejected then, thought Ellie. 'Wonderful idea. Any chance of you staying longer?'

'Maybe.' Sadie's tone was wary. Ellie tried to answer it.

'It's just that being away from home has been good for my perspective on things and this might be the time to talk about them.'

'I suppose so.' Sadie's voice was flat.

'In fact I could call your brother and see if he's got time to come out too.'

'Right.'

When Ellie did call Dom she was more

straightforward. It was how she had always been with her son. With Sadie she was forever second-guessing. Dom simply dealt with facts at the point of their arrival.

'Can you come, Dom? There's a lot we all need to talk about. I wouldn't ask if it wasn't important.'

'Sure, Ma. I can get a cheap flight from Stanstead. Maybe juggle things for about four days. Are you OK?'

'Yes, I'm fine now I'm dealing with things.'

★ ★ ★

Before Dom and Sadie arrived Ellie wrestled with how and what she should tell them. News of a marriage might strike her children as too precipitate; Ellie was gently amused by the thought of a woman of her mature years being able to shock her children, but she certainly didn't desire to hurt them. She agreed with Salvatore that, for now, they would say only that she was seriously thinking of settling in Italy. As it turned out they were far more perceptive than she'd allowed.

Sadie asked her outright, 'And would this settling in Italy have anything to do with a relationship with a certain Palazzo owner, by any chance?'

And Ellie was too transparent to lie. To her

relief, Sadie had got up and hugged her saying, 'I'm glad for you, Mum and, if it means anything, I really like Salvatore.'

Ellie did not however, talk of marriage, for that was still far from being a possibility at this moment.

Telling them about Max was altogether more difficult. He had gone away on Friday morning so at that point they only had an abstraction with which to deal. His part in the removal of the cottage and the assault she kept to herself for now.

'Are you sure Dad didn't know?' It was one of the first questions Sadie asked.

'I haven't talked to Max's mother but no, I'm sure he didn't.' Ellie sighed. 'I know we didn't always communicate perfectly but I do believe he would have told me.'

Sadie's shoulders relaxed.

'What's he like, this Max?' It was Dom's turn.

Ellie paused trying to encapsulate a description that was as near objective as she could reach. She couldn't do it.

'I can't pretend I really know,' she said. 'Complicated might be the word. There's no doubt,' she searched for the words, 'his origins have made life difficult for him.'

'And he's made the move to meet us?'

She looked at her son, who resembled her in so many ways.

'Yes. I think it's going to be very important for him.'

Ellie was pleased that Dom and Sadie had each other. They spent the day in the gardens talking, they slept in the afternoon and then they resumed their time together in the library, before supper. At intervals they would call her in to fill the gaps in their father's history and to tell them more of what she knew about Max's mother. It was painful at times, exposing Andrew in his weakness, but as Ellie sought to find a balance she found a comfort herself. They sat together on the large leather sofa, surrounded by Salvatore's books, and the aura of years of printed wisdom seemed tangible. Ellie found herself able to remember all the things she had loved about Andrew.

'These are things Max needs to know too,' she said at one point to them. 'I hope you can be generous with him.' It was a difficult thing to ask, indulgence for someone so destructive. But as yet, Sadie and Dom still didn't know just how destructive. Ellie had made it clear to Max that he was to be responsible for the telling of that chapter.

'You need to explain about the Bank, I won't do it for you, but I will tell them if you won't. As for the attack on me, that is a matter that can remain between us alone, if you want.' She remembered the expression of relief on his face and was lost in the moment.

Sadie pulled her back. 'Mum, why shouldn't we be generous?'

Ellie just shook her head and put an arm around her daughter. 'I know you will,' was all she said.

★　★　★

Salvatore set out to see Father Giovanni the next morning. It had rained and the air smelt of the sweet decay of leaves. Ellie was amused by his desire to act so quickly — she'd said he was 'seizing the bull by the horns'. He knew the phrase of course but the image of it unexpectedly fired him. He remembered Greek pottery with the friezes of athletes leaping across bulls' backs and liked the comparison. Ellie saw him as her champion, unlike Maria. However, she'd felt it was best that he was not there when her children met Max. As Salvatore set off for his meeting he was determined to focus on the positive in his life.

When he arrived at the church it seemed empty, but Father Giovanni slipped out of the shadows of the side chapel and came towards him, arms extended. The welcome brought hope and encouraged Salvatore to hold nothing back. By the time the meeting was over the sun was high in the sky and Salvatore was once more looking forward. Because of Maria's aversion to a church wedding so many years ago, the Father's advice was that the marriage was never sacramental and that Salvatore was free to wed Ellie in the church. There was a matter of some time to make the proper searches into their circumstances and validate this; perhaps it would take two months after finalising the divorce before a declaration could be made by the local tribunal and the paperwork arranged. Salvatore had, some time ago, questioned his solicitor about civil laws and knew that what he needed to do now was to concede to Maria's wishes and conclude the divorce. And with his agreement this would only take a matter of weeks. Father Giovanni had nonetheless counselled leaving some time for thought before Salvatore committed to another relationship. He had asked that he should meet them both together for an exploration of their intent, but Salvatore knew that there were really no obstacles in his way now.

The lightness he felt was only marred when Ellie later described to him Max's meeting with her children. When Max confessed his part in the repossession, 'angry' was too small a word to describe Sadie's reaction. Ellie had tried reasoning with her, saying she had always felt uneasy about the outstanding debt and so this was the position in which she would have found herself, regardless of Max's actions. But it was not enough for Sadie. She left for Rome with bitterness in her wake. Dom was quiet, hurt but struggling to understand. At least, with him, when he left for home Ellie had some hope of future resolution.

★　★　★

Actually, it was barely a month after Dom and Sadie learned about Max's treachery that all of them returned and were sitting around a table once more. Salvatore watched Sadie chewing on her food, and on the resentment towards Max that she couldn't disguise. Conversation was hampered by the need not to touch inflamed parts. He felt for Ellie as she tried to fill the thickened air with chat.

'For God's sake!' Sadie slammed down her cutlery on the tabletop. 'Don't you think we should actually talk about what needs to be talked about here?'

Salvatore scanned the table; Ellie and Max were alert, their eyes wary. Dom affected detachment, leaning away from the table, arm across the back of the chair.

'What is that, Sadie?' asked Salvatore.

'Just how Max thinks it's all right to behave like he has.'

Salvatore watched Max, knew him well enough to see fear. Perhaps he was computing the odds of Ellie having told Sadie the whole story.

'How he can just take a huge part of my mother's money from her and expect to be the bloody prodigal son.'

'I didn't — ' Max began.

'As good as. The bank wouldn't be clawing it back now without your vindictiveness!'

Salvatore could see Ellie twisting her napkin, hesitating, mouth half open. He couldn't help but be proud of Sadie for her transparency. He'd wanted to challenge Max himself but Ellie had stopped him. She wanted no further discussions. He'd respected her for trying to end the cycle of bitterness but wondered if he could have been as sure about the straight path. At least she would have some money left over from the sale, but Salvatore made it clear he wanted nothing from Ellie but herself; he'd encouraged her to think of it as belonging to her children. Not that they knew that.

'Sadie.' It was Dom, putting a restraining hand on her arm. 'It's up to Mum how she wants to handle things, and she made it clear, didn't she?'

'All this goddam Christian forgiveness. I'm sick of it. Sick of pretending he's some damaged child who doesn't know any better.'

Salvatore watched Ellie's face contract; her heart too probably.

The glass silence was broken by Max. 'Actually Sadie, thanks to your mother, I do know better.' It was not said victoriously but plainly.

She watched him; Sadie's face was resolutely expressionless, but Salvatore saw the contempt in her eyes. The brows raised fractionally, the nostrils flickered.

'I came here to discuss some ideas with you all.' Max looked around the table. 'So I'm glad Sadie kick-started the process really.'

Salvatore felt a communal outbreath, not quite relief, nearer disbelief. Max looked straight at Ellie.

'I know the knock I gave you over the cottage — '

'Understatement of the bloody century!'

'Sadie!' Ellie quelled her daughter. 'Let him speak.'

'And, to be honest, I couldn't believe the way you just let it go.'

'Couldn't believe your luck,' Sadie was muttering. Salvatore wondered if Max had heard.

'At first I was just relieved about that but when it sank in that you weren't out to get back at me, that you even had time for me, I had to think again.'

Even Sadie listened now. Max was explaining that in the past weeks he'd been sorting out financial matters. 'Salvatore knows I've been sidelined in the family business for months now.'

Salvatore nodded.

'I've negotiated a settlement for getting out and it's more than generous, it means I can pay off your debt, Ellie.' He held her gaze. 'You can get the cottage back too if you want.'

Ellie became the focus of four pairs of eyes and ears; Salvatore's own waited to know if Ellie would be tempted back. As he studied her it was as if he saw a light flood her mind. No hesitation.

'No, I don't want that.'

Sadie gasped but Ellie held up a hand. 'But the cottage is the inheritance of Andrew's and my children.'

There was a moment while everyone tried to interpret Ellie's words. Of course the first reaction was from Sadie.

'Am I hearing this right? You and your bloody principles — this is too much!' She jerked out of her seat, sending the chair squealing across the flagstones and stalked out. Salvatore marvelled at Ellie, still and composed.

Dom leaned forward. 'She'll be OK.'

Ellie nodded. 'I know. She just doesn't understand.'

Salvatore felt they all needed some clarity. 'Ellie, will you accept Max's offer to settle the debt?'

She hesitated.

'You must, Ellie. Give me a chance to put things right between us all.'

Max was more assured than Salvatore had seen in a long time. Ellie sat, head in hands, eyes closed for what seemed an age. Salvatore was tempted to break into her thoughts and offer advice but, as he waited, he realised how much he respected this woman and how much he loved her integrity. Dom was silent too; a lifetime with Ellie had no doubt taught him the value of speaking at the right moment, unlike Sadie.

At last she said, 'If that's what you want, Max. But it's a great deal of money. To be fair, that should give you an interest in the cottage.' She turned to Dom. 'I'm trying to think what your father would have wanted. If he'd known about Max.' Her voice trailed off and she looked at him helplessly. Dom reached for her hand across the table but didn't speak.

'Can I say something?'

'Of course, Salvatore,' said Ellie and he heard Max and Dom murmur their assent too.

'I think that for Max, if he'll allow me to interpret, this is not a matter of property and money but discharging his debt.'

Max nodded.

'For you, Ellie, it's a matter of moving forward with your life. You don't want to go back to live in the cottage, for which I am very grateful.' Ellie smiled back at him and shook her head slowly. 'And, as you'd already discussed with me, you want any proceeds of the sale to go to your children eventually.'

Max intervened. 'That's what should happen, Ellie. You don't owe me. I owe you, big time.'

'I don't think you're entirely right there, Max. Your father would have wanted you to have something.' Salvatore saw Ellie groping for a coherent idea, and the right words. 'And I'm the one left to see you do.'

'That's seriously skewed logic, Ellie.' Max got up and paced the floor. 'The only thing he left to pass on was his debts. I'd be taking from you and Dom and Sadie.'

'Hear, hear!' The voice was Sadie's; she was standing in the doorway.

Max gave it scant attention. 'Maybe,' he

was almost speaking to himself, 'if I pay off what was basically my father's debt I can be free. The sins of the father and all that . . . ' He refocused his attention on Ellie. 'Anyway, you have given me something. You've forgiven me. You haven't given up on me.' Salvatore could hear the threadiness of his breath and the shake in his voice. 'That cancels any debt you feel you ought to repay for my father.'

Even Sadie was silent, Salvatore noted. Dom was the first to speak.

'Mum, why does it have to be all or nothing? If Max pays off the debt, buying himself a share, and you leave some or all of your money in the property, then the cottage could be a place for us all. I think Gran would have liked that.'

Sadie moved back into the room then; they all sat once more around the table. Salvatore mostly observed, occasionally rising to pull a blind or light a lamp as daylight faded. They talked on into the evening, moving towards some agreements. Salvatore listened to myriad financial permutations, none of them forced by Max, until some common ground was reached. There was to be a sharing, in a way that everyone would be able to have use of the cottage, but there was room for withdrawal. Ellie would have some funds to bring to Italy with her. Salvatore sensed the potential for problems but he felt peaceful, there was an aura of goodwill around the settlement.

★ ★ ★

It would take time for all their constituent parts to find a pattern to inhabit. Salvatore sensed a growing calm in Ellie, happy that her mother's home would continue to provide a sanctuary for Sadie and Dom. But her children's relationship with Max was still a work in progress. He had to admit that Sadie was making an effort and he was glad that she was trying to keep her feelings reined in for Ellie's sake. She was growing up. Max in turn was careful not to antagonise — perhaps he saw in Sadie the anger he'd so recently known.

What followed was a waiting for the resolutions by legal process; first the cottage, then his divorce, and finally his declaration from the church tribunal. Ellie and he talked with Father Giovanni who gently urged them to not hurry into marriage. Salvatore liked to think of it as a betrothal period: the waiting to be truly united gave them time to know each other well. Sometimes though, it felt as if they were treading water. There were days that Salvatore could see that Ellie missed her home. Then she applied herself intently to the business and poured her creativity into that. On those days he tried to help her by listening, by speaking to her always in English. Salvatore had to keep reminding himself that these moments were not cracks, not signs of another impending failure. It would have been a test for anyone to be living side by side, building a new relationship and a new business all at once. And the business was beginning to do well. The Garden Design side had every chance of flourishing thanks to Ellie's belief in him. She had come up with an inspired idea to create garden houses out of growing plants and he had the skills to see it through to reality. In both the good and the bad they began to understand each other more finely.

★ ★ ★

It was a milestone when Dom, Sadie and Max came to visit in the New Year and they were at last able to talk of wedding plans as a reality. Salvatore had returned from a job and walked into the tiled and scrubbed kitchen where everyone was gathered. Francesca was there too, fuelling the talk with pastries and coffee. A smell of cinnamon and almonds rose up in the steamy atmosphere. It seemed the right time to tell everyone and the news was greeted with enthusiasm.

'It's got to be a huge gathering — I know of loads of people to invite!' Sadie gathered him by the arm and drew him into the room. 'It's going to be lovely. We all need a bit of fun, a real celebration.'

'Hold on, don't get ahead of yourself, Sadie. The business is doing well but we don't want to blow all the profits at once.' Ellie pinched her daughter's cheek.

'We can do lots of it ourselves, can't we guys?' Sadie's question brooked no negativity. 'Max has still got contacts in the flower business, Dom and Francesca are wicked cooks. I know someone who can sort the invitations and the photography.'

'Just a minute, Sadie. Don't you think it's rather up to Salvatore and me to decide on our wedding celebration?'

Sadie made a mock attempt at looking suitably chastised and the gathering laughed at her. She hung on Salvatore's arm and widening her eyes at him, mewed, 'Oh tell me, tell me Salvatore. Don't you want a lovely little party?'

He hugged her, detached himself and went to Ellie who was leaning against the sink holding her coffee. He put his arm around her waist and took a sip from her cup.

'We haven't really dared to talk about plans for quite a while, have we, Ellie?'

She shook her head. 'But we did have a few thoughts about it. We know what we don't want, don't we?'

Salvatore nodded back at Ellie's question and then said, 'We don't want to marry in a registry office as we both did before. This marriage is to be blessed in church by God.'

Sadie made a face but it was good-natured and, knowing her better now, Salvatore had a sense that her derision was a mask. He wanted her to understand the anchor of his faith and hoped she would one day.

'And we do want a party, with family and friends and neighbours. Personally, I want as many people as possible to know how much I long to be married to your mother.'

Was there a moistening of Sadie's eyes? Salvatore tried not to look as though he'd noticed. There were certainly catcalls and whoops from the others; a raising of coffee cups and a waving of buns, crumbs showered like confetti.

'You can all do as much to help as you'd like. We'd love that.'

Salvatore leaned back and he and Ellie watched the young babble of guest lists and dresses and invitations. He regarded his wife-to-be, saw the hope in her eyes and stole a kiss.

18

April

The sun streamed in upon tables and silver-ware. The flowers were carefully un-arranged — acid green and bergamot blues in the hall, warming into crimsons and burnt oranges in the Palazzo dining room. Ellie wondered if she had really just experienced what she had waited for all these months. But it had been necessary, the waiting; time with Salvatore that built trust. They had explored and played and worshipped together. They were building things too: the garden business was really taking off and Dom had brought them into the twenty-first century by designing them a website. It was wonderful to have found such an eager market for their garden houses; the formal architecture growing out of substantial box and holly and cypress. Ellie was rather proud of the name she'd come up with; 'Third Nature.' Salvatore said he liked it — it appealed to the philosopher in him, the idea that the creation of structures sprang from an entirely natural instinct but needed that extra dimension to bring them to fruition.

She wanted that fruition in their union too. She had said to him, after their talks with Father Giovanni, 'This time there will be no loophole, no possible way this marriage can be ended when I marry you in your church, declaring that I know exactly what the sacrament of marriage means.' And now it was all over, the moment that made her into a married woman once more.

When Ellie entered the church it had seemed so gaunt, so overpoweringly inhuman in scale, that she was struck with a sense of having made all the wrong decisions. As she walked the aisle, Dom and Sadie at her side, she saw Salvatore turn to her. Then the cavernous arches into the apse and the jangling gilt of the altar decorations became filled by a new spirit. When she heard their own voices relay the sacrament and commit to a lifetime together she prayed, there and then, for death to be far off. Now, in amongst the press of people and sound of voices in the Palazzo, it seemed entirely banished.

Someone chinked a glass and called for everyone to be seated. Ellie settled into her place, melting on to the seat amongst folds of lavender-grey silk. The fabric came from Nerine; one of the little treasures she had given Ellie in those last days. 'I must have got it in Ceylon. A miracle the moth hasn't had it after all this time.' Ellie was glad to recall her voice on this day, glad Nerine was with Salvatore and her in the weave of their relationship. She thought of the time when Nerine and she had made portraits of Max and was reminded of some words of Alberti, that only he who has tried to draw both a laughing face and a crying face can realise the difficulty of distinguishing the two. Ellie pondered the sweet ache she felt, the similarity of sorrow and joy, as she sat amongst the babble of guests.

Their table was filled with family. Salvatore's children, although they had met a few times before, were still at the stage of being charmingly polite to her. Not so Max; he was now daring to be close enough to disagree. Perhaps it was the emerging student in him: with encouragement he was due to begin a university course in the autumn. She watched Dom, Sadie and Max sitting quite near to each other. Was she willing it or was ease beginning to develop between them after these few months? She was pleased that they had made a way to share some time together; that day when she'd been so clumsy trying to divide the cottage up between them, she really hadn't been trying to patch things up with money, all she wanted was to repair her family. A sigh escaped from her. Perhaps even there would come a day when there would be no secrets from each other.

Dom was with his girlfriend and Ellie smiled at their closeness. If she was honest, she hoped her own step into a new marriage might encourage her hesitant son. Sadie was alone — she had long left Paul to his wife and child — having learnt too much about the devastation of absent fathers. Now Zio Ercole was at Ellie's side, kissing her energetically and taking her from her reverie.

'Dearest Ellie, you are a blessing. Enjoy long life!'

She laughed and it was not just mirth but joy. Salvatore was still meeting and greeting, circulating the tables and settling people in their places, but every now and then he would seek her out with a glance. Finally, he was at her side. Too soon the wedding breakfast was eaten and she hardly tasted it. Salvatore was on his feet, thanking those who needed it, talking with his usual ease. And then he said he wanted to talk about his marriage, how he knew it would be fruitful even in this late season of their lives. 'Speak for yourself, old man,' she laughed.

He smiled back, took her hand, kissed it and then talked of the things they loved together, of gardens and painting and literature. 'And now I want to give my wife two gifts; a Pomegranate and a Mulberry tree, a pair to plant here, in our home together.'

Francesca bore in the small plants, swathed in ribbons. More gifts; that morning he had given her a beautiful small reproduction of *Primavera* to recall when they had first met and a new cycle had been set in motion. They'd been blind to it then, but that early Cupid had begun to insinuate himself into their picture. Ellie watched Salvatore almost distantly, his words were separated from any time or background and she loved him anew.

He was speaking of the symbolism of the pomegranate in painting, its iconography of rejuvenation. There he was, smiling at her and telling everyone how much they shared a love of these ideas.

'Ladies and gentlemen, you may not know that the mulberry is a particularly special plant because it bears flowers and fruits together. It also develops its bloom very slowly but then matures so fast that the fruit bursts forth with dramatic vigour. It's a perfect illustration of the Renaissance concept of *Festina Lente*, Make Haste Slowly. In fact,' he aggrandised the words, '*Ripeness is All*, one must give everything its due time and consideration, let ideas flower, and then seize the moment! Do not ever let the fruit drop to the ground and perish.' He turned and Ellie found herself being helped to her feet.

'I first met Ellie in the spring of two years ago. It has taken both of us time and consideration to get to this day.' He held her hands and faced her, talking to her alone, 'My dearest Ellie, I may be past my first flowering but you have rejuvenated me and I have picked the choicest fruit.'

As they kissed — hard to do when you're smiling so much thought Ellie — she could hear thundering applause.

★ ★ ★

She watched him in the half-light, walking towards the bed. He was throwing off his clothes with a flourish, a small smile tilting the corners of his mouth. It awed her, this lack of shame; marked him as masculine more clearly than his body. There was no passionate fumbling to undress each other. She was under the covers — clean and ready. Ellie shivered slightly. The fresh sheets touched her skin and made her conscious of how she filled the space. Not Maria, not beautiful, not wild, not confident.

He slid in by her side. 'Let me warm you up, wife!'

His hip pressed against the softness of her thigh and she smelled the aroma of him; warm earth and lemons. 'I can smell the sun on you.'

He laughed and she watched, so close to the olive skin and the deep brown eyes of her husband. They kissed in the way they had learned over many months; today they were touched with urgency but he broke away, to look into her face.

'I have no words to describe how much this moment means.'

She was quiet, remembering and forgetting her past all at once. Her expectations were drowned; taken by the current.

He was around her and she responded, opened herself to his warmth upon her cool flesh. Salvatore waited and regarded; adjusted to her rhythm. She felt the press of dark notes; saw the covering sheets fly and her skin as it gleamed under his. The sweetness of giving herself broke over her. She was defenceless; a sponge to soak up all the pain. Their loving absorbed the blood of the past; there was nothing but an exchange of presents.

Further into the night she had spoken to him. 'How do you feel after making love?' She knew she was a coward, trying to generalise and depersonalise the question. What she wanted to know was how he felt with her. He'd propped himself up on an elbow, a warm, dark presence against white sheets, brought his face close to hers and, holding her chin, kissed her as a parent may kiss a child but without power, without condescension. She simply felt a deep sense of her necessity, and his gratefulness.

'I feel I've travelled. Taken a journey into a beautiful country.' He smiled and stroked her neck. 'In this case England.'

It made her laugh. 'Did you take the train?'

'No, I walked naked with the breeze behind me.'

She pushed him gently, feeling easy, and turned to lie back on the pillows.

'And you? Answer your own question.'

She watched the ceiling in the dim light, seeing small movements; the plaster mouldings shifted back and forth, breaking up like pointillist paintings. She knew this was a defect of sight, nevertheless the sensation was real and she believed it. In the half-land between fact and feeling she answered him.

'What do I feel? I feel as if I'm at last in my body. For a long time, you know, I didn't take it with me when I had sex.' She laughed gently. 'Not like you, travelling free! I've spent years being outside my body, not being responsible for it. But,' she turned to look directly at him, 'being able to give it away, to you, means it's been returned to me.'

He moved back slightly to focus on her and questioned her with his expression.

'Sorry. That's rather veiled.' She smiled. 'I just want to say thank you, Salvatore. It's been a long time since I felt this way. Feeling that I am able to give freely, nothing's taken from me forcibly, and knowing that what I give is returned.'

'My darling Ellie, I am the one to thank you — for another new beginning.'

As she drifted into sleep Ellie saw the figures of the Graces dancing before her eyes in their unbroken cycle. Then she herself came to rest inside Venus.

We do hope that you have enjoyed reading this large print book.

Did you know that all of our titles are available for purchase?

We publish a wide range of high quality large print books including:
Romances, Mysteries, Classics
General Fiction
Non Fiction and Westerns

Special interest titles available in large print are:
The Little Oxford Dictionary
Music Book
Song Book
Hymn Book
Service Book

Also available from us courtesy of Oxford University Press:
Young Readers' Dictionary
(large print edition)
Young Readers' Thesaurus
(large print edition)

For further information or a free brochure, please contact us at:
Ulverscroft Large Print Books Ltd.,
The Green, Bradgate Road, Anstey,
Leicester, LE7 7FU, England.
Tel: (00 44) 0116 236 4325
Fax: (00 44) 0116 234 0205

Other titles published by
The House of Ulverscroft:

HIDDEN RAINBOWS

Maxine Barry

When Persis Canfield-Hope finds her grandmother's diaries dating from 1938, she decides to follow in her footsteps and cross Australia from coast to coast by train. On board, she meets the charming Dane Culver who has a hidden motive in befriending her — involving a fabulous and purloined jewel! Also on board is Rayne Fletcher, an insurance investigator, who is out to nail fraudster Avery McLeod — so falling in love with him was not on the agenda. Unfortunately, however, the real criminal has an agent on board — who is determined that neither Rayne nor Avery will live to see the journey's end . . .